FYRE &
STONE

THE
RESURRECTION
MEN

Fyre & Stone

The Resurrection Men

Steve Downes

EST. 2019

BLKDOG

www.blkdogpublishing.com

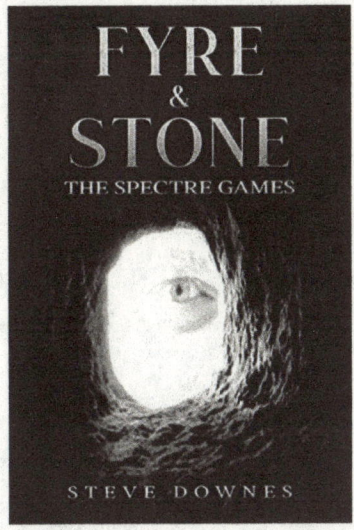

Book one in the Fyre & Stone series.

Two men from the same city, but very different worlds.

Sebastian Fyre is a wealthy young Lord with an unshakable belief that he can communicate with the dead. John Stone is a tough policeman who grew up in the Victorian slum tenements of the city he now patrols.

A series of brutal murders across the city throw these two men into a reluctant and volatile partnership.

Fyre and Stone attempt to hunt down a conspiracy of killers, while trying to avoid becoming prey themselves.

For Niamh,
for her unending support and love.

CHAPTER 1

A dense fear gripped him, like an ice-glove wrapped around his beating heart, squeezing tighter and tighter until his chest felt like it would implode in pure pain.

His carriage had stopped with no warning, on a sunken lane that led from the main road up into the low hills.

He had heard the rumours of strange events in this part of rural Ireland. He had read about disappearances and speculated with friends and colleagues about the nature of the seemingly random set of people who had been reported missing over a number of years.

Other rumours had reached his ears, darker and more unbelievable than the simple explanations given by the police. This stretch of the County Cork coastline had always been synonymous with supernatural occurrences. Ghosts frequented every castle. Pagan spirits, the Pooka, lived in the long-lost tombs and the mounds that littered the landscape. Even the sea was filled with dangerous mythical beasts.

In recent days he had taken to carrying a small pistol. The gun was wrapped in a thick handkerchief in his coat pocket.

After he had called for the driver several times and poked his head out of the window of the carriage, he nervously unwrapped the pistol and sat it on the empty seat beside him. His hands fidgeted and his legs shook from the fear, as if that fear were rising from the ground, into the carriage and through his body.

His mind was a muddle, but he was still able to weigh up his options. The driver was not his usual man; that had made him nervous anyway. He was scarcely able to understand the man's heavy west Cork accent. So the few words the driver did say to him, by way of explanation, were lost. He could sit here, hope the wretched man was just relieving himself in the undergrowth and would return. He had the gun, and a small lamp was lit inside the cab. He could lock the door, although the lock was flimsy and the door itself looked none too solid.

His other options ran through his mind at a panicked pace. He could mount the box seat of the carriage and steer it through the night. His newly acquired country home was a few miles along this coast, and the main road couldn't be more than a few hundred yards behind where he had now stopped. Why the driver had chosen to turn off the main road was a worry. He looked at the pistol again. He didn't want to hold it in his hand. Guns made him nervous. He was a pacificist in voice, but a coward at heart. The thought of violence made his stomach churn.

The next option he considered was to unharness one of the two horses. He was a good rider, and although his age was very much against him, he was sure he could trot the animal along the dark road toward home.

The sudden, loud, neighing of the horses snapped him out of his worried thoughts. The carriage shook for a moment, and he heard the distinctive sounds of the horses galloping off. The carriage stayed where it was. Without thinking, he gripped the pistol and opened the door. He leaned half his body out and yelled into the pitch-black night.

'I have a firearm, I insist you cease this madness!'

There was no answer.

'Do you hear me?' he yelled once more into the darkness.

With a shaking hand he waved the loaded pistol around. As his eyes adjusted to the night, he could make out that a strange blueish glow was reflecting up off the sea. The moon and the stars, although partially hidden by cloud, turned the Atlantic into a dark violet mirror. This allowed him to see the length of the coast, trailing all the way back to Kinsale Bay, and curving around a great headland in the other direction. But this ghostly light did not quell his fear. All around him the land was like coal, with no distinction between plant-life and natural rock.

Weary of just sitting in the carriage, he dropped onto the rough trackway. He could feel the stones through his shoes, the unevenness of the track forcing him to hold onto the carriage frame with his left hand, while still gripping the raised gun with his right.

He rounded the rear wheel and almost fired a shot at a flickering shadow. With his heart pounding in his chest he leaned his back to the carriage and tried desperately to get hold of his senses.

His eyes adjusted more. Below him, at the bottom of the winding hill, the distinct crown-shaped silhouette of a church steeple stood out.

He knew this building. He had attended a service there once. He remembered that a small village was spread out further down the slope, ending in a fishing harbour. To his left was a jet-black wall that he knew to be the boundary of the game wood of Castle Barry. If he could just make it to the village, he would be sure to find someone who could help him. The coast road snaked around the bay and cliffs. His newly acquired home, a rarely visited square block of granite and unkempt gardens, was at the end. He had not wanted the house, or the land. They had been forced on him in a will, and he longed to sell up and be rid of this place.

In the moments that he leaned against the carriage, almost crying with ebbs and flows of terror, he desperately

Steve Downes

wished to be back in Dublin. The safety of his small townhouse called to him.

His other senses suddenly became more accustomed to the night. He could smell the wet gorse and the salt of the sea air. They were both unfamiliar scents to him, and he disliked them equally.

A sharp, unnatural noise forced him to raise the pistol again, which he had lowered to his side while gulping in deep breaths of air. His hand shook uncontrollably and this time the trigger gave way under his finger.

The shot rang out.

At first there was a short high whine, followed by a dull heavy echo. He was running and falling before he had time to think, and before the sound of the shot had stopped echoing in his ears.

In his peripheral vision, something was keeping pace with him. Something to his left, and to his right. Just black shapes against the black background, but with enough outline for him to know that they had a humanoid form.

In the village, a few hundred yards below where William Egan's carriage had stopped, a figure was watching the night from the topmost walkway of the Protestant church. In times past, the church walkway had been used to look out to sea; fearful eyes watching the dying storms, hoping to catch a glimpse of a fishing vessel.

The eyes of this watcher were not aimed toward the dark waves to the south. They were looking north, their cold stare peering into the black canvas of the scrublands.

The watcher heard the gunshot ring out.

The echo from the stones of the church steeple made it difficult to pinpoint exactly in which direction the shot had been fired, but the watcher already knew where to fix their gaze.

There was a single lantern lit over a disused blacksmith's workshop, just where the village stopped, and the rocky wasteland rose into the hills. The watcher knew the lantern was there because they had lit it minutes earlier.

4

The watcher on the walkway waited for movement. A shadow appeared out of the pitch and seemed to float effortlessly across the roadway. Where it passed close to the lantern, it caused the flame to shimmer very slightly.

William Egan fell from the darkness into the thin circle of light. He stumbled around for a moment, dropping his firearm, and fumbling to reclaim it. He waved the gun wildly into the hills behind him, then began to run again, toward the church.

The watcher in the steeple saw Egan running toward the wall that circled the church graveyard. The gate was locked, or at least appeared to be. A heavy chain had been wrapped around its two halves, and Egan tried for a few frantic seconds to pull it apart. Had he been in his right mind or had the light been better, he would have seen that the chain was not locked to the gate, but just loosely knotted on the inside.

He placed his pistol on the shoulder-high section of wall that held the gate. The watcher on the steeple above mouthed the word, 'Foolish,' and smiled. A gloved hand reached up from inside the graveyard and silently slipped the gun away.

In his panicked state, Egan didn't even try to retrieve the pistol from the wall. His attention moved from the gate to the two near-shapeless figures that were advancing on him from the road.

He let out a scream that seemed to wake the night itself. A sudden gust of wind drew up, as if in response to his yelp, and the chain from the gate fell away to the ground, helped by some unseen hand. The church gate opened from the weight of his body, and he tumbled into the graveyard beyond.

The watcher on the steeple walkway had seen enough. From inside their coat, the watcher drew a small black covered notebook, made a mark on a page with a thin pencil and slipped the notebook back into their pocket. The watcher turned away from the scene below, safe in the knowledge that they knew what would happen next. There were other matters to attend to. This little distraction with Egan was of no real concern, it was only a means to an end.

In the graveyard below, William Egan's panic had reached a fevered state. He could see moving shapes in every hedgerow, disembodied faces appeared and disappeared from the darkness, and muttering voices seemed to rise from the graves themselves.

As a stream of cold sweat ran down his face, he raced for the church doors. His body hit the heavy wooden frame with a thump. He banged on the doors with his fist, making a dull echoing noise. He didn't wait for a reply, he ran back along the path toward the gate. His eyes darted around, peering across the graveyard for dangers. A movement to left caused him to wildly lash out with his arms, and the screech of a cat, moving between the headstones, took on the wail of a banshee in his terrified mind.

He watched the feline move like a weightless shadow across the graves. He stood there, in a moment of unnatural frozen silence. The night air was now so cold that it made the sweat on his body feel like a floe of ice on his skin. It was now he remembered the pistol, left on the wall by the gate. If he could just get there, only a matter of tens of yards. His heavy breathing stopped for a second. He held the cold air in his lungs. His head moved to the right like a clockwork device. He could see it.

This was no shadow, no flickering illusion, no feral feline.

There was a human creature advancing on him. Following the path, moving above the ground, as if floating. Whatever it was, its faceless form was wrapped in an ethereal mist. The creature itself appeared to be made of black, swirling smoke.

He ran again, his mind lost in shock. He heard screams, terrible childish pleas for mercy. His broken consciousness did not realise these screams were coming from his own mouth.

He stumbled into the sea of gravestones. The ground here had deep sunken rectangles where the topsoil had dropped into the subterranean grave cuts. The stones above the graves had moved into awkward angles, making them appear like broken teeth in the jaw of some ancient dead monster.

Egan's foot tripped up on a buried stone. He fell forward, gashing his forehead on a piece of rusted ironwork. He didn't notice the heavy flow of blood down his face, even when it reached his mouth and ran across his lips.

Whatever was behind him was close now. He could feel its movement, hear a rapid trample of weeds and grass, and he could see other shadows closing in on him. He fell again, but this time he could not get to his feet. From the shapeless form a disembodied hand clawed out at him. It had seemed to have razors for fingers, which raked through his jacket and made thin lacerations on the skin below.

He could go no further. His body was exhausted, and his heart threw one last sharp warning across his chest. He tried to speak, but the blood from his wounds had poured into his mouth, and all he could do was spit it out with a gurgling sound.

He was surrounded. Faces appeared out of the silk-like shadows that circled him in perpetual movement.

William Egan tried to rise from the ground, but his heart could take no more. He fell backwards, without making another sound. The open grave behind him, topped with a seventeenth-century marker, received his body. He fell several feet into the freshly cut soil.

He lay there, seriously injured, his heart beating its last in a desperate attempt to survive. He was conscious, his eyes able to see, his ears able to hear, as those above filled the grave with loose soil.

The Chief Surgeon worked deep into the night.

Around his vast surgery, various lamps sent up a flickering light show that made the furniture and very walls appear to be moving independently.

Above the slab he was working at, a single steady white light shone done, enabling him to make precise cuts into the corpse lying there.

A hunched figure slowly walked into the surgery. He was carrying a paper folder, and was moving forward with fearful steps.

'What is it, Michael?' the Chief surgeon asked, without looking up from his work.

Michael stuttered his response, 'Um …er, Doctor Barry wants your notes, sir, …. sorry, sir.'

'The good doctor is working late tonight, as are you, Michael.'

'Yes, … sir.'

'We seem to have a glut of fatalities of late.'

'The Lord works … in mysterious ways … sir.'

'He does indeed. The notes are here, beside me.' Still the Chief Surgeon didn't look up. Instead he lifted a bloody organ from the body and carefully placed it on a metal dish.

Michael, his face contorted with fear and disgust, moved forward. Unsteady on his feet, he moved around the Surgeon and, trying not to look down at the slab, he reached out for a pile of paper on a side table.

'Not those!' the Chief Surgeon snapped.

It was now that Michael noticed a second pile of papers. He lifted this second pile, just as his eyes caught sight of the dead face of a young woman, her eyes absent from her skull.

Michael ran a few paces backwards, and hurriedly put the notes into the paper folder.

'Try and get some sleep, Michael,' whispered the Surgeon, as he continued to work, a thin smile across his face, 'the night is always darkest before the dawn.'

CHAPTER 2

Stone raced along the wide street, his eyes firmly fixed on his quarry. The pavement had been planted with tall, thin young trees and their branches whipped into his face as he ran along. The target he was chasing took a sharp left turn and Stone darted across the road to follow.

'Trying to get home are you," he panted, 'not today.'

He gave an extra burst of speed to get ahead. Although he was fit and his wiry strength rarely let him down, his feet protested gravely. His shoes had been new just a few months ago, but they were cheap, the leather thin, and the soles had cracked within days. He had done a lot of legwork in the last few months. He had needed to do the legwork. It was a matter of survival.

Stone skidded to a halt outside one of the tall redbrick terrace houses that lined this part of Dublin's middle-class suburbs. In the corner of his eye he spotted a flash of black scrambling up one of the more mature trees.

He adjusted his jacket and looked around the street to see if anyone was watching. In the distance some traps were moving back and forth across the main Drumcondra Road, but the street he was on was eerily empty. Satisfied he was alone, Stone took in a deep breath and walked over to the base of the tree.

'Come on down. There's nowhere for you to hide now.'

Stone tested the base of the tree, it was too thick to shake, and he suspected the branches were too thin to support his weight.

'Why don't you just give it up? I've been chasing you for two days. We've been through a lot, you and me, over rooftops, down drains and through the back gardens of every house in this village. Give it up, old friend, come down. What do you say?'

'I'd rather not, I like it up here," the voice that replied did so in a smooth whisper.

Stone sighed and looked up into the tree at the black cat.

'You know,' he said disheartened, 'I was hoping never to hear your voice again.'

'Me or the cat?' asked Fyre, in his normal tone.

Stone kept his eyes on the black cat. The lady who was employing him to return the creature to her had been very specific; the cat was not to be hurt or distressed in any way. As for Stone's physical pains or mental anguish, she didn't seem so concerned.

'What do you want?' asked Stone.

'We have a job.' Fyre replied casually.

'I don't work with you any more, we have ceased our professional relationship. I'm an independent private investigator now.'

'I can see that,' mocked Fyre, 'Do you think perhaps the cat doesn't like its owner and that's why it ran away? Maybe it is better off on the street, fending for itself.'

'I'm not interested in whatever you have to say, no matter what smart wordplay you use. Go away, Lord Fyre!'

Fyre leaned against the garden wall of one of the fine redbrick terrace houses that lined the street. He watched Stone for a moment, as he called to the cat and made 'swish-swish' noises at it.

'It's a lot of money,' Fyre stated.

'I don't care, I don't need it. I'm doing just fine.'

'When was the last night you had a decent meal? Or a wash and shave?'

Stone winced. He still kept his back to Fyre and his eyes on the cat in the tree. The last few weeks had been tough. It had been over year since the Spectres case; their fame had proved to be fleeting, and the work which followed was well paid but often pointless. Fyre's methods and character had simply become too much for Stone. He had taken a gamble with setting up his own detective office, and the gamble clearly hadn't worked.

He looked at the cat staring down at him in a smug sort of way. He hated this animal. Just as he hated the part of himself that had dreamt of a better life.

Fyre didn't wait for Stone to answer, 'It's not like the other jobs, no things that go bump in the night this time.'

'I don't care,' said Stone through his teeth.

'They paid a large sum in advance, I have your half here.'

'I have a job, now go away, you're upsetting the cat. Come down, you little furry bastard!"

Fyre took a few steps forward so that he was now in Stone's eyeline.

'Our client wishes us to investigate a missing person and possible murder. The fee is exorbitant and comes with all expenses. More than enough for you to pay your outstanding debts and begin again. With or without me.'

Stone shook the tree, despite knowing it was pointless.

'What about the danger?'

'Danger?'

'I got shot in the arse last time we worked together.'

'That was not my fault, you flirted with the wife of a very grumpy man. And it was only rock salt.'

'It hurt like hell!' Stone looked into the face of his old partner and sometime friend for the first time in months. Fyre's boyish good looks and modern attire made him stand out in a city of conservative faces.

'One more job, and if you no longer wish to associate with me, I will understand.'

Stone held his dirty hands to face and rubbed his tired eyes.

"No ghosts!' he stated.

'None that I know of.'

'No cups flying around rooms on their own?'

'Not ever a saucer, dear chap.'

'And I get my money now?'

'This moment.'

'Is it in some posh townhouse or out in the suburbs?'

'Actually it's down on the south coast.'

'What! You want me to leave Dublin?'

'It has been known to happen. There is a train service and coach from the station. I've made all the arrangements.'

Stone half-heartedly shook the trunk of the tree again, the cat mewed at his effort.

'Why ask me now? Why not do the job yourself?'

'I fear I lack your skills, old friend, and the letter from our new client was addressed to both of us, as was the bank draft inside.'

Stone didn't need any more time to think about it. He knew that, despite lying to himself about his financial situation, he was out of options. He held his palm out to Fyre, who dropped a large bundle of pound notes into it, as well as a train ticket.

'It leaves this evening at five from Kingsbridge.'

'This client of ours, when do we met him?'

'That may prove an issue, you see out client is the man who is missing and also he has stated that he suspects he may have been murdered. It's all in his letter. I'll read it to you on the train.'

'This sounds like a ghost hunt,' muttered Stone.

'You find his body, alive or dead and I'll take care of any ghosts, should any crop up.'

Fyre grinned his most annoying grin and raised his cane sharply upwards. There was a loud squeal and the black cat dropped in an ungraceful fashion into Stone's arms.

'You might as well collect from the old lady. I will see you on the train at five. We have a private compartment.'

Stone watched Fyre as he walked across the street to where his carriage was waiting. Bertie the driver tipped his hat to Stone. Stone nodded back with a smile and yelled, 'Still employed by this madman, Bert?'

'Better on the coattails of the devil than in his path, sir.'

Stone watched the carriage turn and slowly make its way along the street toward the city.

He held the cat to his chest and petted it lightly. It didn't seem to object to Stone's attention now that it was caught.

'Come on, you stupid moggy, you and me are the only sane creatures left in all of Ireland.'

Fyre pulled the blind down on his side of the carriage. The morning sun was streaming across the city and reflecting off every window it could find.

He had lied to Stone, but it was a white lie. Their entire working relationship had been based on such lies. Stone didn't ask many questions about Fyre's ability to tap into the supernatural world, and he didn't ask Stone about his less than moral methods of gleaming information. Stone had a habit of breaking into secure building and breaking the fingers of the occasional low-level criminal.

'Home, sir?' Bertie called out from the plate.

No, Bert, take me to Dublin Castle.' Fyre had to lean forward to be heard as the carriage rattled along the cobbled suburban road.

Bertie, who was privy to much of Lord Fyre's and Mr Stone's dealings, halted the carriage. He opened the hatch into the cab and spoke softly in his heavy Dublin accent.

'Are you sure, sir? They haven't been so welcoming in the Castle of late, what with all this trouble in the country.'

Fyre laughed, largely to himself. Bertie's statement was true. While, after the Spectres case, Stone and he had become minor celebrities, the faceless machine of government that ran the nation had eased them away from any official positions.

'I still have some influence there, and I fear, Bert, that we will need all the help we can get on this next case.'

'Mr Stone doesn't know all the facts then?' Bertie asked, with a huge knowing grin on his face.

'Has Mr Stone ever known all the facts?' Fyre asked back, with an equal grin.

'Ignorance is bliss, sir,' replied Berite. He closed the hatch and geed the horse forward once again.

Fyre leaned back in his seat, and through the far window of the cab he watched the red brick houses of Dublin's northside drift by.

He had, over the last few days, admitted to himself that he needed John Stone, much more than Stone needed him. Not just because of his incomparable skill set, but because he was fearful of facing what was to come without him. The first vision he had had in over a year came to him the night before the letter had arrived. It hit him like a sledgehammer in the chest, knocking him from his feet and sending his limp body back onto his bed. Horrible things came out of the darkness. Distorted creatures, tortured by disfigurement, silently howling at him. The seemed to be no sense to it, a waking nightmare filled with the broken faces of people he knew were trapped between one life and another. The shock had taken him to the very brink of his sanity. He had been alone in Drumcrow House, that bleck pile of granite that overlooked the distant city and seemed always to weigh down on his shoulders.

By the time Bertie had trotted up from town with the mail, Fyre was beginning to recover from the experience. He was meditating, with his back against an ancient standing stone, one of a fragmented circle that stood on the grounds, when Bertie called to him from the yard.

Fyre had read the letter by Matthew Barry with great care. If it had arrived to him without the dreadful vision that preceded it, then he may have dismissed its contents as the ravings of a madman.

But, the details in the letter had a frightening similarity to the vision he had just endured. Matthew Barry had begun his plea to Fyre and Stone by stating that if this letter reached them …

'… I may be dead by the time you are reading these words. I have enclosed payment in full for your services, and have entrusted this letter to a lowly servant, a boy from the local village, whose mother, I suspect, was taken in the same way that now threatens me.'

Fyre had read the rambling description of abductions.

'Many have disappeared over recent years, many more than were taken by the malignant spirits in the past.'

He knew that he would have to show the letter to Stone. But he would do that on the train, went it was too late to back away from the case.

He mulled over one sentence in particular from Matthew Barry's letter.

'They began by taking the living, those isolated, even ostracised by the community, but now I have become aware that the recently dead too are disappearing.'

Somehow Fyre knew this to be the crux of the matter. That jumble of spirits that forced their way into his consciousness on that first night, were now invading his mind daily. It was the vison in the early hours of this morning that convinced him to seek out Stone.

It had not been as horrific as the other; it was almost gentle in fact. Fyre was standing at the great bay window of Drumcrow, looking down on the city as the summer dawn crept over the grey and redbrick lines of urban life. Like all of his visions it came fast, his mind was dragged from his body. His perception raced down the hillsides, across the country into the town. His mind stopped at a row of dark slim townhouses in the village of Rathgar. He recognised this suburb, Bertie used this road to ferry him to and from the city centre. Standing at the gate of one of the houses was a middle-aged man. He was short, plump around the stomach and wore a top hat and long-tailed coat, the kind that had gone out of fashion two decades ago.

Fyre knew the man. Not by name, but he knew he had met the man at some social occasion. He could instantly recall speaking to him, just polite small talk, in Dublin Castle. It had been one of the gatherings his overbearing mother had insisted he attend, before the drama of the Spectre case.

In the vision, the man, with no name as yet, tried to enter the gate of the townhouse, but could not. It was as if an invisible force was pushing against him. For the briefest of moments his eyes met those of this desperate man. Fyre knew that his life had been forfeited, and only recently.

Bertie steered the carriage through the narrow streets of the city centre. He crossed Grattan Bridge, leaving behind the shrill voices of the street-side sellers and entering the more affluent Southside. Along Parliament Street, Fyre observed the change in shop windows from one side of the river to the other. On the north there had been open-fronted butchers, nameless shops with assorted pots and pans strung up outside, and the now obligatory pawn brokers, that seemed to litter the poorer parts of the inner city. Along Parliament Street stood tailors, dress makers and tobacconists, with trays of silver smoking accoutrements gleaming in their windows.

Stone had told him that Dublin was really two cities, unwittingly glued together and constantly trying to pull themselves apart. It took Fyre a long time to understand what he had meant by that, but now it was obvious that the whole country was pulling itself apart.

Before Fyre could contemplate anymore, Bertie pulled the carriage up outside City Hall, which itself stood up against the large dark walls of the Castle. The Castle had been the administrative centre of British rule in volatile

Ireland for centuries now. By one community it was looked to for peace, justice, and the maintenance of the status quo. By another community was seen as the enemy, walled up inside their fortress.

To Fyre, the Castle seemed to represent everything he loathed about his own upbringing. Like Drumcrow, it seemed to him to be his family's history carved in blocks and mortar.

'I'll wait for you here then, sir?" asked Bertie.

Fyre smiled at him, 'I suspect I won't be long, Bertie; no is a very short word, even for mindless bureaucrats.'

'No bureaucrat worth his salt would ever be so idealistic to use simple terms like yes or no,' came a familiar voice from behind Fyre.

Fyre spun on his heels and smiled a grin of joy at seeing the face of Trevor North. North had been Stone's friend and partner in the Constabulary, and he had, innocently, been dragged into the Spectre case.

'North! Good to see you.' Fyre extended his hand. North took a step forward, using his cane to help him and shook Fyre's hand as if he were a lifelong friend.

'How's the leg?' asked Fyre, feeling a pang of guilt.

'Not bad,' North replied, his cheerful disposition was something Fyre had sorely missed.

'Good, good; what are you doing here?'

'I'm one of those mindless bureaucrats I just heard you mention. I moved here six months ago, a sort of promotion.'

'Sort of?'

'Yes, more money, less work and they wanted me to stay out of trouble.'

'I hope it's working?'

North grinned, 'I am more mindless and bureaucratic than ever.'

Fyre was not much of a conversationalist, and there was an awkward moment of silence, broken by North, who seemed oblivious to the man's nervous disposition.

'And what are you doing here? If I may ask that, your lordship,' he grinned again.

Fyre laughed out loud, he detested the use of his

official title, but he could see that North was joking with him.

'Actually, you could help me with something. I need to see the guest sign-in ledger from August two years ago. They do keep such things here?'

North snorted a laugh, 'We have them from sixteen ninety-four. But why?'

'I'm looking for the name of a man I met here once.'

'That sounds like a John Stone answer.'

Fyre smiled knowingly, 'Yes, it does, and John Stone is also on the case, a little unwillingly.'

'That I can believe. He does everything unwillingly. You'd better come with me.'

CHAPTER 3

Melisa Barry stood behind the substantial frame of the window in her husband's office. The scene in the large formal gardens below was tranquil. She lifted her eyes and looked out over them. A range of dark hills framed a thin crescent of blue sea, and in front of this, a patchwork of fields and fox covers formed a bright and dark green quilt. Her eyes fell again to the gardens below. They were divided into four even quadrangles, each surrounded by a tall, whitewashed wall, with arched gateways and iron gates providing access from one to another.

From immediately below her, a group of men were filing into the first walled garden. They were distinguished by the way they were all dressed in snow white shirts and matching trousers. Over their shirts, some of the men wore white or grey aprons, the type used in industrial kitchens and workshops.

The men, around forty of them, spread out across the garden. Some, in small groups of threes or fours, walked along the gravel paths, talking in what seemed to Melisa to be hushed tones. Others stayed alone, walking under the shade of the willow trees, or sitting on one of the many iron-cast seats that dotted the garden. In a second garden, divided by a slender wall, a smaller, but similarly dressed group of women emerged from another wing of the vast building.

Melisa could now see a second group, following the women. They were men dressed in black uniforms, with, what looked like, a thick whale-skin aprons covering their torso and upper arms. These men all had gloved hands, and each carried a long thin baton. She noticed their hats, which struck her as rather comical. They were truncated top hats, with a whale-skin flap running down the back and sides to cover their neck and ears, and a wire mesh protruding from the rim, which could be pulled down over the face.

No doubt, she thought, that directly below her, another group of these guards had marshalled the men out into their garden area. Melisa watched the men and women mill around their gardens for a while. She observed their ticks, twitches, and small fits. She watched some of them laugh out loud, seemingly at nothing. Others cried incessantly, but most of them just walked around, as if unaware of their surroundings or any other people.

Melisa's legs were tiring; she had been standing at the window for an hour now. Her husband had asked her not to come to the asylum unless it was necessary. He had told her that he feared the sights and sounds there would upset her. She had railed against this, and had assured him that she was a modern woman, capable of understanding and sympathising with whatever sights and sounds such a place could throw at her. She had seen such sights before, but Charles didn't know that.

She had been educated at Girton College, Cambridge, and although, as a woman, she could not receive a degree, it had been widely acknowledged that her work in modern medicine and chemistry was among the finest research of any undergraduate in the university. Despite her work being published, albeit under a pseudonym, she had found it impossible to forge a meaningful career in the five years since she had left college. She had nevertheless continued to work, driven by her desire to succeed, another aspect of her life that she felt is necessary to hide from her husband.

Charles had been the one ray of light in a dark cloud of years of frustration. He was an odd character, even by the standards of eccentric landed gentry families. He had grown up a child of privilege in southern Ireland. The family had been the dominant landowners in this part of county Cork for centuries. Several vast estates spread out across the Irish landscape, from the low mountains to the north, to the rough cliffs of the Atlantic coast, large and small farmers had to lease their land from the Barry family. It was an old and profitable way of living, but, as Melisa knew, a way of life that was dying.

Melisa had met Charles in Cambridge. Even then, as an undergraduate, he had stood out from the rest of his peers. The sons of lords, dukes and the new monied industrial super rich, were arrogant, loud, and sometimes boisterous to the point of crass. Charles had resisted following in the footsteps of his father, grandfathers, and other ancestors. He had not become a judge, or an MP, or even an officer. Despite his deep personal belief in God, he had shunned approaches from several religious institutions, sometimes dismissing them offhand to the point of insulting them.

Charles was a solitary and gifted academic. Shy to a fault, especially during his time at Cambridge, he found it difficult to make friends. The drunken revelry, the gluttonous clubs and the sycophantic parties dedicated to the social hierarchy of the student body, were not for Charles.

As an outsider herself, for many different reasons, Melisa had found solace in the reading halls and libraries of the University. It was in one of those halls she met Charles, reading a medical textbook. Their attraction to each other was instantaneous, and she made sure it blossomed. She had help in that respect from an unexpected source. The patron of her research was one, Lord Barry, Charles's father. This patronage was no secret, but there were other reasons for her persistence with Charles. He seemed to find his confidence around her. His usually bumbling manner seemed to settle into the calm, assured stature, of a gentleman. He became a different man, and Melisa made sure he stayed that way.

As the first year gave way to the second and then the third, their relationship cemented itself into a solid form. Charles's standing at college increased greatly. He became a leading member of several academic clubs, a firm favourite with his professors and even the noble names of the student body, those same brash boys from the first year, showed him a newfound respect.

Charles was conscious of Melisa's own academic accolades, but he was unaware that her own standing in Cambridge was significantly raised by being associated with him.

'A woman still needs the name of a man to be someone,' she had told a colleague in Girton. Her resentment of this fact was something she kept from Charles, at the time, and, even now, years later.

Melisa's mind had wandered. She had hardly noticed a third, much smaller, group of people enter into one of the upper gardens.

The group in there were dressed differently from the other patients and guards. There were four men, each in a grey and black sack cloth garment which covered their feet and seemed to tie around the back of the neck. Melisa's keen eyes could see several leather straps on the garments. Some were dangling loose, others were tightened so fast that they restricted the men's movements.

The four men waddled, and half fell across the lawn of the enclosure. They were followed by two guards, each with their face cages drawn down and their batons held across their shoulders, as if ready to strike.

She took a slight, almost imperceptible breath, as she spied her husband. Charles walked a few paces behind the guards. He was dressed in a smart dark suit, which hugged his athletic figure and accentuated his six-foot-two stature. He was a young, handsome man, with soft green eyes and a kind face that seemed to smile, even though he rarely did.

Melisa let a smile cross her lips, as she watched Charles stand with his hands clasped behind his back, a trait he had picked up from his rather eccentric father. Melisa had first met the rest of Charles's family between their second and third years. It had been a wonderful, and sometimes daunting, summer in Ireland. The Barrys, like all old monied families she had known, were filled with character and the full gamut of temperaments. Lord Barry was much like his son, but with more confidence. Lady Barry had died when Charles was a boy, but he had two sisters, both older and both married into land-owning families. There were several uncles, aunts, cousins and even a grandmother, who had been particularly unwelcoming to Melisa.

Charles had, on that first stay in Ireland, largely protected her from exposure to his overbearing family members, chief among them his two aunts. When her time at Cambridge was done, and Charles had received his degree, they got married. Their guest list had been small, until Charles's father had invited half the aristocrats in Ireland. Melisa and Charles wilted under the attention, but persevered because they knew Charles had been offered a position to study for a doctorate in his college.

The next three years had been the happiest either of them had known in their short lives. Cambridge now felt like home, and the young couple were able to grow socially, to the point where a permanent career within the university looked likely for both of them. All things come to an end, good and bad, Melisa told herself the day she packed to return to Ireland. Charles had been offered the position of chief administrator in one of the country's flagship asylums. It stood, like a sprawling barracks for a large army, just a few miles from Castle Barry.

Melisa had had to leave behind much of her own work, but she had found a renewed source of interest in Charles's own work, and it was this passion for discovery that led her to come to the asylum today. She moved across the floor, stretching her stiff legs and back. As she leaned against the far side of the enormous window, a movement in the enclosure where Charles was, caught her eye. Below, one of the patients had lunged forward. Both of the guards stuck out with their batons and a number of heavy blows landed on the restrained man's head and upper body. Melisa winced. She wanted to pull her gaze away, but she was unable to. She watched the patient's body crumple under the assault. Despite the impact of the blows, he still tried to reach forward.

Charles stood, emotionless, a few feet away. He observed the beating the guards dished out, then raised his hand as if to signal that the man had had enough. They stopped hitting the poor man. He lay on the ground for a minute or so, then rolled up onto his knees and crawled away into a corner.

Melisa felt sickened, not by the savagery of the treatment, but by the coldness of Charles's reactions. It was a coldness she had hoped was gone from his character. Charles had spoken about the need for discipline,

'It is necessary to be cruel on a Monday, so you can be kind for the remainder of the week,' he had said to her once.

Since their return to Ireland, he had often spoken to her about broken minds being like rudderless ships, and he, as their captain, must find a way to steer them to safety. She was unsure if he believed his own words, or if he had simply adopted the methods of those around him.

When Charles left the garden, leaving the patients and guards to their daily exercise routine, Melisa moved away from the window and idly perused the volumes of medical books lining the office.

'Something wrong, my dear?' Charles said as he walked in.

Melisa jumped slightly and turned. She was always able to hide her concerns, her true emotions and even her intentions. It was a skill that she found came easily to her, and, as a woman, she could use her charm, her smile, and other aspects of her nature, to her advantage. She smiled at her husband and rushed over to embrace him.

'No, no, no, dear, let me disinfect my hands.' He stood back, with his palms held up, as if a schoolboy waiting for inspection.

'What on earth have you been doing, Charles, dear?' she smiled at him.

His face flushed a little, but only so much that she would notice.

'It's been a difficult morning.'

He washed his hands and forearms in a basin in the corner of the office. He was fastidious in washing and drying his skin, before replacing his jacket and fixing his collar.

'Now?' asked Melisa with laughter in her tone.

'Now,' he replied.

She rushed at him and caught him a huge hug around his waist. He, laughing at her silliness, embraced her gently and kissed her on the forehead.

'What brings you to my lair?' he asked, 'has father arranged yet another party?'

'Yes, he has actually, down at Garryhinch, in the orangery. He's debuting his new toys. Everyone will be there.'

'Of course they will,' said Charles absentmindedly, 'It's free.'

'But that's not why I'm here.'

Charles paused, he could see the excitement on her face. 'Why then?'

'I made a breakthrough … I found something.'

As the morning became the afternoon in southern Ireland, two uniformed men from the Royal Irish Constabulary, pulled at their collars to try to get some relief from the heat.

'I thought it was supposed to be cooler by the sea?' asked one of them.

'Is it not the other way round?' the second constable was scanning the long winding road that led to the grand house. He could see a dot of black moving in the distance.

'How would it be the other way round?'

'Well, people go to the seaside in summer, don't they, so it must be warmer, stands to reason.'

The first constable shook his head, 'No, you go to the sea to cool down, it's supposed to be cooler here.'

He wiped his forehead with his handkerchief and

looked up at the dark granite of the house. The sun was reflexing off the glossy stone and seemed to be magnified onto the gravel drive where the two of them stood.

'Do you think that butler wears that suit when the master of the house is out?'

'Quiet, Frank, we've got company.'

Frank followed his colleague's gaze along the tree-lined coast. A thin road wound its way around the small headlands and bays. There was a carriage, moving at speed and the driver, high in the plate, was wearing a black uniform.

'Maybe that's our missing Mr Egan?' asked Frank.

'I don't think so,' said the second officer, a tone of concern in his voice, something his colleague hardly picked up on.

The carriage only slowed when it hit the loose gravel of Garretstown House. The uniformed driver hopped down from the plate and attended his sweating horses. A man in his mid-forties, dressed in a dark suit got out and strode over to the policemen.

'Careful Frank,' said the second officer, 'let me do the talking.'

'Who is this fella, Cieran?'

'Quiet now.'

'Gentlemen,' he said, his strong English accent seemed harsh to their ears.

'Hello sir, may we help you?'

'Holt, Dublin Castle,' the man produced a warrant card.

'Constable Cieran Murphy,' said Constable Murphy, 'and Frank Owens.'

'Also an officer,' said Frank, he held his hand out to shake Holt's.

Holt ignored Constable Owens' hand and looked up at the façade of the building.

'I'd worked that out,' he said plainly, 'I'm here to take over this case.'

'Case, sir?' said Constable Murphy, as he pushed Frank's hand down, 'What case would that be?'

'Missing person, one William Egan. That is why you are here, yes?' asked Holt.

Constable Murphy gave a little snort of laughter, 'Yes, sir, Mr Egan's valet sent a message to the local barracks early this morning, saying that Mr Egan hadn't returned home.'

'You don't seem too concerned about this, Constable....?'

'Murphy.'

'Ah yes.' Holt grinned at him.

'Not really, sir, there are a lot of grand houses around here, a lot of parties. Mr Egan is probably a little the worse for wear from red wine, sir, couldn't make it home. He'll turn up in due course.'

'I doubt that,' said Holt, almost to himself. 'Anyway gentlemen, I'll take things from here.'

'I'll have to speak to my sergeant about this, back in town.'

'He has already been informed,' replied Holt, 'this matter is out of the hands of the local police. Goodbye, gentlemen.'

Murphy mounted the small trap they had at the side of Garretstown house. The grounds of the place were ruinous, much of the garden overgrown and all but the front of the building looked dilapidated.

'What was that all about, Cieran?' asked Owens.

'Trouble, lots and lots of trouble. Come on, we've got to get back to town.

Detective Holt watched the policemen rattle away down the coast road.

In the distance, above the thick treeline, he could see the steeple of a church, and beyond it the towering roof of a much larger grand house. He checked his pistol, which he kept under his jacket at all times. He instructed his driver to take the carriage to the side of the house, where it could not be seen from the road.

William Egan's valet, an older gentleman with grey hair and a suit that looked far too big for his elderly frame, hobbled down the stone steps of the house.

'Hello, sir, may I help you?' he asked.

'Yes,' said Holt softly, 'just this one thing.' He spun on his heels and shot the valet in the forehead at point blank range.

'That will be all,' he said and stepped over the body.

CHAPTER 4

John Stone was a man who lived on his instincts and wits. As a young boy his mother had died, and the circumstances of her death were now unclear to him. All of his early life was just a haze of patchworked memories. For most of the time he had believed she had died of neglect, starving herself so that he might have enough food to survive. He had avoided the workhouse, the institution of abuse run by religious orders and, for a time, a prison cell. Stone was able to survive on his own from an early age, a thief, a runner, and, as he grew older and stronger, a gangland bullyboy. Something in his nature didn't suit that lifestyle. In the end he was glad he had got caught.

He stood in one of the deep stone arches that ran the length of the engine shed of Kingsbridge station. With the shadow of the arch covering him, he could watch the comings and goings on the platforms without drawing any attention. He absent-mindedly reached down to his pocketbook. It was stuffed with the notes Fyre had given him earlier that day, minus the price of a good meal and new shoes. With his left hand he checked the pistol under his jacket. Not a day had gone by, since the weapon had been given to him by his old

Constabulary boss, that it was not by his side.

In recent years Ireland had become more dangerous than ever. Violent crime was at an all-time high, and Republican tensions made for a paranoid society. The Irish Republican Brotherhood had moved from ideology to militarism, the British and Unionists in Ireland had retorted in their own brutal way. Violence was creating violence. Stone was aware that he could be thrown into jail without trial, just for carrying a gun.

He watched two uniformed police constables walk the length of the passenger concourse. The large crowd moved out of their way, like a wave, closing again behind them. The tension in the city was reaching a boiling point. Perhaps, he thought to himself, it's better that I go with Fyre on this mad ghost hunt.

Stone saw Fyre entering the concourse. He stood out among the drab suits and black dresses of the throng.

'One thing is for sure,' Stone whispered in the shadow, 'we won't sneak up on anyone.'

Fyre walked slowly across the floor, his cane tapping the ground lightly as he moved. His eyes were fixed on the large ornate tiles of the station concourse. He seemed to completely ignore the stares of the passengers as they passed him.

Stone was unsure if they were staring because they recognised him from the papers, or because he was dressed in a custard-coloured suit, with a top hat to match and red gloves and cravat. He giggled. Then stopped suddenly.

Fyre was standing still in the concourse, his head held high, in contrast to the crowd around him, who all appeared to walk in a head-stooped gait. Fyre's eyes were glazed over, his head moving in a slow side-to-side motion, as if scanning the station for an invisible enemy.

Stone had seen his friend do this before. It unnerved him. Fyre claimed he could see the dead, contact spirits, and even speak with them.

'Death,' he had told Stone in one of his talkative moods, 'is a door, sometimes it opens briefly to allow a soul to move from one room to another. Mostly it is closed, keeping our reality from whatever lies beyond.'

Stone listened, carefully noting each word, while pretending not to care.

'Sometimes, the door is stuck ajar, just enough for those who have passed on to reach out to us. All we have to do is open our minds.'

'What about when these ghosts try to kill us?' Stone had asked.

'The dead don't murder people, they have moved beyond the base emotions of our world, they are shadows casting themselves on our perceptions.'

'Why?' Stone had asked, he found himself often asking 'why' of Fyre.

'Why indeed? Perhaps they are trying to help us avoid their fate.'

Fyre found that he had little control of late. His visions had become dark once again. They were more vivid, more frequent, and, at times, more terrifying than ever. He tried to control his fear. This was something he had become quite adept at, but it led him to become distant from his own emotions. He was a worried man. Something potent was trying to engage him, something more than the spirit of a departed soul. He moved his head from side to side slowly, seeing through the clothes and flesh of the crowd.

The living stood out like iridescent lights, some a bright young white that moved smoothly across the floor. Other were a darkening yellow, an older, fading light, and some were a flickering dirty flaxen colour. Fyre could see the aged, the sick, the dying as they moved around him. But he could see much more than that. It was only a few moments, but the vision allowed him see another colour. A series of black shades, moving above the whites and yellows of the living. The souls of the recently departed, clinging to the living in a hopeless battle against the inevitable.

Some of the shades he could see were little more than whisps, formless smoke, dissipating before his eyes. But there were one or two others that were different. Darker, thicker clouds formed over some living persons. He could see body shapes, faces appearing and disappearing into the melee of smoke, as if screaming in silent pain.

As his eyes moved across the concourse and his vision narrowed, near to the point he knew it would stop, he spied a new brighter light. He watched the light move closer to him, its glare forcing him to narrow his eyes, even though all this was happening in his mind.

As the bright light approached and the crowd of passengers thinned, in-between trains arriving and departing, he began to see the familiar shade of a spirit. This was no formless shape, no wavering face, appearing for a moment then dissolving into smoke. Fyre could see a small child, no more than a toddler. The vision hung over the light of the living, buzzing like a moth around a flame. Fyre could see the face of the child, its sunken eyes, its gaping mouth, and a tiny hand that reached out to him, coming within inches of touching his own face.

'Fyre! You alright?'

Stone stood right in front of him. The vision was gone. 'John,' he managed to mumble.

Stone was outwardly a sceptic about all of Fyre's claims. But he had seen enough in their short association, that inside he knew there was something going on. Something he couldn't explain with logic. Something he couldn't fight with his fists or his gun.

'If you'll forgive the cliché, you look like you've seen a ghost,' Stone grinned.

'More than one.'

Stone had a sinking feeling, again. Without thinking about it, he touched the pocketbook and pistol.

'Is it like the last time?' he asked.

He knew Fyre would know what he meant; just over a year ago the spirits of murdered women had appeared to Fyre. This is what he claimed anyway, although he could offer Stone no tangible evidence.

'Yes ... and no. There's something different happening. Connections I haven't made yet. I fear that something sinister is about to reveal itself and I'm not sure I know how to prepare for it.'

Stone could see that his friend was genuinely worried.

'I've got a gun, and you could always poke them with that silly cane of yours,' he jested.

Fyre gave a half-hearted smile, just as a guard's whistle sounded.

'That'll be us,' said Fyre. 'I had Bertie take all my bags down earlier this morning. What about you? Is your luggage onboard?'

'Luggage!' exclaimed Stone, 'How long is this going to take?'

Fyre rolled his eyes, 'I would imagine it will take a week, or perhaps more.'

'A bloody week outside of Dublin!' Stone's raised voice drew some interesting looks from the passing crowd.

Fyre spoke softly, trying (but failing) to hide his frustrations from Stone.

'I would have thought that you, Detective Stone, would have surmised that we were not going to seaside for a daytrip.'

'Well, you *surmised* wrong,' said Stone through his teeth.

A second whistle was sounded, and the guard began to call for a last boarding of the Kinsale train.

'Right,' said Fyre, 'it is of no matter, I have packed enough clothes for both of us.'

Fyre walked off in the direction of the train. Stone followed him, complaining all the way.

'I'm not wearing your clothes, I'd look like an idiot.'

'Meaning I look like an idiot?' asked Fyre idly.

'No! … well, yes, but no. Oh, for crying out loud, Fyre, you could have told me!'

The District Asylum was a vast building. Its upper floors were bathed in light from windows large and grand enough to grace any great country house or royal palace. The corridors were wide, and the ceilings seemed impossibly high.

Stretching out from either side of the main block, two four storey wings formed a U-shape around the gardens. From the tip of one of these wings a chapel jutted out into the surrounding lawns. The chapel was neo-gothic in style, fitting in seamlessly with the rest of the asylum buildings.

Inside the chapel, the tall unadorned windows let in a plain light that moved across the red titled floor as the sun circled the building.

'Chaplain?' came a questing voice from the darker reaches of the nave, where the sunlight had not yet penetrated.

The chaplain was standing in deep contemplative silence, watching the linear divide of sun and shadow move across the floor. The light was just a few inches from his feet. He was only aware of time passing because of the approaching line of illumination. His thoughts were profound, concentrated, and worried.

'Chaplain?' a young, nervous voice asked again.

'I'm here, Michael, come into the light, it's not good for you to be walking around in the darkness. … It's not good for anyone.'

Michael appeared in the bright sunlight, like a small goblin caught above ground for the first time. He squinted and held his palm up over his eyes.

'There you are, sir, I've been sent from the Chief Surgeon's office.'

The chaplain was a man of few words, outside of his sermons which could be long and rambling. He was a busy man, he gave service twice a day, once for the women patients, once for the men. On Saturdays he gave service for the staff, which, Doctor Barry insisted, was mandatory for everyone to attend.

He delighted in quoting obscure parts of the Bible to his flock. He delighted even more in the free hand he was given to explain such quotes at length. His explanations were often of his own devising, but, as his role here fell under no bishop or primate, he was free to indulge his fantasies and conspiracies.

Since Doctor Barry had arrived, the young lord-to-be was a revelation. He had new, untried, and interesting methods of dealing with patients, even those with the most severe mental disorders. The chaplain had taken Michael under his wing from the first day he was elevated from being a regular patient to being a trustee. It was something Doctor Barry openly encouraged.

With a gentle smile on his face, the chaplain took in his ward. Michael was short, thin, but had knotted muscles on his arms and chest. He appeared misshapen, as if he was put together wrong. His head was far too big for his body, his jaw jutted out and his teeth were crooked and coated brown. His eyes were sunk deep into the sockets, and, although they shone a sapphire blue, they darted around constantly and made his appearance even more disturbing.

'Tell me, Michael, what do you think of our esteemed Chief Surgeon?'

'Not for me to say, sir,' replied Michael, his nerves making his voice quiver.

'Come now,' said the chaplain, as he stepped into the light, 'this is a safe place, anything you say to me will never be heard by another living soul.'

Michael had to look up at the chaplain. He was six-foot-four, thin, middle-aged but handsome, so that a guess at his actual age could only be framed between fifty and sixty-five.

He had long, kind face, with a pointed nose and thin pink lips that seemed to smile constantly, even when he was in full flow on the pulpit.

'Well, as you asked me, sir, I think it's very unnatural. I think the dead should be left alone, sir. They should return to God as whole as they lived. If you know what I mean, sir.'

'I know exactly what you mean, Michael.' The chaplain reached out his hand and patted Michael on the shoulder.

'I suppose our esteemed Chief Surgeon wants you to bring over the late Miss Downey?'

'Err, yes, sir, he does.'

The chaplain spun on his heels and looked to the back of the chapel, where a handcart was covered by a long linen sheet.

'Did he say anything else?' asked the chaplain.

'I find it very hard to understand what the gentleman says, what with him been foreign and all. The gentleman ... I mean doctor, said something about cause of death.' Michael stuttered his words.

'Doctors cure people,' the chaplain said the first words so softly that Michael didn't quite hear him, 'as for the cause of death, I would have thought that the belt she managed to obtain and wrap around her young neck was evidence enough.'

'Yes, sir, I helped cut her down when they found her.'

'You're a good man, Michael,' the chaplain said.

Michael stood in the light behind the chaplain for what seemed to him to be an age. The chaplain stared off into the shadows of the Chapel, and Michael could hear him humming to himself.

'Sir?' he finally became brave enough to say.

'Ah, yes, you'd better take the young Miss Downey off for her appointment.'

'Yes, sir.'

'No doubt the other patients are locked up for the afternoon?'

'Oh, yes, sir, that's why Doctor Barry says to do it now, so that wheeling her through the building won't cause any distress to anyone, sir.'

'I see,' said Chaplain, then muttered to himself, 'how considerate of Doctor Barry.'

'I suppose he thinks it for the best, sir.'

'Yes. Tell me, Michael, did Doctor Barry order you to bring Miss Downey to the Chief Surgeon?'

'Yes, sir.'

'Himself, in person?'

'Yes, sir.'

'Interesting.'

Michael cautiously stepped by the chaplain and began

to move the gurney down the aisle.

He stopped abruptly beside the chaplain and asked, 'Sir, if I were to die in here, you won't let him cut me up like what he'll do to this lady here, now?'

The chaplain gave him a comforting smile and replied, 'No, Michael, I assure you, when you meet our maker, you will be wholly you.'

'Thank you, sir, that's been irking me something terrible at night. I've had terrible dream and all.'

'So have I, but dreams pass.'

'They do, sir, oh is there anything you want me to say to the Chief Surgeon?'

'I have two daughters, virgins both of them. Let me bring them out to you and you could do what you like with them. But do nothing to these men because they have come under the shelter of my roof.'

The chaplain spoke with reverence, his voice rising at the end.

'Is that from the good book, sir?'

'It is, Michael, can you remember it.?'

'Oh, yes, sir, I remember everything, everything anyone ever says to me. Doctor Barry says my brain works differently.'

'That is does.'

The chaplain watched Michael wheel the body of the young woman out of the chapel and into the corridors of the main building.

'I fear Doctor Barry's brain is working differently too,' he said to himself, as the shadow of a large crow resting on the window threw a fluttering blackness over his face.

CHAPTER 5

F yre was quiet as the train pulled away from the
platform and parts of suburban Dublin drifted by the
window.

Stone had seen all of this before. His intelligent mind
made constant calculations about everything around him, but
somehow Fyre remained an enigma. Stone wanted to believe
everything he said, but his logical way of thinking wouldn't let
him admit that, not even to himself.

'You see that tunnel over there?' Stone asked. He
pointed out of the window.

Fyre turned his head and peered out. 'Is it the Phoenix
Park tunnel?'

'Yes. I used to hide out there as a kid.'

'What were you hiding from?' Fyre asked, but from the
tone of his voice, Stone could tell that his mind was far away.

'Dragons.'

'I see … what?'

Stone laughed. The train was now clear of the city's
edge and began to pick up speed. As Fyre had promised they
were in a private compartment and being separated from the
throng of third class and the stuffiness of second class made

Stone relax into his seat. He was able to sink into himself for the first time in weeks.

'A penny for your thoughts?' asked Stone.

Fyre didn't answer for a few moments; he continued to stare out of the window. He reached into his jacket pocket and produced the letter from Matthew Barry.

'Read this.'

Stone read the letter. Then, without a word in-between, read it again.

'This fella sounds crazy.'

'That's what I thought.'

'Floating dark spirits, the dead walking among the living, voices from the graves. Frankly, Fyre, I think dragons in the Phoenix Park tunnel sounds more likely. Are you really taking this job on based on this?'

'There's more.'

'Visions and spirits?' asked Stone.

Fyre snorted. Stone was trying not to let his natural cynicism creep into his voice, but he was failing.

'Yes, visions. But as I said, these are different, I'm not sure about spirits.'

'Different how?'

Fyre turned his head away from the window and smiled at his friend. 'Am I under interrogation?' he asked jokingly.

'Once a policeman, always a policeman.'

'Alright then, officer. The last time I had visions like this, it was the spirits of recently murdered women.'

'So you claim.'

'Yes,' replied Fyre as calmly as he could, 'So I claim. But these apparitions are somehow more organic. It seems to me as if they are not dead at all, but they're close to it.'

'So the living are appearing in your dreams?'

'Living, but not really living, as if they were halfway between life and death. Trapped, disfigured, … tortured.' He paused and then added, almost to himself, 'In purgatory.'

'That doesn't sound good. Could this letter have sparked these … visions?'

Again Fyre had to ignore Stone's natural cynicism.

'No, the first vision came before the letter arrived.'

'Coincidence?'

'You know, Stone, I don't believe in coincidence. Everything is interconnected, we only have to see beyond the apple we are eating to perceive the tree.'

'And beyond the tree to see the forest?'

'How did you know that?'

'You're sometimes so predictable,' Stone laughed. Fyre joined in. Behind their intense working relationship they had nurtured a close bond that neither of them would openly admit to.

'Have you eaten?' asked Fyre..

'No,' replied Stone.

Fyre opened a small wicker basket, he opened it to reveal a spread of sandwiches, pickles and potted preserves.

Stone ate greedily, while Fyre picked at a few crumbs of food. They both watched rural Ireland fly by the window, occasionally a gust of wind would drive a grey plume of smoke from the engine across their view, but largely the scenery outside was lush and pretty.

'There's a round stone tower of there,' said Fyre absentmindedly.

Stone was busying himself with the paperwork Fyre had brought with him in a large brown envelope.

'I often wondered what it would be like to live in such a tower. High above the world, locked away in splendid isolation.'

Stone didn't answer. He glanced up from his reading and saw the finger of stone protruding from the patchwork greens of the landscape. He had seen round towers like it, there were several on the outskirts of Dublin. He knew they were monastic sites, ancient and abandoned. He didn't understand what Fyre meant by splendid isolation, he had always associated these places with fear, paranoia and a world cloaked in superstition.

'This is interesting,' Stone said as he spread several official documents across the table. 'Where did you get these?'

'A mutual friend.'

'North?'

'The same. He has a secretary who copies documents for storage, these are those copies. He assured me that no one would notice they were gone.'

'According to this, Dublin Castle were very interested in the finances of the Barry family.'

Stone ran his fingers down the lines of bank account numbers.

'Specifically their finances in the last three years, which appear to have taken a dramatic upturn.'

'Very dramatic, if I'm reading this right; just a few years ago they were broke.'

'I believe the phrase is land rich – cash poor.'

'Very cash poor. And yet, they have been the main contributor to several large public projects. Hospitals, workhouses, old soldiers' homes, the list goes on and on. There's no way they could afford all this.'

'There's more,' said Fyre, 'Lord Barry has hosted several large family weddings, gala dinners, balls, and has bought back or bought up vast amounts of prime land around his estates.'

'Did he find a pot of gold somewhere?'

Fyre reached down to seat beside him and took a second large envelope up to the table. He emptied the contents.

'Newspaper clippings,' said Stone.

'Engagements, weddings, births. In the last six years the Barrys have been very busy. A large extended family has been married off to other wealthy families in droves. And they have benefited from the deaths of several landed gentry, even when their connection with them was tenuous.'

'That could explain where all the money had come from.'

'Perhaps,' agreed Fyre, 'what is doesn't explain is how

a minor, largely forgotten noble family have unexpectedly become the most influential family in the whole country.'

'That's why Dublin Castle was interested?' asked Stone.

'I guess so. There is one more strange thing about all these reports gathered by the Castle.'

'Go on.'

'The investigation was closed down, suddenly, about two months ago.'

'You think this Lord Barry could have pulled some strings?' asked Stone: he was aware of how Ireland's upper classes remained as powerful as they clearly were.

'No, someone else did. In London; the order came straight from an office in Whitehall.'

'Maybe Lord Barry has a friend in Civil Service,?'

'This order didn't come from government, it came from the Lord Chamberlain's Office, with a Royal seal.'

Stone was confused. It was one of those rare occasions when he could not immediately put the lines of a puzzle together. Fyre could see it in his face.

Fyre leaned forward, 'It means, my friend, that someone in the Royal circle wanted the Barry family left alone.'

'Oh dear!'

Fyre smiled, 'Oh dear, indeed.'

Melisa disliked Rathmullen house intensely. It was almost two-hundred years old and was showing its age. But, as much as she disliked the house they now lived in, it wasn't Castle Barry, and for that she was grateful.

'Are you going to tell me what's going on?' asked Charles as their carriage pulled up in front of the house.

'Not yet, I want you to see it for yourself.'

The house was once a grand affair. Built before Castle Barry, which stood a few miles away, it was the first grand house in the area and had been in the Barry family's possession since the seventeen-fifties. When they had first arrived back in Ireland for Charles to take up his post,

Melisa's heart had sank on seeing Rathmullen House.
Charles, in his quiet but overbearing way, had insisted they
live there. At first Melisa had thought that it was to keep her
from the extended family and all the drama that went with
them, but as time went by she realised that Charles's decision
was purely financial.

The faded red brickwork of Rathmullen, clad by
eroded limestone and punctuated with two rows of dark
windows that appeared too small for the scale of the house,
grew in Melisa's mind to represent the Barry family itself. All
of the glory of the neo-gothic castle further down the valley
was for show, but the reality was Rathmullen House, a
crumbling home filled with damp and dusty relics.

As they got out of their carriage, Charles waved over
to two men in brown clothes, who were carrying planks of
wood through the nearby outbuildings of the house.

'Are those the men your father sent to do the repairs?'
Melisa asked. She knew it would take more than two men
with hammers and saws to restore Rathmullen House to its
former glory.

'Yes, father said there would be enough in the annual
budget this year to start the renovations of the house.'

'That means we're staying here then?'

Her question was very loaded. They had had several
arguments about the house. Charles had become angry,
which was unlike him. But he had assured her each time that
the family's fortunes were on the up, and that if she was still
not happy they could find somewhere else to live.

'We have enough in savings now that we could
probably get a small townhouse in Kinsale.' Charles spoke as
if he was trying to be offhand.

Melisa wasn't going to let this comment go by
harmlessly.

'Then we could move, to a less ...' she hesitated.

Charles jumped in with the same old argument they
had had before, 'It's just, Father gave us this place for free ...'

Melisa cut him off before he began to repeat the whole
story again. He knew she was unhappy, and she understood,

but disliked, his often-neurotic sense of family loyalty.

'Never mind that now. Come inside and let me show you what I've found.'

Charles beamed at her, he was acutely aware of the sacrifices she had made for his sake. A townhouse in the busy port of Kinsale was little reward, but, right now, it was all he could offer her.

As the young Barrys climbed the steps into the house, the workmen spied on them through a windowless frame in what would have once been the stables.

'Do you think he's like the old man?' asked one of them.

'I doubt it, Mr Potts,' replied the second man. He was large, over six foot and barrel chested.

'Looks like the old man, Mr Grey,' said the first man, who was skinny, short, and spouted a grey and black beard that looked like tangled wire. His face was unnaturally lined and his teeth black and rotten down to little more than stumps.

'Looks can be deceptive, Mr Potts; it's what's inside that matters.'

Mr Potts sniggered and said, 'Yeah.'

'Do we have to go up on this blasted roof?'

'We do indeed, Mr Potts, can't have anything nasty happening to young Lord Charles' pretty wife, now can we!"

Mr Grey's accent was a forced London cockney twang over what was once a west of Ireland voice.

Mr Potts had an English accent too, but with a strong Midlands drawl. .

'She's a curious one, Mr Grey.'

'That she is, Mr Potts, that she is.'

Several miles away on the rocky coast, Holt was walking around Garretstown House. He checked each room, carefully observing the contents. The house had four floors. The basement consisted of a large open kitchen, several pantries, and a completely empty wine cellar. The top floor was empty too, several small rooms with undressed single beds.

The main two floors of the house had been kept in good order. Although the furniture and fittings were old, they were well looked after. Holt could see that William Egan and his valet had taken two rooms on the second floor. Several large suitcases had been recently packed, and it appeared as if Mr Egan was planning to leave the house.

Without causing much disturbance, Holt searched the belongings of both men. The only thing of interest he found was a series of letters between lawyers. These gave him no new information. He already knew all about William Egan and his sudden and reluctant acquisition of Garretstown.

From the main bedroom window, he watched his driver drag the body of the old valet to the back of the house.

Holt wanted to set a trap. Killing the old man wasn't necessary, but it left no loose ends. He had found that, in his line of work, it was better to leave a trail of dead bodies than a trail of evidence. He reloaded the missing bullet in his pistol, then began to change from his plain suit and put on the clothes of the dead valet. He knew that this ruse would almost certainly not work, but he was counting on it not working. He wanted to cause a panic. To flush out his prey.

Across the small bay from Garretstown House, Constables Murphy and Owens were climbing through the undergrowth to reach higher ground.

'This seems a bit much, Cieran.'

'I just want to have a look. Here, here's a good spot.'

They reached a flat point on the path that followed the treeline along a low hill beside the road. There was a gap between two acorn trees which gave an excellent view of the front of the house.

'He's gone inside, he could be hours. Let's get back to the barracks, Cieran,' panted Constable Owens as he leaned against the trunk of a tree.

'Somethings not quite right with that fella.'

'He had a warrant card!'

'That could be a fake.'

'You think?'

'Quiet, Frank, someone's coming out.'

They strained their eyes and watched a man in a black suit emerge from the side of the house. He stopped in the drive and looked around for a few moments before leaning down and grabbing the dead valet by the legs and dragging him away.

'Bloody hell! Is that the old fella?'

'Yeah,' said Constable Murphy, not taking his eyes off the movement a few hundred yards away.

'You don't think he' s …'

'If he's not dead, Frank, then he's a very deep sleeper.'

'What'll we do? Do we go back down there and arrest him?'

Constable Murphy didn't answer for a long moment. He watched the man dragging the obviously dead body away, until he could not see him anymore.

'No, we go back to the barracks and talk to the sergeant. I knew this would be trouble.'

CHAPTER 6

Stone had never been so far from Dublin. When he stepped off the train at Kinsale he said to Fyre that the air tasted strange.

'No soot being pumped into your lungs, my dear friend,' replied Fyre.

'I don't like it.'

Fyre hailed a hackney cab from roadside outside the train station. At first the driver seemed unwilling to take them the fifteen or so miles out to Castle Barry, but the sight of Fyre's pocketbook bulging with fresh notes changed his mind.

'This Matthew Barry, who is he exactly and what does he do?' asked Stone, as the carriage trotted along a coast road, then turned sharply to follow a wide shallow river.

'He is the current Lord Barry's nephew. His mother married a merchant who made a small fortune from importing cheap materials from the Americas. And, as far as I know, he does nothing.'

'A rich layabout?' asked Stone with a raised eyebrow and a wry grin.

'If you are suggesting that he and I are of the same ilk … then I am afraid you are correct. He seems to have spent most of his time at parties. Educated at Eton, a short spell at Trinity, an even shorter one at Oxford, after which he seems to have settled into spending his late father's money.'

'Has he spent it all?'

'Apparently so, Lord Barry acquired his house, along this coast, for a very miserly sum. It seems Matthew Barry-French, to give him is full name, moved into the Castle, under the strict watch of his uncle. He states in his letter that his mother-in-law had died, and he feared she was going to leave him her house.'

'Why would he fear that?'

'He doesn't say, only that he pleaded with her not to leave it to him.'

'I read that bit and I still think the man sounds crazy.'

'I have to admit it does sound strange.'

'What about his wife? She's not mentioned in this letter.'

'Elizabeth French. It seems young Matthew partied a little too much. There's nothing much about her. Other than she no longer lives with Matthew Barry. Her whereabouts weren't mentioned.'

'And all this is in the report by Dublin Castle's spies?'

Stone was only too aware, that in this age of paranoia in Ireland, spies were believed to be everywhere. Sometimes that was true.

'Most of it is in the report, but the gossip lines of the idly rich filled in the rest. Madam French, Matthew Barry's mother-in-law, still lived in the house until her death a few weeks ago.'

'What's the house called?'

'Garretstown House.'

Stone sat in silence for a long period, watching the countryside go by.

Finally Fyre spoke. 'You think this is another wild goose chase, don't you, John?'

Stone kept his eyes on the passing landscape. They had turned away from following the river inland, crossed over a headland and were now driving down toward the coast once more.

'I'm getting paid, aren't I?' Stone replied.

'You still think you could have saved that girl?' asked Fyre.

'I don't think about it at all,' Stone answered quickly.

'You're a terrible liar, John.'

Stone watched the cliffs of a rugged coast come into view; his eyes never left them.

'I know,' was all he said.

They travelled the rest of the journey in silence. Neither of them was uncomfortable in silence, and both of them were deep in their own thoughts.

Inside Rathmullen House, Melisa and Charles made straight through the hall and into what was once a fine drawing room.

'You've certainly changed this place,' Charles said. It was only now that he realised how much time he had been spending at work. His passion for his innovative techniques at the asylum had meant he worked all the hours he could. He would come home, have dinner with Melisa, who often had to sit up until near midnight, and then go straight to bed. Six days a week, with the exception of Sundays; this seemed to be his life now.

As he looked around the long room filled with glass tubes and laboratory equipment, he suddenly had a realisation that he was neglecting his wife, and her work.

'I've been working here most days, I barrowed some books from your father's library, and he ordered some from Dublin for me, but they haven't arrived yet.'

'Where did you get all the equipment?' Charles reached out and touched an elaborately interconnected set of glass tubes, the coloured liquid inside bubbled at his touch and he snapped his hand back.

'You are silly, Charles, and very inattentive. Especially of me.'

'Oh sorry, my dear, I forgot, father allowed you to take what you wanted from my mother's collection.'

'She was more than a collector, Charles, you do your

late mother a great disservice. She was a dilettante pharmacist, but talented.'

'Not as talented as you, dear.' Charles's eyed more bubbling beakers. 'Is it safe to leave these like this?'

'Quite safe,' replied Melisa. 'Your mother was a genius. It is hard to believe she was completely self-taught, she was far more talented than I. I inherited her notebooks too.'

'Father said she wanted to publish a book, someday, but everyone one in the family was against it.' Charles grinned at her, knowingly. 'As you'd expect from my family.'

'Indeed.' Melisa smiled, but it was a laboured smile. 'I think she could have written a book, and one that would have changed our view on medicine.'

'Father said that she was more interested in witchcraft than medicine,' Charles said, idly.

'Do you always quote your father in reference to your mother?'

'He's the only reference I have.'

Melisa could see that this question had disturbed her husband, so she quickly moved on.

'Well, in this case, your mother was on to something. You see we're discovering that a lot of the herbs and weeds used in European witchcraft actually have strong medicinal properties. Those crazy old women from the storybooks weren't as mad as they seemed. Perhaps a few of them in your fancy new asylum aren't mad either.'

Charles's face took on a stiff look of disapproval, 'I doubt that,' he said seriously.

'Oh Charles, cheer up, you've become such a Barry!'

'Darling, don't say that.'

'Look here, in your mother's notes.'

An ear was pressed up against one of the doors of the drawing room of Rathmullen house. The person listened with great care to Melisa explaining to her husband how his mother had discovered natural chemicals that could alter human perception, and even alter the physical state of a human body.

'I thought most of these herb mixtures damaged the mind?' asked Charles. He couldn't really make head nor tails out of his mother's notes, or from Melisa's typed additions.

'Yes, and no,' she was getting frustrated at his lack of ability to grasp what she was showing him.

'So is it yes, or no?'

'Charles, you've got to get your head out of Cambridge and their stuffy old ideas. Not everything is black or white.'

'Some things are grey?'

'Yes, grey, if you like. The mind is not always logical, you said that, and neither is nature. The two can work as one. There are holes in your mother's research, largely because she couldn't put her theories into practice. But you and I can.'

Charles let out a nervous laugh. 'Are you saying what I think you're saying?'

'I'm saying your mother was on the brink of discovering cures for illness we thought incurable.'

'You're saying you want to experiment on my patients, with flowers and parsley.'

'Don't be so crude, Charles. I'm saying we have a chance to make people's lives better. This is groundbreaking.'

'You cannot just use a patient like a test tube.'

'You do!'

'I'm trained for this. I'm employing new techniques to unlock the human mind.'

'How is that different from this,' Melisa hadn't noticed that both their voices were rising with annoyance.

'It just is.'

'That's not a reason.'

'This is witches on broomsticks and boiling frogs' legs in cauldrons; it's not the same.'

'And I suppose beating people with sticks while you look on is better!' Melisa screamed.

There was a tense silence in the room. Charles took in a deep breath.

'I think we have both said enough here,' he said.

Melisa wanted to scream at him more. But she held her voice and turned away from him.

'I won't let this go, Charles, If I were a man you would listen to me.'

Charles didn't answer, he walked out of the room and out of the front door of the house.

Melisa watched his carriage pull away. He would stay late tonight at work; he always did that when they fought. It was becoming an increasingly common occurrence.

She closed her main notebook and patted it on the cover as if it were a beloved family pet. Slowly she walked over to a door which led to the servants' hallways at the back of the house.

'Did you hear all of that?' she asked.

A thin voice whispered back, 'Yes.'

'Ready that next patient. We're close. I can feel it,' spoke Melisa through the door.

'As you wish.'

Murphy and Owens arrived back at their small, two room station house in the nearby village.

They had both grown up in the area, work was scarce at times, and they found that enlisting in the rural Constabulary was better than slaving in the fields of the many large estates that ringed this coast.

There were downsides to the jobs. As constables of the law they were naturally mistrusted by the local communities, who had a long history of isolation and hatred of British rule. Both men found themselves ostracised from their own people, and increasingly, as tensions rose across the country, from their own families.

'The Sergeant's carriage is here,' said Owens.

'He's not due to be here today,' replied Murphy, much to himself, 'there's definitely something up.'

The sergeant, who moved around from parish to parish, was just inside the door. He was a large, gruff, Cork City man, a Presbyterian who took his religious convictions into every part of his life.

'Where've you two been? I've been sending messages to you all morning,' the Sergeant asked.

It was hard for Murphy to gauge the Sergeant's mood from his tone, he always sounded displeased, but now there was a positive concern in his question.

'We've been up at Garretstown House, a missing person. The new owner didn't come home last night,' said Murphy.

'I'm sure he'll turn up,' the Sergeant replied quickly, 'and we have more pressing matters. There's a man from London about, a detective Holt.'

'We just met him,' blurted out Owens.

'Really? Where?'

Murphy and Owens exchanged concerned glances.

'That's why we came back from Garretstown, actually. He turned up there, with a driver and a warrant card, said that this missing Egan man was his case,' said Murphy.

'And you just left him there?' asked the Sergeant, his voice rising in an unaccustomed manner.

'He had all his papers sir, said he's come from Dublin Castle,' replied Owens.

'Oh there's word about him from the castle all right, an arrest warrant for him, all the way from Scotland Yard, no less,' the Sergeant wiped his brow with his handkerchief, 'he arrived in Kinsale yesterday, brandishing the same cards and papers.'

'So he's a fake?'

'No,' said the Sergeant, 'he's a real detective, from the real Scotland Yard, but a week ago he shot three men dead in a house in west London.'

'Bloody hell!' said Owens.

'Oh, dear,' said Murphy.

The Sergeant looked at his constables with real concern on his face, 'Has something happened?'

'That's why we're back here, we were going to telegraph you for help, we think someone up at Garretstown is in trouble, real trouble,' replied Murphy.

After they had explained in great detail their meeting with Holt and their spying from a distance, the Sergeant had to sit down for a while to gather himself. He was a panicky man, who found rural police best suited to his nature when he was dealing with lost cattle or stolen carts.

'What are we going to do?' he asked Owens.

Cieran Murphy, whose nature was a lot calmer than his colleagues', took the lead on their course of action.

'First, send a message to Kinsale for more men, then we three will go out to the house and see if he's still there,' said Murphy.

'What do we do if he is still there?' the Sergeant asked, as if he were asking a superior.

Murphy picked his words carefully. He was getting frustrated at the whole situation.

'Then we arrest him. That's our job.'

'Shouldn't we wait for more men?' asked Owens.

'It'll take at least an hour and a half for men to get from Kinsale to here. Garretstown is only four miles away, we'll go there now, and see what we can do,' Murphy said deliberately.

'Are you sure?' asked the Sergeant.

'We have family living along that coast, we can't let a madman with a gun run around … can we?' Murphy stressed the last few words.

After a pause, the sergeant checked his sidearm with a shaking hand and replied, 'Yes, yes, let's go and see what we can do.'

CHAPTER 7

F yre paid the driver and tipped him handsomely. The
man had barely said 'thank you' before he urged his
horse on and left them at the gate.

Stone looked up at the towering gatehouse of Castle
Barry. It was three storeys high and looked like a medieval
castle with turrets, battlements, and a thick wooden gate,
studded with metal bolts, that stood over twenty feet tall.

'If this is their front entrance, what's the house like?'
asked Stone.

'Pretty impressive, I've heard. I've seen sketches of it in
a book of Irish grand houses. It seems that every generation
of the Barry family has added something to the house. It has
sort of spread with age, like an old man with a paunch.'

Stone pointlessly pushed at the massive door with his
hand.

'What do we do now, Fyre? It's locked. I thought these
estates were always open? Irish upper-class hospitality and all
that nonsense.'

'So did I,' mused Fyre, 'I telegraphed a reply to
Matthew Barry before we left Dublin; he should be expecting
us.'

While Stone wandered around the side of the building, Fyre stood still, his eyes transfixed on the neogothic battlements of the gatehouse. He could feel a presence, one that had been with him since his first vision, the night before Matthew Barry's letter arrived. This presence wasn't like the lost spirits of the departed that he had felt many times before, it was softer, more like a background hum that occasionally spiked.

Fyre tried to focus on the inaudible voice in the back of his mind, but it simply wouldn't come forward.

'Fyre!'

Fyre realised Stone had been calling him from the side of the gatehouse.

'Have you found something?'

'Yeah, there's a low wall here, it's covered in brambles, but I think I can scramble over.'

Stone disappeared again behind a wall of grey masonry. Fyre grinned as he heard Stone give commentary as to his slow progress over the wall and through the undergrowth.

The door of the gatehouse opened, and the face of an elderly man poked out.

'Can I help you, sir?' asked the man in a heavy Cork accent.

'Ah yes, good man, I'm a guest of the Barry family, are they at home?' Fyre asked.

'Oh yes, sir, his Lordship is at home, and other family too. I'll just get the carriage hooked up and take you down to the house, sir. I wasn't told you were coming, sir, I do apologise, I was at my tea.'

'That's quite alright, we arrived late.'

'We, sir?' asked the man, opening the gate a little more and looking about from someone else.

Just before Fyre could answer, Stone called out, 'Oh feck it!'

Fyre smiled, 'My colleague, he likes to do things the hard way.'

'I see, sir, you'd better come through.'

Fyre walked through the gate. On the inside there was a small door which was opened to a modest kitchen. Fyre could smell bacon burning in a pan and said to the gatekeeper, 'You'd better take that off the stove before you hook up the horse.'

'Ah yes, sir, I will do. Just a moment.'

Just as he spoke they could hear Stone battling through head-high reeds and saplings.

'Your friend, sir, does he need a hand?'

'Oh no,' replied Fyre, 'he's an expert at this sort thing.'

Stone popped out of the thicket, nursing a cut right wrist. His eyes widened as he saw Fyre standing in the small semi-circular courtyard, smiling at him.

Fyre looked at his dirtied clothes and scratches, 'Pull yourselves together man', he gloated.

'Fyre, you …'

'Stone! Keep calm, we have a lord to meet.'

It was a mile along a winding gravel road from the gatehouse to the main castle. Stone sat in the open trap with a sour look on his face. Fyre peered around, taking note of everything they passed.

'Notice anything odd?' Fyre asked as they trotted along the road.

Stone's quick mind had been working while he huffed. He didn't directly answer Fyre, instead he asked the gatekeeper a question.

'Are there many staff working on the estate? It seems to be wild with plants and devoid of people.'

'Not too many now, sir. There were hundreds back in the day, but there's only a handful now.'

'Does his lordship pay well?' asked Fyre.

There was a long silence, and the gatekeeper's voice betrayed his change of mood.

'Yes, sirs,' was all he said. He didn't speak again until they reached the castle itself.

Whatever grandeur and scale Stone had been expecting was surpassed as they rounded a corner of oak trees and caught their first full sight of Castle Barry.

'Bloody hell,' Stone said under his breath.

'Fit for an Irish prince,' Fyre commented.

The castle did, as Fyre had said, spread out across the landscape.

At its centre, Castle Barry had a tall tower, adorned in an identical style to the gatehouse. The neogothic look continued across the main body of the house, but Greek palatial windows and half-columns broke the medieval illusion. To the right of the main block of the house stood a second large granite block. This second block had small windows, and a colonnade that wrapped around it and continued through an archway and into a wide yard. To the left of the main building a vast glass and iron greenhouse stood, its metal pinnacles and cast-iron flying buttresses mimicking the look of the castle. Beyond the greenhouse was another wing of buildings in the neogothic style; they formed stables and small houses, as if they were a terrace in a city street.

'Impressive,' said Stone as he got down from the trap.

'A mess, if you ask me,' whispered Fyre, so the gatekeeper would not overhear him, 'too much money and not enough taste. I believe the other side of the house is in a completely different style.'

'You know, Fyre, for a posh fella, you really don't like rich people,' commented Stone.

Fyre didn't reply. He half-smiled and pointed his cane to a figure emerging from the main door of the house.

'Official reception?' asked Stone, sarcastically.

The figure came closer. He was dressed in a butler's uniform, with a cropped haircut, which rode up the back of his scalp just a little too far not to be noticed. He stopped short of Fyre and Stone and nodded his head.

'Gentlemen,' his Germanic accent barely covered by an educated English intonation.

'Good afternoon,' replied Fyre, 'I am Lord Fyre. This is my colleague Mr Stone.'

'Hello,' said Stone, as he subconsciously tried to brush

some of the dirt off his coat.

'We are expected,' Fyre went on.

'I am Max, the butler. I'm afraid I was not informed as to your arrival.'

Fyre had silently suspected that their arrival at the behest of one family member might not be overly welcomed.

'I did send a reply to Mr Matthew Barry, giving him the time of our arrival.'

If the butler had any qualms about this statement, his emotionless face showed nothing.

'I see,' he said, 'if you would wait here for a moment, Mr Matthew Barry is in the lounge, I will fetch him.'

'Fetch him!' muttered Fyre to Stone, with a raised eyebrow.

Fyre watched the butler march back across the yard and into the house.

'Is it normal to be left out in the yard like this in one of these houses?' asked Stone.

'No.'

'We did cash his banker's draft, so he must know we're coming.'

'Yes.'

'You're tense,' stated Stone.

'How do you know?'

'You always revert to one-word answers when you're tense.'

Fyre rolled his eyes at Stone, 'Clever!'

'Someone is coming,' said Stone. He took a step behind Fyre, as if hiding behind his well-dressed figure.

'Gentlemen,' said a tall, thin man dressed in a casual tweed suit. He was sporting a flat cap and had a pair of thigh-high riding boots on. A few steps behind him the butler walked, with his hands clasped behind his back.

'Mr Matthew Barry?' asked Fyre.

'Yes,' replied Matthew Barry, he didn't extend a hand or exchange a nodded head; something which both Fyre and Stone noted in their minds.

'And you are the famous Lord Sebastian Fyre and

Detective John Stone. I've read about you, and those murders in Dublin. Who would have thought it, old men killing women for sport.'

'It wasn't just old men,' said Stone flatly.

'Indeed, what can I do for you?' asked Barry.

This question took Fyre a little by surprise, but Stone jumped in.

'We have a letter from you,' said Stone, stepping forward and not caring so much about his soiled clothes, 'you said your life may be in danger, you employed us to investigate a missing person case.'

'A rather unusual missing persons case,' added Fyre.

Stone watched Matthew Barry's face go through a quick set of reactions. It was only a split second, but he saw confusion, near panic and then resolution. Barry turned to his butler who spoke up.

'We have a lot of missing persons around these parts, there is a long history of people falling from the cliffs or being lost in the wilds.'

'And have you been in these parts long?' asked Stone in his usual aggressive manner.

The butler didn't flinch, 'I have been in the service of the Barry family for ten years now, since I arrived from my previous employment in South Africa.'

'This letter,' said Barry, spinning on his heels, his face adorned with a friendly grin for the first time, 'may I see it.'

Fyre took the letter from his pocket and handed it to him. He read it from start to finish, then folded it and held it to his chest.

'I'm afraid, gentlemen, you've been on a wild goose chase.'

'You didn't write the letter?' asked Stone.

'Oh, I wrote the letter, you have my bank draft after all. I'm afraid I was very tired and emotional when I wrote this.'

'Tired and emotional?' asked Fyre.

'He means drunk!' said Stone coldly.

Barry laughed a fake laugh, as if deeply embarrassed.

'I'm afraid Mr Stone is right, I was drunk. My uncle, Lord Barry, is helping me get my life in order. This letter was written at a particularly low point. It's all nonsense.'

'So, there is no case? You're not in fear of your life?' asked Fyre.

Barry laughed again, more heartily this time. 'No, dear chap, as I said I've put you on a wild goose chase. I can only say sorry, but I did pay in advance so perhaps we can chalk this one down to the demon drink and move on. I'll keep the letter, if that's alright; it could be a little awkward for me. You can keep the money of course and I hope you have a nice trip back to Dublin. Now, if you will forgive me gentlemen, I have to speak to my uncle.'

'Then we'll say goodbye, Mr Barry,' Fyre held out his hand and this time Matthew Barry shook it.

Fyre's handshake was unusually firm and just a moment too long to be comfortable. Stone didn't offer his hand and Barry immediately walked away.

The Butler called over the gatekeeper, who ferried Fyre and Stone back down the long gravel drive and left them just outside the main gate, which he closed behind them.

'Well, that's the quickest case we've ever had,' said Stone.

'He was lying,' stated Fyre, as he began to walk down the road, away from the main gate.

'I'd worked that out on my own,' grinned Stone, 'he'd never seen the letter before, that's why he read it the whole way through.'

'That's right, he wasn't aware of the letter. We've put someone's life in danger.'

Stone raced after Fyre.

'What? Whose life is in danger? Is it me?'

'No. The letter says it was entrusted to a local boy from the village. Whoever he is, his life is now in danger.'

Fyre marched on down the road, with Stone walking beside him.

'Hang on a minute, I have questions.'

'Of course you do.'

'One, who is this boy? Two, how do we find him? Three, who is he in danger from? And four, how do you know he's in danger?'

Fyre stopped his progress and addressed all of Stone's questions at once.

'I don't know who the boy is, or how to find him. But, I'm guessing, starting in that small village would be a good idea. This is really your area, so I was hoping you would pitch in. Secondly I believe whoever that fake gentleman was could be dangerous to this boy's wellbeing.'

'Matthew Barry?'

'He was not Matthew Barry. No true gentlemen would refuse to offer formal greetings or hospitality to a guest, especially someone with 'lord' in their name. And when I shook his hand just then, I didn't feel the fear.'

'Feel the fear?'

'Matthew Barry's letter was full of fear, it was not scrawled by the hand of a drunk. It was carefully written by a man fearing for his life and for his soul. That man who shook my hand was not the author of that letter, ergo, he was not Matthew Barry.'

Fyre continued his march to the nearby village. A steeple could be seen rising above the trees a few hundred yards away.

'What about the butler?' asked Stone, as he walked along side.

'He seemed cold,' replied Fyre, 'even for a butler.'

'Do you think we'll get a better welcome in this little country village?'

'I doubt it, but one of us had better come up with a plan soon,' stated Fyre.

'How so?'

'It's getting toward evening; there are no trains here, no cabs for hire. The nearest hotel is in Kinsale.'

'What!' yelled Stone.

Fyre didn't reply for now, he had seen something up ahead.

'Quiet, John.'

Stone was almost shaking with anger. 'You dragged me all way down to the middle of nowhere, and we haven't got a place to stay, or eat?'

'A minor oversight in my planning. I had presumed that the Barry family would obey the unwritten laws of Irish hospitality.'

'You presumed!'

'It's not that farfetched. Now be quiet.'

'Why should I be quiet?' said an angry Stone.

'Because there's a funeral up ahead.'

CHAPTER 8

Holt watched the approaching carriage follow the long coast road that led to Garretstown House. He told his driver to position himself in an archway at the side of the house, while he stood at one of the large first floor windows. He was dressed in the valet's clothes; they were ill-fitting, but he had managed to tuck them in so at first glance no one would notice.

He steadied himself at he opened the door. Outside, the small carriage, with its top folded down, had pulled up and a plump, well-dressed man was tethering the horse to a post.

'Good morning, Mr Egan, sir,' said Holt, 'I was getting concerned for you.'

Mr Egan looked up from his work, he took an almost imperceptible moment to take in Holt and the front of the house, then quickly replied, 'No need for concern, my dear chap.'

'Do you wish me to continue to pack for our return to Dublin tomorrow?' asked Holt as he stood to one side to allow Mr Egan to enter the house.

'Oh yes, Dublin, I want to catch the morning train, so

let's pack everything up.'

Egan took a few steps up into the doorway as he spoke, then without any warning launched an attack.

Holt was on guard for the first blow of Egan's cane. He managed to deflect it away from his face and harmlessly into the heavy wooden door. Egan moved far swifter than Holt expected for a man his age and shape. His second blow was a well-placed elbow into the side of Holt's head which sent him reeling out of the main door. As Holt half-fell down the steps he pulled out his pistol and let a badly aimed shot ring out.

'What the hell was that!' exclaimed the Sergeant as he pulled the trap to a halt just around the bend from the headland where Garretstown House stood like a low monolith against the dark sea.

'Gun fire,' replied Murphy. He subconsciously checked his sidearm. 'Drive the horse on,' he added. Murphy was uncomfortable with guns, they had only been recently issued to all members of the constabulary, and he felt they were symbolic of Ireland's current woes.

After a moment's reluctance, the Sergeant urged the horse forward and they quickly rounded the bend to catch sight of the house just a few hundred yards along the coast.

Holt scrambled to the door, but had to immediately duck back behind the frame as Egan discharged his own gun toward him. The bullet passed out of the door harmlessly and Holt was able to fire back, but Egan has already dived into one of the state rooms. Holt shouted to his driver for help, but didn't wait for a reply. He dashed into the house, smashed his way through a door to the drawing room and dived for the floor as more shots rang out.

Egan fired two shots over his head, they stuck the high cabinets at the back of the room and sent shards of porcelain raining down on the prone figure of Holt. Holt rolled under a table and heard a third shot ring out, this time it seemed to be aimed away from his position.

There was a short silence.

'It doesn't have to be like this,' shouted Holt, as he checked his weapon. Five shots left.

'We can talk,' he went on, all the time edging to one side of a large settee, 'I can help you.'

There was no reply, only a single gunshot rang out again. The bullet broke a glass case to one side of the room.

Holt stood up and aimed the gun at Egan, who was standing in the doorway.

'That's six, you're out.'

Egan's face was full of panic. He pulled the trigger. The gun clicked, but there was no shot. He pulled it again, the result was the same.

'Don't run,' said Holt, he could see in Egan's eyes that this was a pointless request.

Egan ran for the back door of the house. Holt didn't fire, even though he had a clear and probably deadly shot. He rushed after his quarry. Egan had reached the back doors of the house, which were heavy glass in strong wooden frames that ran the height of the room. He rattled the handles, but to no avail. As Holt slowed to a walk and raised his pistol, Egan tried to smash the glass door with the butt of his own gun, but it didn't even make a crack.

'It's no use, I have you,' said Holt, 'whoever you are.'

'Go to hell,' said Egan, his voice slipping from a cultured Dublin accent to an unrecognisable slur.

Before Holt could say another word, Egan's eyes fell on a large and ornate sword which sat on the wall below an equally ornate round shield.

'Don't,' stated Holt, the muzzle of his pistol following Egan as his hand reached out for the ancient weapon. Holt was about to try and reason with the man one more time. Egan had other ideas. He grabbed the sword and rushed at Holt.

A single shot rang out.

Holt looked down to where Egan lay dead at his feet. The sword clanged on the floor just inches from him.

'You idiot,' whispered Holt to himself, 'it's not even a real sword.'

'Don't move!' yelled a voice from the doorway.

Holt didn't move his body, his eyes darted to the left, he could just make out the black uniform of an Irish policeman.

'I'm a copper,' said Holt.

'You're a wanted man,' replied Owens. He had his sidearm out, held high and aimed directly at Holt. His right hand was shaking, so he raised his left hand to steady it.

Holt turned his body slowly, his gun still down by his side, a wisp of smoke drifting from the barrel. He looked into the eyes of the young constable.

'I don't think you'd shoot me, young man. I don't think killing is in your nature. Not like this fella,' he nodded his head downward to indicate to the dead man.

'Don't test me,' said Owens, his voice now shaking and his hands even more so.

'I'm going to walk out the door, get my driver and leave now,' stated Holt.

'I can't let you do that, you murdered this man … and others.'

'Sort of true, but …' Holt laughed, 'why am I bothering, you wouldn't believe me anyway. I'm going now.'

Holt took a step forward.

'Don't move again, or I will shoot you!' Owens screamed.

Holt stopped, but smiled and replied, 'I don't think you will, it's not in your soul.'

'It's in mine,' said a third voice.

The hair on the back of Holt's neck stood up. He could sense the barrel of another pistol at point-blank range behind him. This voice was different, more assured, more dangerous.

'Yes, I think you would,' replied Holt. He dropped his gun to the floor.

'You're under arrest,' said Murphy, his pistol just inches from Holt's head.

Fyre watched the funeral cart approach the church gates then drive straight by and up a country lane. There were only a few mourners, a dozen or so, mostly older women, one older man and one young boy, no older than fifteen.

'Where are they going?' asked Fyre of Stone.

Although Stone had grown up in the city, he knew well what was happening in front of his eyes. He also took great pleasure in filling in the gaps in Fyre's knowledge, it was rare occurrence.

'It's a Catholic funeral, that's a Protestant church. Before the emancipation act Catholics couldn't be buried inside the town boundaries without paying, so they started burying their dead in old places. Ruined churches, old abbeys, even castles.'

'Separated in death as they were in life.'

'Seems a bit silly, doesn't it?'

'Very.'

Fyre starting walking behind the funeral procession.

'Where are you off to?' asked Stone in a whisper as he followed.

'I can hear a voice, very faint, very frightened, but very much here.'

'We don't have time for ghosts and voices.'

'Time is irrelevant to the dead,' stated Fyre and he walked on.

Stone was extremely uncomfortable over the next half an hour.

They stood at the back of the small group of mourners. Their presence could not help but be noticed by everyone, particularly given Fyre's outlandish attire. Despite Stone's lack of faith in religion, he made the sign of the cross as the priest rattled out prayers at a breakneck speed.

Fyre found Stone's reaction to the funeral rather odd, his usual cold demeanour seemed to crumble slightly as the prayers were read and the cheap plank-wood coffin was lowered into an unadorned grave.

As Stone had said, the graveyard was on the outskirts of the town. It stood in raised circle, surrounded by a thick drystone wall. There were grave markers of all kinds sprouting up from the long grass. Large stone tablets with grand inscriptions and heavily carved mortis mori stood side-by-side with simple wooden crosses and uncarved stones.

Beyond the graveyard itself, a large green mound blocked the view of the village. To Fyre this mound looked like it might once have been the base of a motte and baily Norman castle, but it could easily be something much older, an ancient tomb of some long-forgot pagan king. Fyre lacked the knowledge to tell the difference between the two; he supposed most people in Ireland couldn't tell the difference either.

When the prayers had finished, the priest didn't bother with shaking hands and exchanging sympathies, he rushed away from the graveyard and mounted a small trap that had been standing by the roadside.

'Is that normal?' asked Fyre.

'No,' replied Stone, 'something's not right here.'

The small group of mourners stayed only a short while longer. As they moved away from the open grave they shook the hand of the young man, who stayed at the graveside, still and emotionless.

The mourners passed by Fyre and Stone as they left the graveyard. The women didn't raise their eyes from the ground, but the man in the group tugged his forelock and gave the slightest of bows to Fyre.

'Let's pay our respects, shall we?' said Fyre to Stone, and he walked forward a step. Before Fyre could move any further, Stone caught him by the arm.

'This boy has lost someone, don't say anything … stupid.'

Fyre swallowed his displeasure at this statement and simply replied, 'Understood.'

'Hello sir, sirs,' stuttered the boy as the two men approached.

'Our condolences. A close relative?' asked Fyre.

'My only relative, my older sister, Ciara.'

'We are so sorry,' Stone said quickly. He was reluctant to disturb this young man's grief any more than they had already, 'We're visitors in this area, we were just up at Castle Barry.'

'You're guests of his lordship?' asked the boy, his voice still faint, as if in shock.

'Yes,' Fyre exchanged scowling glances with Stone, 'and no, we were supposed to be guests of Mr Matthew Barry, but it seems circumstances have changed.'

The boy's face suddenly lit up, as if he had woken from a dream.

'Oh, you must be Lord Fyre and Mr Stone?'

'Yes,' said Fyre, his mind putting the pieces together quickly, 'and you're the young man who delivered Mr Barry's letter to the postmaster in Kinsale?'

'Yes, Sean Downey.'

Fyre shook Sean's hand again, followed by Stone.

'That's a bit of luck, we were just about to look for you,' Stone had no doubt that Fyre would make some mystical reference to this meeting, but he knew in a small community it was just a coincidence.

'Can you tell me what happened to your sister?' asked Fyre.

Stone threw him a withering stare.

'My apologies,' said Fyre before Sean or Stone could speak, 'my colleague here thinks we are imposing on your grief, I hope that is not the case?'

'No,' stuttered Sean, 'not at all. I don't really know what to say, it's all happened so fast.'

Sean Downey began speaking, his voice still distant, as if in a dream. He told Fyre and Stone about his family. His mother had died just a year ago of consumption, his father had died several years ago in an accident on the Barry estate. Lord Barry had paid for the funerals and the small cottage they had rented was given to them as compensation.

His sister had taken a maid's job in a nearby house, while he worked on the farm of Matthew Barry's home, just a few miles further down the coast.

'They are good jobs,' said Sean earnestly, 'we were glad to get them. When Mr Barry moved back to the castle last year, the house was taken over by his lordship, all the staff were let go except me and one other gardener. We keep the gardens going. They really only use the place for parties and picnics and such.'

All the while Sean was speaking, Fyre had his eyes fixed on the open grave of his sister.

It was very strange; even those who died peacefully in their sleep whispered to him, like the passing breeze of a spirit as it moved from one world to another. But, here at the grave of this young woman, he felt nothing. It was as if she were devoid of a soul. Whatever voice had been trying to reach him earlier in the village, it was not this young woman.

Sean continuing speaking about the Barry family, interrupted only by Stone edging the conversation toward Matthew.

'When he gave you the letter, did he tell you anything of its contents?' he asked.

'No, nothing, just that I was to tell no one. I rode into town early in the morning and was back before breakfast.'

'Was there anything unusual about Mr Barry at the time?'

Fyre woke from his daydream at this question. How like Stone, straight to the point.

'Yes, I thought so. But maybe my own mind wasn't really thinking right, Ciara had just been put into the institution, just a few days earlier. I thought Mr Barry was acting very odd, he was sweating and nervous, but he wasn't drunk.'

'Was he often drunk?' asked Fyre.

Sean hesitated.

Stone added, 'You can be honest with us.'

'Yes,' said Sean simply.

Fyre changed the direction of conversation; he could see the distress on Sean's face.

'This institution, this would be the new asylum they built around here a few years ago?'

'Yes, sir.'

'Was she sick?' asked Stone.

'They said so. After old Miss French died in Garretstown House, they found my sister in the attic, screaming. Just screaming, so they took her up to the big place for a rest. That's what they said it was, a rest. That was just a few weeks ago.'

'Why did the priest rush off like that?' asked Frye.

Stone took and intake of breath. Sean's eyes filled with tears immediately. Fyre, in his innocence, knew he had said something to upset the boy, he looked to Stone for an explanation.

Reluctantly Stone answered the question, 'She committed suicide. No more questions for this young man, let's head back to the village and see what we can do from there.'

They were a sombre trio as they walked down the country lane back toward the small hamlet in silence, the early evening sun beginning its decent behind them.

CHAPTER 9

Melisa had grave doubts in her mind, but she had come too far now to turn back. All of her life had been a struggle to find her way. It was not only the fact that she was a woman that had held her back. The ghosts of her childhood and her life before Cambridge still haunted her. If Charles knew what she was really doing with his mother's research, then he would be more than a little upset. The thought of losing Charles was unbearable. She loved him. It had been a slow, progressive love, that grew out of necessity at first, but became a genuine emotion.

Melisa couldn't begin to explain to Charles the complexity of her life before she had met him, or the passion that had been renewed in her from his mother's work. She had made a deal, it seemed like a reasonable compromise at the time. Now, as she began to realise the power that could potentially be unleashed by her research, it felt more like a deal with the devil.

Melisa changed her clothes, she had kept her laboratory dresses and aprons. She had always disliked the drab garb which seemed to cloak British and Irish women, like a silencing veil. The laboratory she had set up was basic compared to the facilities at Cambridge, the equipment was old, but serviceable. She had several heavy, leatherbound ledgers piled on a side table, these contents, among other things, Lady Barry's notes, compiled over several decades. Lady Barry had not been greedy about sharing her work with others interested in the chemistry of the human brain. And while many of the learned men she contacted indulged her because of her title, the correspondence Melisa found showed that she was largely dismissed. There was one doctor who seemed to recognise the value of her work. Melisa had carefully read through the letters, back and forth, from Doctor Keogh of Portraine. Not only was this eminent professional interested in Lady Barry's work, but he also actively put in into practice with patients in his asylum.

There had been some controversy over the doctor's death. He seems to have been caught up in a vile case habitual homicides in Dublin, just over a year ago, and, rather unfortunately for Melisa, he committed suicide. She read through Doctor Keogh's letters and notes. They were scant on details, and he seemed more interested in Lady Barry's progress than on reporting his own. The letters between them ceased on a certain date twenty-five years ago. It was a date Melisa recognised. Her husband always went into mourning weeks before that date, the loss of his mother still effecting his emotions, as if she had died just days ago.

She took a deep breath, she knew, that on the back of Lady Barry's brilliant work, she was within touching distance of making a drug that could alter the human mind. This would not just alter it, but save it, a new person from the ashes of the old. She thought of those poor wretches up in the asylum, beaten and chained. What if a mind could be brought back from the brink of insanity? What if a criminal, even a murderer, could become a good person?

Melisa felt that she had to take the risks she was taking; what choice did she have? She had made the deal with the devil.

Fyre, Stone and Sean Downey walked slowly down the

graveyard lane toward the village.

Sean was quite talkative, and Fyre, who usually found chatty people bothersome, was able to talk with him freely. Stone kept a stoic silence, but was listening to every word.

'There's been a lot of strange things happening here in recent years,' Sean said.

'We specialise in strange happenings,' commented Fyre.

Stone just rolled his eyes.

They had reached the bottom of the lane, and the sun was now very low in the sky, sending a red glow out across the sea as if it were boiling the water far out to the west.

'I read about you in the papers, I used to get them after Mr Barry had read them,' said Sean, as all three of them subconsciously stopped to admire the sunset.

'Mr Matthew Barry,' said Fyre, his eyes were still fixed on the red lines rising up from the darkening blue sea. 'Do strange things happen around him?'

'Well, Mr Barry was always a bit strange, I suppose, but in a nice way. I always found him a pleasant, for a posh fella … er, no offence sirs!'

Stone snorted and replied, 'Trust me, at least one of us doesn't take offence at that.'

'Neither of us does,' Fyre assured Sean.

'The real trouble started a few years back, just before I went to work at Mr Barry's house. It was when Lord Barry's son returned from England, and they opened the asylum. They said it would bring plenty of work for the local people, and it was a good job too.'

'Why so?' asked Fyre.

'It was about that time that Lord Barry began to close off the estate and let people go.'

'By people, you mean the staff?' asked Stone.

'Yes, sir, he closed off the workshops, the stables were moved to Mitchelstown, there were no more hunts, or parties held in the castle. Can't be more than a few locals working there now, and them is mostly groundsmen.'

'Lord Barry still hosts parties though?'

'Yes, sir, but they're all held down the coast at what used to be Mr Matthew Barry's house, Garryhinch House. That's why he keeps the gardens up and running. That's why I still have a job, sir.'

'I see,' said Fyre, his mind had begun to wander, and a strange sensation was rising in his senses.

'This still leaves us with our problem; how are we going to get back to Kinsale now?' asked Stone.

'I could take the trap from the head gardener, but not until the morning, sirs. And anyway, it's dangerous to travel these roads at night.'

'Robbers? Republican gangs?' asked Stone.

Sean hesitated in his reply, 'No, sir, other things.'

'Other things!' Stone had an inkling what the boy meant by 'other things' but he didn't want to say the words out loud. He looked up to see if Fyre was going to comment, but Fyre had wandered away and was walking toward the Protestant churchyard.

'These other things,' asked Stone as he slowly followed his colleague, 'would they have anything to do with graveyards and the things that supposedly come out of graveyards at night?'

Sean didn't know quite what to say, so he just nodded.

'I knew I should have stayed in Dublin, chasing cats.'

They followed Fyre in silence for a few moments. He stopped at the iron gate of the graveyard.

Fyre placed his hand on the rusted green paint of the gate and closed his eyes. From his time in the far east he could recall the first time he heard voices coming from stonework. There was an inaudible babble of ancient tongues, not directed to him, more like a wax cylinder recording of long dead peoples.

Although he could not hear their words, Fyre could feel the sensation of thousands of souls. They were no longer present in this world; they had long passed onto another place, but they left behind a snapshot, a memory, ingrained in the places they knew well. This is what Fyre heard in his mind at first.

'What's the gentleman doing?' whispered Sean.

Stone was about to answer, then realised if he told the boy what Fyre thought he was really doing, that would sound insane.

'He's listening,' Stone finally managed.

'Does he hear voices?'

'Sort of.'

'My sister said she heard voices. When they found her after Miss French died, she was convinced that the dead were coming to get her.'

Stone could see the sincerity in the boy's face, there was fear too, a real, deep-set fear.

Fyre's mind searched through the mire of whispers. Somewhere inside the graveyard there was another type of voice, a pleading, panicked voice.

'Where is he going?' Sean asked.

Stone checked the gun under his jacket.

'Come on, we'd better stay together, it's getting very dark now.'

Stone entered the graveyard behind Fyre, who was walking slowly along the narrow pathways between graves.

Sean hesitated.

'Don't worry, the dead don't scare me, it's the living I'm worried about.'

'They scare me, sir,' replied Sean.

Stone laughed and asked, 'Do you want to stand out here guarding the gate on your own.' He turned and walked after Fyre.

A moment later Sean was at his heels.

The sun had gone down beyond the horizon and only a thin blue light from the western sky allowed them to see their way. In the eastern sky, stars were beginning to form constellations and a half moon was shining like the white-hot centre of a forge.

Fyre had stopped at a grave and was touching the stone with his hand.

'Ghosts?' asked Stone sarcastically.

'Have you got a match?' asked Fyre, his voice serious

and distant.

Stone retrieved a box of long matches from his coat pocket and stuck one. The orange light burst out and gave a momentarily frightening visage of their own faces.

Sean jumped back a step.

'This is Miss French's grave,' he said.

Stone held the match closer to the grave. It was an old stone, with several names carved on it, dating back as far as 1779. On the bottom of the carving, freshly made, was the name Elizabeth French.

'Coincidence?' asked Stone of Fyre.

'I've told you before, John, there is no such thing as coincidence. When was this lady buried, Sean?'

'A month ago, no wait, six weeks. That's how long my sister was in the asylum.'

Fyre pointed his finger straight down for Stone to follow it. Stone moved the match.

'This is freshly dug.'

He lifted a handful of soil and smelt it. 'Very recent.'

'I don't think Miss French is in this grave,' said Fyre.

Stone wasn't quite following, but he had heard rumours of such things in the past.

'You mean someone stole her body and there's no one in there?'

'Oh,' replied Fyre, his voice still sounding far away, 'there's someone in there alright.'

Just then the flame reached Stone's fingers. He cried out, sending a nearby murder of crows into the air with a terrifying screech.

Despite Stone's protests, they now had no choice but to avail themselves of Sean's hospitality.

The walk back to his cottage took them through the single street of houses that constituted the village. They came across no people, and the only signs of life were the thin black smoke columns rising from the low chimneys above thatched roofs. A single lamp was lit in a small triangular space which marked the centre of the village. A brightly coloured iron water pump stood there beside a stone marker, which looked out of place.

'Have you lived here all your life, Sean?' asked Fyre as they walked.

'Yes, sir, I travelled to Cobh once, to see the tall ships in the harbour.'

'The ones that go to America?' asked Stone nonchalantly. His mind was still processing everything that had happened in the last few days. He had quickly concluded that Fyre was withholding information from him.

Sean answered and there was an innocence to his voice. Although physically he could pass for a grown man, his tone betrayed his childishness. 'Yes, sir, I want to go someday myself. If I can save enough for the fair. Start a new life. They say there are whole mountains of gold waiting to be dug up.'

'I've heard stories of mountains of gold before,' said Fyre, 'they are only ever told by poor men.'

They reached the cottage, it was a small stone-built affair, with a wooden door and two windows to the left and one to the right.

Sean lit a fire of turf and dried sticks, and Fyre and Stone sat down on two of the three plain chairs gathered around the hearth.

'I'm afraid I don't have offer much in the way of food,' Sean said with a genuine degree of embarrassment.

'Anything you can offer us will be most welcome,' said Fyre, 'and of course we will reimburse you for the trouble.'

Sean looked at Stone with a confused face.

'He means we'll pay you for the food and accommodation.'

'Oh, sorry, you really don't have to. You were in need, and I was always taught to help someone in need.'

'It's a fine attribute,' said Fyre. He then saw the same look of confusion of the boy's face and added, 'You were taught well.'

The cottage only had three rooms, the living space doubled as a kitchen, while one bedroom stood to the left and another to the right. Sean busied himself preparing supper for his guests.

Stone wasted no time; he didn't like being kept in the dark.

'So, get on with it, what ghosts have visited you this time?'

Fyre took a moment to answer. 'My dear friend, if you were not my friend I would consider you quite the bore. There are spirits here, yes. There are spirits everywhere, they leave traces like echoes in an endless cave. Some are louder than others and some are clinging to this world, with a violent grip.'

'And what are these spirits saying?'

'Why do you care?'

'I care about my own wellbeing,' said Stone sternly.

'Is that all?'

'Enough games, Fyre!'

'Very well, I believe that spirits of recently deceased people are trapped somewhere nearby. They are calling to me, not from beyond the grave, but from this world, as if their path has been blocked. What all this has to do with Matthew Barry, I have yet to ascertain'

'Ghost jail,' whispered Stone.

Fyre giggled, 'Yes, I suppose it is as good a term as I can give you.'

'And that business at the graveyard?'

'That felt more conventional … for me, of course. A distressed soul is in that grave, one that should not be there.'

'I'd imagine all the souls in those graves are distressed?'

'You would imagine wrongly.'

The meal Sean prepared was indeed simple, but both men were hungry and made no complaint about it.

'Tell me about Gerretstown House,' Stone said to Sean.

'There not much to tell,' Sean replied. 'Missus French lived there, mostly alone after her husband died. That happened before I was born.'

'What happened to him?' asked Fyre.

'They say he walked out to the cliffs one day and never

came back.'

'This lady, French, was she related to the Barrys?' asked Stone.

Sean didn't seem to mind answering questions.

'Oh yes sir, the French family and the Barry family have been marrying into each other for generations. It's a bit of a joke around here.'

'I bet they don't find it funny,' Fyre said.

'No, sir, they don't.'

'Missus French's niece is married to Mr Matthew Barry, I believe the idea was the house was going to go to him.'

'But it didn't,' said Stone.

'No, sir, it went to the Dublin man, a cousin, I think.'

'I suppose the house and the land with it would be a fair sum to the Barry family, in a way it could support a lavish lifestyle?' Stone asked Fyre.

'Maybe,' replied Fyre in an unconvinced tone.

Before Stone could question Sean more about the Barry family and their lifestyle, a tapping noise caught the attention of all.

'Are you expecting anyone?' asked Stone.

'No, sir.'

Stone drew his pistol from inside his jacket. He could see the fearful reaction on Sean's face.

'Don't worry, I used to be peeler.'

'I know, that's what worries me,' Sean said.

A second noise, like a series of scratches running down the tin roof of the cottage, made all of them stand up.

'Whatever it is,' said Fyre, 'It isn't friendly.'

Steve Downes

CHAPTER 10

Lord Barry stood at the window overlooking the formal garden of his home. He had listened to his nephew's long-winded and rambling speech about the two men who had unexpectedly turned up at the castle gate. As was his way, his lordship said very little in reply. He waved away his nephew's apology and gave him instructions to prepare for the latest party at Garryhinch House.

Lord Barry had other things on his mind, away from the social graces of his position. He watched his nephew make his way across the pathways of the formal garden, toward the stable block. That young man's character had changed a great deal since he had come to live under the direct supervision of his uncle and the rest of the family. This pleased Lord Barry. Above all, the family name must be protected.

A thought occurred to Barry as he stood there, watching the evening sky darken. There had been little sport of late in his life, little amusement. His business affairs had kept him away from idle thoughts, just as the work he assigned his nephew kept him away from his less than moral habits. Barry smiled and reached over to the bell push that stood out from the wall of the drawing room. Somewhere in the bowels of the house a summoning noise was sounding. It further amused him when he realised he didn't know what that sound was. Was it a bell, a buzzer, a din like a crow cawing? He wondered if any member of the family knew what the summoning bell sounded like. He supposed not.

Within moments a polite cough at the door told him that Max was standing there, waiting for instruction.

'Max, who were the two men in the front yard just now?' It seemed an absent-minded question, but it was purely rhetorical.

Max replied with the names of Lord Fyre and Mr Stone.

'Ah, of course, those two men.'

'Will there be anything else, your lordship?'

'Yes, Max, take a letter.'

Stone opened the front door of the cottage just enough so that he could see into the small front yard outside.

The place sat in a slight dip in the landscape, with the road surface beyond at shoulder height. To the left and the rear of the building was a small stretch of farmland before the darkness of the woods surrounding the Barry estate. To the right, the road followed the hill downwards to the small village and looped around the church before joining the main coast road.

The moon had risen and was almost full. Stone could see clearly into the night.

'Anything?' asked Fyre, who was standing close behind him.

'No, they might have gone round the back. Is your back door locked, Sean?'

'I don't have locks for the doors, front or back,' he replied.

'Great,' Stone rolled his eyes, then said to Fyre, 'You'd better take a look out the back door then.'

'You're the one with the gun,' replied Fyre drolly.

Stone lifted a large walking stick from behind the door

and handed to Fyre with a grin.

'Noble,' commented Fyre.

Stone told Sean to stay inside. He left the front door open, so that what little light there was from the fireplace spilt out, but it only illuminated the first few feet of the pathway.

To his left, Stone could see a lamp lit above a large stone building, one of the few two storey buildings he'd seen in the village. There appeared to be no other light, except the moon reflecting off the sea in the distance.

A movement made his heart leap. His hand, holding the gun close to his chest, followed his eyes as he spun around. A flickering shadow moved across the elevated roadway to his right. The shadow moved far too fast to be a person along the road. It was accompanied by a noise, like the swish of a whip cracking through the cold night air.

He was about to scale the small bank up to the road surface, when Fyre's voice cried out. It was a yelp of pain. Stone was running before he was thinking. He ran around the side of the cottage and found Fyre lying in the back yard. His instinct was to run to his friend's aid, but he stopped himself and swept the darkness with his pistol following his eyes.

Despite Fyre's groans, Stone kept his eyes fixed on the darkness, convinced that whatever attacked his friend could still be close.

Fyre was up on his knees by the time Stone had scanned the yard and beyond.

'Are you alright?'

'Yes, I think so, there's some blood on my head, but I think I'm alright.'

'Who was it?'

Fyre didn't answer at first, he dragged himself to his feet and wiped a small dash of blood from his forehead.

'It wasn't a person.'

'An animal?' Stone was still watching the darkness.

'No, it was something else, something in the air, a creature, or something else.'

'Pull yourself together, Fyre. What the hell was it?' demanded Stone. As he spoke, Sean appeared at the back door, armed with a large knife and another walking stick.

'It's the Puca,' spoke Sean, the fear in his voice patently obvious.

'It wasn't friendly, that's for sure,' said Fyre.

They both retreated to the back door and slipped inside.

On seeing the police arrive, Holt's driver had done as his boss had instructed. He hid in the woods beside the house and observed. He watched as Holt was led away in handcuffs, and as the body of another man was lifted into the back of the trap he had arrived in.

After a long hour, the carriage and trap moved off and darkness began to fall over the now silent house. The driver, unsure of what to do next, made his way back to Garretstown House. He found the door unlocked and the signs of the firefight between his boss and the small fat man, who had arrived on his own.

The driver owned his life to Holt, he trusted him, and he did what he was told. He fished in his overcoat pocket for a sealed envelope that had a single name written carefully on it. Holt had told him that if plans went wrong, he was to hand-deliver the letter to the person whose name was written on the envelope. There would be no going out to deliver letters tonight. Although the weather was clement and the night had stars and moonlight, the road was too dangerous to travel in darkness, and the sound of the nearby sea crashing against the cliffs made him nervous.

The driver risked lighting a lantern and checked every room of the house, as they had both done when they arrived. Satisfied he was alone, and that the police would also not risk the road at night, he lit a small fire in the back kitchen hearth.

As the night wore on, the need for sleep forced him to bed down beside the dying fire. Holt had not permitted him to have a firearm, but he had found several large knives in the kitchen. Choosing the largest knife as a potential weapon, he lay down and tried to get some rest. Holt had made their journey from London to Dublin at breakneck speed. They were being perused by the Metropolitan police, and what little information his boss gave him seemed to suggest that all they had worked for was close. Holt was on the trail of a sinister criminal organisation, one that had deep roots in high society and government. The driver had seen many things in his short life, terrible things. He and Holt were both guilty of cold-blooded murders, but then so were those who stood against them. A feeling came over him. As he lay there on the floor his hand subconsciously reached out and pulled the large knife closer. He was on his feet by the time the unnatural noise outside was obvious to him.

He instinct was to run, he knew all too well the danger he was in. Without Holt, without protection, this supernatural threat could take him. He had seen what these dark forces could do to a man.

He panicked.

He ran.

Perused by something. Something fast. Something dangerous. Something that easily matched his speed.

Something that cut through his clothes and skin like the claws of a ghostly bird of prey.

Stone didn't get much sleep. He sat in a chair most of the night. His eyes only closed for an hour, when Fyre took a turn at guard. In that hour he had a dream. It was a recurring dream.

At a fireside, similar in size to the one he was sitting at now, the flames licks upwards, doing a strange dance of orange and white light. There was a lush carpet, he could feel the fibres against his legs and feet. He was a child, barely more than a toddler. Above him was a large chair, he could see the frame of his mother sitting there, the flickering fire making her features move as if they were liquid. He tried to stand up, but found he had no power in his tiny body. He tried to call to her, but found he had no voice. He desperately tried to see her face, to remember it, to find comfort in it. But, no matter which way he turned, or how frantically he tried, she seemed to be permanently looking away from him.

Stone woke with a start, Fyre's hand was on his shoulder. It was daylight and his eyes burned for a second before they adjusted.

'Bad dreams?' asked Fyre.

'Just the same one, the same one I've had for nearly two years now.'

'You know I could help you understand that dream,' said Fyre earnestly.

'Why don't you stay out of my dreams and in the real world?' replied Stone grumpily.

'As you wish, my friend, there are some who think the dream world and the real world are mirrors of each other.'

'I don't like mirrors. Where's the boy?'

'A cart pulled up outside. Sean said it was the head gardener from the Barry's other house along the coast, Garryhinch.'

Stone got out of the chair; his joints ached from lack of sleep.

'That thing that attacked you last night, you don't think it was a ghost, do you? This Puca thing?'

'I've told you before, the dead are benign, they don't come back from the grave and attack people. Whatever that thing was it wasn't alive or dead. I've had this strange feeling for weeks now, Stone, a feeling like there are voices, souls calling out to me.'

'You heard those voices before. The murdered women in Dublin,' said Stone.

'I told you this feels different, these souls are not dead, they're …. trapped.'

Sean came in. On the raised road outside the cottage's window, Fyre and Stone could see the cart pull away.

'We're keeping you from your work, young Sean, we'll get you in trouble,' said Stone.

'More trouble,' muttered Fyre.

'Actually no, I've been told to stay with you, as a local guide,' Sean said. He smiled and shrugged.

'Told by whom?' asked Fyre.

'His Lordship, apparently. There's a carriage coming

for you at two, and your luggage arrived from Kinsale and was brought up to the castle.'

'That's interesting,' said Stone.

'And there's this,' Sean said, holding out a sheet of white paper.

Fyre unfolded it and read it carefully.

'Well?' asked Stone, 'An invitation to go away?'

'Not at all, an invitation to a garden party, and an apology. Signed by his lordship himself.'

'We're not going to go, are we?' asked Stone. He had hoped it was an invitation to leave the area; he felt this whole situation was out of his control, and he hated that.

'Of course we're going to go. His lordship wishes to apologise in person. It's not until four this afternoon, but he's sending a carriage around at two so we can wash and dress for the occasion.'

'Occasion?' questioned Stone.

'It's one of his daughter's birthdays, he always gives a big party at the orangery for her, or for any of the family,' Sean told them.

'Will we bring a present?' asked Stone, sarcastically.

'We'll bring questions, plenty of them,' replied Fyre, 'But first we need to go to Garretstown House, the one mentioned in Matthew Barry's letter.'

'We're going there to find answers?' Stone asked, as he checked his jacket for his sidearm.

'No, dear friend, we're going there to find the questions. I fear we're a long way from answers.'

Fyre grinned at him and raised the walking stick Stone had armed him with last night.

'I'll bring this!'

CHAPTER 11

Charles Barry watched the police carriage wheel away from the asylum. The patient they had deposited into his care was deemed criminally insane, at least according to the letter he was now holding in his hand. Charles was a man prone to worries and doubts. He held such concerns inside like a fist gripping a tightrope for dear life. He opened the letter once again. It had the seal of the British government and had been stamped by Dublin Castle. He noticed that the ink was significantly dried, and the paper rustled from lack of freshness. Whoever this man was, the authorities had been searching for him for some time.

The two detectives who had arrived from Dublin earlier in the day had not furnished him with much information about their prisoner. They seemed unwilling or unable to answer basic questions, and constantly referred him to their orders.

'Just obeying orders,' whispered Charles to himself.

Charles found it suspicious that both detectives had been recalled, via telegraph, as soon as this man was in custody. But neither they nor the local police questioned the order.

Charles was a worried man for many reasons. His wife's unhappiness, and her seemingly unshakable obsession with his late mother's work, upset him greatly. He could see history repeating itself, and he had hoped so much that his life could be lead without such family history rearing its ugly head.

He was good at putting things out of his mind, throwing himself into his work, just as he did at Cambridge before he met Melisa distracted him from his darker thoughts and memories.

Charles left his office and walked through the tall, elegant halls of the asylum. No expense had been spared on the building. Marble floors, stucco ceilings and finely carved doors and frames in regular lines had cost the Barry family a significant fortune. Where the money had come from and how his father was managing the family's business affairs was a matter of great concern to Charles. His father, an outwardly cheerful man, was secretive and manipulating behind the closed doors of Castle Barry. And those doors had now been closed for years, since the death of his wife. Lord Barry only entertained, in other, smaller houses.

Charles agreed with his wife, in how much they both hated the social obligations his father heaped upon them. He had hoped that this lucrative job running the asylum would provide enough money for a home of their own and financial independence from his father. Somehow money seemed to drain away. He suspected Melisa was spending far more of his income than she claimed. On quite what and why, was another cause for concern. Melisa's own demons from her past seemed to have returned. He pretended he didn't know her secrets, but he knew enough, enough to make him fear losing her like he did his mother.

It was lockdown in the asylum. After breakfast the patients were allowed to wash, and those with more liberties were allowed to dress themselves. He met only two people on his way to the high security rooms. The first was a guard, dressed in his black uniform, with his long baton hanging from a leather strip at his side.

'Good morning, Doctor,' the guard tipped the side of his hat.

'Good morning,' Charles said/ His mind was elsewhere, but he could see by the way the guard stopped in the corridor that he had more to say.

'The new prisoner is comfortable in room 102, sir, he gave no trouble. Didn't say anything actually.'

Charles's face remained stoic.

'We have no prisoners here, officer, we only have patients.'

'Oh yes, sir, I forgot,' mumbled the guard.

'Don't forget again,' said Charles sternly and walked away.

'Yes, sir.'

Charles walked on, his footsteps echoing on the ornate floor. Occasionally he could hear voices in the distance, ghostly whispers of screams as if they were coming from the walls themselves. As he reached the secure wing of the building, the furthest away from his office, he met a second man.

Michael was a ward of asylum. He had been a patient in the old asylum, which had stood on these grounds for seventy years in an old estate house belonging to a rival landowning family to the Barrys. Local history had shown that it did not bode well for any family to stand against his own. The Barry family had used every means possible to make a miniature empire in this part of Ireland. They had bullied, bankrupted, and besmirched the reputation of any Anglo-Irish family that dared threaten their position. If none of those tactics worked, the Barrys married into those families and made them their own. Such methods had worked in their favour for two hundred years.

'Good morning, Doctor,' stuttered Michael.

'Michael,' Charles barely looked at the man. He was still incensed at the guard he had passed moments ago.

'Just on an errand, sir.'

'Oh yes,' said Charles absentmindedly, 'Shouldn't you be washing for the day?'

'Already done, sir,' replied Michael nervously.

'Good man,' Charles was about to walk away, when a thought occurred to him. He liked to know everything that happened in his hospital, and too many of the senior staff were conducting their own research without his permission.

'What errand are you engaged in?'

'Sir?' Michael cocked his head in confusion.

'Where are you going? And who told you to go there?'

'Oh sorry, sir, I have to bring bandages up to the second floor, the room for Patrick Healy, the postmaster's son.'

'Has he hurt himself again?' Charles knew the patient in question; he was suffering a severe mental breakdown, brough on by a vast consumption of homemade poteen. His father had committed him several weeks ago, and the young man was prone to violent outbursts and self-harm.

'Oh yes, sir, banged his head on the walls. The Chief Surgeon is up there now, it was him that sent me for the bandages, you see.'

Charles noted that the Chief Surgeon was one of the staff he mistrusted the most. The man seemed to take delight in the more macabre aspects of his job.

'You'd better run along then,' said Charles.

Michael gave a low, unnecessary bow, and half-ran, half-skipped along the long corridor.

Charles wanted total control over who was employed at the asylum, but he suspected his father's hand was involved in assembling the staff already here when he arrived. The board of directors were very much his father's people, lawyers, bankers, and members of the extended Barry family.

'Melisa was right,' mumbled Charles to himself, as he reached the secure heavy doors that separated this wing of the building from the rest, 'we should never have come here.'

Charles had insisted that the secure wing was as brightly lit as the rest of the asylum. Light was vital to his theories on curing mental illnesses. He hated the darkness.

He was disappointed to see that the curtains were half-closed, and immediately told the guard on duty to draw them open. Charles checked the ledger which contained the names and details of each of the more volatile patients kept here. Their latest entry had not been logged. He jotted the name down himself and made the note, 'yet to be assessed,' beside the name of 'Holt.'

He then went to room 102, and drew back the observation panel in the door. Mr Holt was sitting on his bed, his back to the window, and a serene expression on his face.

'I have been expecting a visit from you, Doctor Barry,' said Holt.

Charles didn't reply to him, instead he addressed the guard.

'Open the door.'

'Are you sure, sir?'

'Yes, open it, I know this man.'

Despite Sean's and Stone's complaints, Fyre would not be dissuaded from his course of action. They reached the village and Fyre looked about frantically for signs of life.

'Where is everyone?' he asked.

Stone was leaning against the church wall, a grumbling in his stomach reminding him that he was hungry.

'It's nine in the morning, they're in the fields, or at sea or cleaning floors in big houses, where else would they be? This isn't London or Paris you know. And even if the locals were about, do you think they're going to just lend you a horse and cart out of the kindness of the hearts?'

'Never underestimate the kindness of the working classes,' replied Fyre, as he saw something coming down the hill.

'And never underestimate the stupidity of the rich,' mumbled Stone.

Fyre didn't hear him, or at least pretended he didn't. He stood in the centre of the road, with his arms outstretched. A trap was approaching at a trot and the driver had to call to his horse and pull the reins to avoiding running Fyre down.

'Hello, could we trouble you for a lift? It's very important,' Fyre called out, as the large horse swayed his head just inches from him.

'It must be if you're willing to get run down like that,' the voice that answered was educated and not local, or even Irish.

'Chaplain,' said Sean, removing his cap, 'This is Lord Fyre and Mr Stone, they're guests of Lord Barry. This is Chaplain Smith.'

The chaplain turned his horse to the side, and looked down at the three men.

'Lord Fyre and Mr Stone, you need no introduction to me. I read about your … um, case, in the papers. Most peculiar. They say you are ghost hunters,' The chaplain gave a genuine laugh.

'The only thing we are hunting now is a lift to Garretstown House,' replied Fyre.

'Are you on the hunt for our murderer?' asked the chaplain, casually.

'Has there been a murder?' asked Stone.

'Oh yes, but you're too late, they've got their man, brought him in this morning. He's locked up in the asylum. But where are my manners? I'm Chaplain Greyson Smith, I work at the asylum, for my sins.'

'Can you tell us who was murdered, sir?' asked Fyre.

'I believe it was that nice man from Dublin, Mr Egan. Met him once, seemed like a decent fellow. His valet was killed too. Terrible business. The local police took the bodies up to the chief surgeon late last night. Terrible business, did I say that already? Sorry.'

'And the man they have in custody?'

'Oh I wasn't told about him, unless he wants to confess to a higher power, then I'm afraid it's a matter for the police.'

'This is an unexpected turn of events,' said Fyre.

'Why do you need to be at Garretstown in such a hurry?' the chaplain asked.

'Oddly, we were hoping to talk to Mr Egan, about his house and how he came by it.'

'I can bring you gentlemen there, if you like, but unless you can speak with ghosts, I'm afraid there won't be much conversation with Mr Egan.'

Fyre smiled, 'We'll accept the lift, nonetheless.'

The chaplain was chatty, and Fyre sat up front in the trap as they trotted along the coast road. Stone had noted how Fyre, despite his awkwardness, bordering on shyness, seemed to be able to exchange small talk to his social peers at will. Stone and Sean sat in silence in the back of the trap. Sean pulled his cap down over his brow and kept his eyes on the road ahead, while Stone watched the stunning scenery roll by.

His mind was temporarily distracted by the sunlit landscape around him. In the evening, this rural place had seemed foreboding and even dangerous. But now, under the morning sunshine, the sea shone a pastel blue, except where it met the jagged cliffs, then it exploded into a pale green, topped with fierce white crests.

The cliffs of southern County Cork appeared to be gouged out of the land, as if clawed at by some gigantic ancient levitation. As they trotted along the empty road, with Fyre's lyrical voice interspersed with the chaplain's gravelly, but gentle tone, Stone could see walls, towers, and shattered remains of what looked like great houses smashed by the violent sea. One large group of ruined walls, tall, with red brick shining in bands around grey stone, caught his eye.

'What was that down there?' he asked, and directed Sean's gaze to the shoreline.

'Copper mines, long closed, The Barrys owned them.'

'Of course they did,' mumbled Stone.

The trap barrelled along the road. On turning onto a sweeping headland they came into a view of a square house, sitting, almost impossibly in a spur darting into the sea.

'The is Mr Egan's house?' asked Fyre.

'Yes,' replied the chaplain, as he slowed the horse so they could take in the scene, 'when the lady French passed away a few weeks ago. Mr Egan came into possession of the house. I got the impression from him that he was quite surprised at the inheritance.'

'What relation were they?' asked Fyre.

'She was an aunt, through marriage. I believe Mr Egan was a widower, and they were not close, or even in regular contact.'

Stone decided at this point to test the waters.

'They must have upset the apple cart, I believe Matthew Barry was in line to get the house.'

They were at a slow trot now, and they were only a few hundred yards from the house. The chaplain was able to turn in the seat and smile at Stone as he replied, 'Well, yes and no. You seem to be clued into the local gossip, Mr Stone.'

Fyre responded, 'We've had our dealing with the Barry family, and it seems we will have again. We've been invited to a party, later today.'

'You and half the county,' The chaplain gave a snort of laughter, 'I'll be there too, but no claret for me; my doctor forbids it these days.'

Stone was going to press more on the subject of Mr Egan's sudden inheritance when the horse reared up and caused the trap to veer toward the road's edge and the bay beyond.

A scream broke through the noise of the wooden wheels and the horse's distress. Fyre gripped the reins to help the chaplain, but Stone was out of the trap and running after someone or something before they regained control.

CHAPTER 12

'Who do you think he really is?' asked Owens.

They were standing under one of the large windows of the asylum. The summer sun had reached full height and was beaming down on them, so much so that both of them could feel their skin reddening where their uniform left it exposed.

Murphy leaned against the cream-coloured wall and kept his eye on the cell door opposite, slightly ajar.

'He's not mad, that's for sure. Not any kinda mad I've ever seen,' he said in reply.

'What makes you say that?'

'He's cold, calculating. He kills without emotion and isn't scared of being here. Almost like he was expecting to be here.'

'Yeah, strange that. Doctor Barry doesn't seem worried about being in there alone with him.'

'No.'

'I would.'

'So would I.'

'I'm surprised you recognise me,' said Holt.

103

'Our previous meeting was not one I would forget easily, Detective Holt. If that is your real title and name?'

'It is. The name anyway. I've been temporarily removed from my position in Scotland Yard.'

'Temporarily?'

Holt grinned.

The doctor stood under the small, barred window, which was above head height. The sun caught his features, and Holt recalled their first meeting in his mind. It had been several years ago, and Charles Barry had hardly changed. His face was an ivory pale, except across his cheeks, which stood out a rosy red, not an unhealthy flush of alcoholism, but more a painted rouge of youth. His lips were thin and bright red and if it wasn't for the kindness of his eyes, his face could seem quite cruel.

Holt had been chasing ghosts when he met Charles Barry back in Cambridge. He had found one. But while Charles Barry remained of interest to him, it was his father who Holt wanted to get close to now.

'I seem to remember you having an interest in the business of my wife,' said Charles.

'Congratulations, she was just your fiancée when last we met.'

'Don't be glib, Mr Holt, why are you here?' Barry's tone changed to a more threatening level.

'Didn't you hear? I murdered several people, in cold blood.'

Charles didn't reply for a long moment. He took a few paces toward the cell door and glanced out at the two policemen stationed outside.

'I did hear that. Mr William Egan and his valet, I believe.'

'That remains to be seen.'

'You deny killing them?'

'I killed two men, who they were is another matter,' Holt's voice stayed steady.

'I recall you asking questions about my wife's family, and about mine. And then spouting some conspiratorial nonsense about dark forces at the heart of British society.'

Holt's grin was fixed, as were his eyes on Barry.

With no answer forthcoming, Charles changed tack.

'I have received instructions to hold you here indefinitely, if necessary.'

Holt's voice altered for the first time, and Barry detected annoyance and anger.

'Instructions from whom? Your masters or mine?'

Barry took the few steps to the cell door. He opened it and stood in the frame, the sunlit making a silhouette of his thin body.

'It is my belief, Mr Holt, that you are suffering from paranoid delusions. It is a condition I have been working on for some time.'

'You intend to cure me?'

'I intend to help you, Mr Holt. We will speak again, soon.'

Barry turned to leave; the policemen outside approached the door, one of them holding a large set of keys.

'Just one thing, Doctor Barry,' called out Holt.

'Yes?'

'Are you one of them?'

'Who are 'they'? Mr Holt.'

'Ask your father.'

The cell door was locked, and the doctor let out a breath of relief. He could feel his heartrate slow back to its normal level.

'We were told to stay just for a few hours, until you were happy he was settled, Doctor Barry,' said one of the policemen.

'You may go; he's quite safe here.'

'It's not him being safe I'm, worried about,' said the policeman.

Barry didn't reply. He clasped his hands behind his back and walked quickly down the corridor toward the main block of the asylum.

'What do you make of all of that?' asked Owens.

Murphy was looking through the spy hole in the cell

door. Holt lay down on the bed, folded his arms across his chest and appeared to be ready to fall asleep.

'Let's get back out to the house.'

'Shouldn't we go the station house, though? I'd imagine the whole district has heard this news by now.'

'Let them gossip. They've little else to do. Come on, let's go, there's nothing more we can do here.'

Stone was used to running on cobbled streets and he found it difficult to keep his footing on the uneven ground of the woods. He could see the figure of a man just a dozen feet in front of him. Whoever this man was he seemed to struggle on the ground too. Within fifty yards Stone was at the man's back. He reached out his arm and grasped the shoulder of the man's jacket, sending both of them off balance and tumbling down into a small gulley.

Stone rolled head over heels into an inch of running water. As the world spun around him, he could see the man rolling down the bank, just feet away.

For a second, Stone lay on his back, panting for air. He turned his head, his heart gave an extra beat as he realised that the man had landed right beside him.

The man's open eyes glared at Stone. It was a wide-eyed glare, a panicked madness, that Stone had seen before. He only had a couple of seconds to take in the man's face before they both moved. He was covered in blood, part of his cheek appeared to be severed, and his teeth were showing on one side of his mouth, just a little too much, as if his lower lip had been peeled away by a sharp knife.

The man was up, but Stone was too quick for him. Stone reached out as he got to his feet and pulled the man backward toward him. He held him in a strong bearhug, hoping to calm him down enough to speak to him.

The wounded man's legs and arms flailed wildly, but Stone held firm. He felt the sharp pain of a bite in his forearm, teeth sank with powerful force into his flesh. He had to release his grip and the man scrambled away, following the path of the tiny stream. Stone let of a yelp of pain on release, and gripped his arm. He knew the skin was penetrated, but he got to his feet and ran again in pursuit. It wasn't difficult to catch the man, he stumbled from side to side and fell several times. Stone could see he had run into a dead-end. The stream disappeared behind a thicket of fallen trees and impassable bushes.

'Stop, I can help you,' yelled Stone.

Instinct told him that this man was in trouble. He seemed to be running from someone or something and was not the attacker Stone had first thought.

The man turned, having tried in vain to get through the blockage. His eyes were darting, and blood now poured into them from a cut on his forehead. For the first time, Stone could see that his face and clothes were ripped asunder, thin gashes across his skin oozed bright red blood on top of darker dried blood.

Like a trapped rat, the man lunged at Stone. Where his mouth had been ripped open, his teeth looked like those of a savage animal.

For a second, Stone, stunned by the man's appearance, froze on the spot. The injured man didn't reach Stone, Fyre had, unseen, ran down the stream bank and stopped himself by slamming into a leaning tree trunk. As the man ran past him, he swung the stick he was carrying and caught him in the temple with a sweet and sickening contact.

Stone and Fyre stood over the stricken man. He was semi-conscious and mumbling to himself, but clearly unable to move.

'Are you alright?' asked Fyre.

Stone felt his bitten forearm. There was a trickle of blood on his skin, and the man's teeth had left bruised marks deep in the tissue.

'Yeah, I'll be fine. What's happened to him?'

'Looks like he's been attacked by a wild animal,' said Fyre, taking the man's appearance in for the first time.

'I don't think so,' replied Stone, 'look at those cuts on face and arms, all straight lines; no animal I know could do that.'

'You're right, a knife then.'

'Maybe, … doesn't look right.'

'He needs medical attention.'

'Let's get him back to trap before he fully wakes up. The chaplain has some spare reins in the back, we can tie him down.'

Fyre and Stone half-carried, half-dragged the man the sixty or so yards back to the road, where Sean and the chaplain were wating.

'Good God, who is he?' said the chaplain, his voice full of shock.

'We don't know,' replied Stone. 'He's not local, then?'

'No,' said Sean, 'he's no one I know.'

'Come on, let's tie him up, he's as much a danger to himself as he is to us.'

Stone helped the others pull the man into the back of the trap, but his eyes were on the woods and house beyond. Now, this idyllic summer scene felt treacherous.

Melisa found it more difficult to move around Ireland surreptitiously than she had in Cambridge or London. Packed streets and busy collages could be the perfect cover for someone who wanted to be unseen in a crowd.

She had found several inventive ways of passing between the house, the asylum, and, if necessary, even into Castle Barry itself.

Today, she decided to hide in plain sight. She had insisted, when they first came to Ireland, that servants be kept to a bare minimum. Charles, who was in agreement with her, had taken this to the extreme. A cook arrived from the castle once a day, a cleaner, three times a week, and a driver for Charles's work only.

Melisa was a keen horsewoman, she readied the small trap with ease, harnessed the horse and trotted it out into the yard. There she stopped as she noticed the two workmen staring at her from the dilapidated servant's block attached to the house.

'Good morning,' she called out, without having to look

over at the men. The men mumbled replies, which Melisa didn't hear. She knew that Lord Barry was having her watched. He was, she knew, even watching Charles. She trotted the trap out of the yard, onto the short drive and through the gate. She would travel to the asylum. If she was questioned, which was unlikely, she could use Charles as an excuse. If she met Charles, she could say she had come to apologise for their recent disagreement. Charles was always more pliant when Melisa played the 'sorry' card.

Her real purposes for visiting the asylum were far more sinister. She steadied her mind, and checked her large bag. All she needed was in there. The only thing missing was another specimen.

She tried to force the doubts in her mind away.

'Has he said anything?' asked Fyre from the front of the trap.

'No, sir,' Sean replied. 'He just mumbling. There's a lot of blood in his mouth; he's cut up real bad.'

'Is there no other doctor close by?' asked Stone.

'No, not for miles, Kinsale would be the nearest. There are several medical staff at the asylum,' replied the chaplain. 'I think it's the best place for him, it's obvious something terrible has happened to the poor man.'

'That's true,' said Fyre.

The chaplain drove his horse on at a speed he wouldn't normally travel, then came up through the village, past the church and Sean's cottage, before he joined a new road that wound up along the hills.

'Is it far?' asked Fyre.

'Oh no, just half a mile along this road. Lord Barry had the road especially made for the asylum.'

'It's seems an odd place to have such an institution. Aren't they normally near towns or on the outskirts of cities?'

'Yes, I suppose so. It was the thinking at the time that patients could be cured by country air and clean living,' answered the chaplain.

'At the time?' questioned Fyre, 'That's sounds like you don't agree with it?'

'Oh, I agree with the principle of it. But, since I came here, I have to say the practice is often not in agreement with the theory.'

'How do you mean?'

The chaplain pointed to a vast, rambling building that came into view as they crested a hill. He smiled as he spoke, his voice with a lilt of remorse, 'A curtain wall, strong doors, barred windows, and cells. More a castle than a hospital. One wonders if it is to keep the patients safe from the world, or to keep the world safe from them!'

'One does wonder,' agreed Fyre.

They moved down the hill and onto the drive of the asylum, stopping at the gates, where a guard took their details and the chaplain gave him instruction to call Doctor Barry.

'The Barry's didn't just build this place, they staff it too?' Fyre asked.

'Just Charles, sorry, young Lord Barry, but he insists on being called doctor. He's a Cambridge man. Did you go to one of the great collages?'

Fyre had to control a temptation to laugh, but he answered plainly, 'Only for a short period, I found education elsewhere.'

'As did I,' said the chaplain and he pulled on his white collar. 'We're here. Hopefully they can patch this poor fellow up.'

'And hopefully we can find out who he is,' added Fyre.

'And who attacked him,' said Stone.

'Or what attacked him,' Sean added in a whisper. There was a silence in the trap as the eyes of the other fells on him.

'I'm just saying …'

'Alright,' said Fyre, 'Let's speak with the doctors first. Help him down and see if we can get him on his feet.'

CHAPTER 13

'I asked for Doctor Barry to meet us here, …' said the chaplain, as they came through the massive ornate doors of the asylum into an equally massive entrance hall, that would be more suited to a palace than a hospital.

'… I'll just go and look for him; you chaps had better stay here.'

As the chaplain's footsteps echoed through the great hall, Sean, who had been almost silent until now, began to mumble under his breath.

'Are you alright, young man?' asked Fyre quietly.

'Just saying a prayer, sir. I was only here once before; they let me see my sister.'

'Just once,' asked Fyre.

'They said it was for the best.'

'Did they, indeed?'

Fyre could sense a tension in the boy, but he could sense so much more. He took a few steps away from the others. His mind began to reach out, involuntarily at first, but within seconds he embraced the sensation.

Sean didn't notice Fyre drift off; he looked behind to where Stone was holding their prisoner up against a wall. The man was half-conscious, but giving no resistance at all. Stone was searching the man's pockets.

'What are you doing?' asked Sean in a whisper, but the echo in the hall made it as loud as if he had announced it.

Stone put his fingers to his lips and continued rifling through the man's pockets. He quickly put the items into his overcoat; two watches, a pocketbook, and several documents. There was also a cardboard carton of ammunition for a pistol, but no weapon.

While Stone was pocketing the man's possessions, Fyre had walked, in a trance, further into the building. He was now standing at the foot of a wide marble staircase, which split in two as it joined the upper floor of the building.

'Fyre!' called out Stone from the doorway, 'are you alright?'

Fyre was not alright. Far from it. His mind was surrounded by consciousnesses. These were not the spirits of the dead. He did not fear the dead. He feared what was calling to him now. There was a sudden realisation that the minds drifting in and out of his recent visions, were not shadows of the departed, but living people, prisoners. Prisoners in this place. Voices rang out from the ether. Screams of anguish, living minds imprisoned in their own bodies. Never before had Fyre felt such sensations. He could see them, not like shades of the dead, but manifestations of minds tearing themselves apart. This was the madness he feared the most. Inside one mind was another, and another … violently opposing each other.

Despite his growing dread at what he was seeing, Fyre knew he could break from the trance at any time. He felt in control. These consciousnesses were not calling to him. They were not even aware of his presence. They were isolated from the real world, and from each other, just whispers of minds, screaming in the darkness.

The great entrance hall, the grand stairs, and even the asylum itself, melted away to nothing. It was as if he were standing in fields before this monstrosity of masonry and marble were erected. There was a girl, just yards from where he was standing. She was young, but her features were obscured and her voice a frail breath.

Fyre knew this kind of vision. This girl was dead. Her soul, like a shadow of a person, reflecting the life she once had in this world.

Fyre approached her. 'Why are you still here, young woman?' he asked, softly. He wasn't expecting an answer. Spirits of the dead were often cryptic, fleeting or even unaware of their encroachment on the world of the living. He watched the girl. Time was meaningless in his vision. He could be watching her for hours or just a moment. Like a dream, in the waking world outside his vision, this could all take just a second to pass.

She seemed preoccupied with a task. Fyre could not make out any clear objects in her hands; it was like watching her through a thick lens of rough glass. In the distance, from beyond the landscape, a black substance moved toward them. Fyre knew what this part of his vision meant. He had seen it before. It terrified him, and, for a brief moment, it took all of his constitution and concentration to hold the vision in place. The whole world around him shook, as if an earthquake rocked it. The landscape shattered, the asylum's walls and doors came into view. The building was not hazy, as the landscape had been, it was solid, real, imprisoning. The black substance gained a little form, not much, just enough that Fyre knew it to be the malignant soul of a malevolent being.

This was not the dead.

'Is Mr Fyre, alright?' Sean asked.

Stone had always outwardly disbelieved in Fyre's claims of supernatural powers. The modern world was full of men and women who claimed they could talk to the dead. There was money in immortality. Secretly he was both intrigued and scared by Fyre's seeming ability to see the dead, to somehow gain knowledge from them. Everything that had happened in their professional relationship so far, could be explained away, but only with great difficultly.

'Sean.'

'Yes, sir?'

'Go outside and sit in the chaplain's trap until we're done here.'

Sean didn't need telling twice.

Stone let their prisoner slide down the wall. He flopped on the gleaming tiles of the floor and almost lay flat. He was still mumbling to himself, but his willingness or ability to run seemed to be gone. Stone took a few steps toward his friend. He stopped. He felt a cold sensation, as if the whole building were made of ice, bearing down on him. In his mind he could see a man closing in on a terrified young girl. He could feel her fear. He could taste the threat of extreme violence.

'Gentlemen?' the chaplain returned to the entrance hall. His eyes widened as he saw the man they had captured, lying alone, and awake on the floor. Stone was a few feet away, staring into space.

Fyre was at the bottom of the stairs, his back turned to the scene.

'Gentlemen, is everything alright, you seem … odd?'

'Just taking in the atmosphere,' Fyre said.

'I always found it a bit acrid,' replied the chaplain, his expression still confused as to why the three men were now standing so far apart.

'I couldn't agree more,' Fyre replied.

He spun on his heels and was surprised to see Stone standing in the centre of the hall, his eyes distant and his body with a slight tremble throughout. Fyre immediately knew what was happening. The monks he had studied under stressed the importance of being ready to perceive the supernatural world. Minds that were unready could break.

'John,' Fyre called out to his friend. 'Can you hear me, John?'

'Your friend looks like he's had a bit of shock,' said the chaplain. He walked forward, holding out his hand as if to take Stone's elbow, but Stone didn't stand still for long. He darted to his left, running at full speed, his cheap shoes making an erratic drumbeat echo down the long corridors.

'Does he often do that?' asked the chaplain.

'One of us normally does, but it's not normal to be

him,' said Fyre, 'If you wouldn't mind looking after our man there for a few minutes, I'd better see to Stone.'

The chaplain looked nervously over to where the man was slumped on the floor.

'On my own?'

Fyre tossed the walking stick he was still carrying to the chaplain, who caught it awkwardly.

'This seemed to do the trick last time, but I'm sure he'll be no trouble.'

'Doctor Barry is coming with men,' said the chaplain, desperately.

'You can hold the fort till then,' Fyre called; he was already running down the corridor. 'Many thanks to you.'

'I'll hold the fort,' said the chaplain to himself, his words bouncing off the walls, 'but who's going to hold me?'

Stone was always instinctive, but this felt different. He raced down the corridor, passing the open doors of large rooms as he went. He didn't really know where he was going, just that it was the right direction. Just like chasing a criminal on the streets of Dublin in his early days of policing, he was chasing down his prey, and nothing focused his mind better than that.

Stone reached a T-junction at the end of the building. He skidded to a halt. Whatever the vision was that had briefly overtaken his mind, it was completely gone now. For a moment he felt a little foolish, but his police training kicked in. To his left the corridor opened out into a large hall. It was brightly lit, with elegant windows, two storeys high, and a colourful floor of red and black tiles. To his right, the corridor was darkened, the same tall windows stood on each side of the wing, but they had been covered with cream-coloured curtains, laced with black. Only narrow slits of light came through, making the corridor seem criss-crossed with blades of shimmering yellow. At the end, stood another ornate doorway, and set in the marble frame a simple double wooden door.

Stone felt as if he had stumbled onto a dark secret. In this building of light, where masonry seemed to defy gravity, this doorway appeared out of place, almost from another time. He glanced back to see Fyre hurrying after him. Not waiting for his friend, he walked to the darkened door and without knocking, went inside.

Fyre too had felt his subconscious drawn in this direction. He worried for Stone; the untrained human mind was unable to cope with the stresses of the supernatural. Even the concept of death itself was beyond most. Fyre knew, from experience, that some ended up at the mercy of religions, and others at the mercy of institutions like this one. It was an experience and a fear he was trying to isolate from the front of his own mind. He slowed to a walk, caught his breath, and followed Stone toward the doorway, bathed in shadows.

Stone knew what this room was. He'd seen one before in Dublin. This mortuary was a cathedral compared with the simple bare walls of Dublin's coroner's offices. The room was vast and well-lit. Those same high windows, that lit the corridors across the building, allowed light to come in from all sides. There were no curtains and no shadows.

Stone's keen eyes took in the scene, even as the man standing in one corner of the room spoke to him. There were eight marble tables, two had sheets covering what Stone correctly presumed were bodies. The other six tables lay empty, clean, sterile, and shining like white shore pebbles on a summer's day. All around the room were metal shelves, holding a wide array of medical devices. There were several identical trollies, also made of polished metal, each meticulously laid out with surgical tools. The man who was speaking to him, was standing, dressed in a snow-white coat, with his back to a long bench of marble, containing large glass jars.

'Can I help you, sir?'

Stone had to think quickly, 'I'm investigating a murder.'

'I see,' said the man in the leather apron. 'The uniformed police have only just left, they informed me that the detectives from Dublin would not arrive for a day, or perhaps two.'

'I'm not from Dublin Castle, I'm ...' Stone wasn't quite sure what lie he was about to tell, he was edging closer to the two occupied tables.

'We,' stressed Fyre's voice as he strode into the room, 'are private detectives, I am Lord Sebastian Fyre, and this is my colleague Mr Stone. Hello, sir.'

'Good day, gentlemen, I know who you are, you're the famous, or is it infamous, ghost hunters.'

'We prefer to think of ourselves as solvers of mysteries,' replied Fyre with a grin.

'Forgive me, I don't get many callers down here, not live ones, or ghosts, anyway. I am Doctor Bohan, the chief surgical officer for the hospital,' the doctor took a small bow toward Fyre and walked to Stone's side.

'What is it, exactly, you do here?' asked Stone, his eyes were still fixed on the two body shapes beneath the sheets.

'This is a hospital, Mr Stone; we make people better,' replied Doctor Bohan, in a deliberate tone.

'They're not getting much better,' said Stone, sarcastically, pointing to the two body shapes.

'I think what my colleague was attempting to ask,' interjected Fyre, 'is what, exactly, do you do in this room?'

Doctor Bohan suddenly whipped off the sheets from the two bodies. Stone took a closer look at both, while Fyre kept his distance.

'The gunshots are from a pistol, very close range for both,' said the Doctor, 'Impossible to say if the shooter was an expert or not, but both were killed by a well-placed single shot. Are these your murder victims?'

'It would seem so,' said Fyre.

'No,' said Stone.

'I beg your pardon?' asked the doctor.

'There was a girl,' said Stone, still dropped looking at the two dead men, ' a young woman. Where is her body?'

Fyre wasn't sure what Stone meant, but he knew to back him up, 'Did you have the body of a young woman here recently.'

'Yes,' answered the doctor, slight confusion evident in

his voice, 'but she wasn't murdered. She died of asphyxiation. Self-inflected.'

'Roisin Black?' asked Stone.

They were interrupted by a voice at the doorway.

'Gentlemen, if you will forgive me for being so curt, but I do not allow visitors to walk around this institution without my express permission. I am Doctor Charles Barry. If both of you would care to follow me.'

CHAPTER 14

Melisa watched the trap with the chaplain and four other men arrive. She was standing in the window of an office that had never been used; it overlooked the courtyard, and she was able to see three of the men half-carry the fourth man into the building.

'Curious,' she said to herself. She waited several minutes. Her nervousness growing. As she had got closer to the solutions of her life's work, the risks had increasingly affected her personality. She found it more and more difficult to hide her real feelings, and her passions, from her husband.

The doubts in her mind would sometimes rise like a sickened stomach, and she would wish one of her two lives away. She wanted her life with Charles, maybe not here in Ireland, but somewhere far away, across the Empire. A new life, another new start.

The doubts disappeared in a flash as she heard the office door softly click shut behind her.

'Did you see who arrived at the main entrance just now?' asked a familiar voice.

'I recognised the young man, Sean, the groundsman's assistant. Pleasant young fellow. He brings fruit to the house on occasions.'

'Indeed.'

'Who were the other men?'

'The one in the fine, but vulgar, suit, is Lord Sebastian Fyre.'

'That man from the City Club murders in Dublin? He caught the killers, I mean. Those poor, unfortunate women.'

'The same.'

'Then the other man, with the rough but handsome face, was Constable John Stone?'

'Former constable. You kept up to date with the events?'

'They were hard to ignore. Even the Barry family take note of current affairs, and normally they never care what happens outside their walls.'

The voice behind was silent for a long, telling moment, then spoke in a gentle but matter-of-fact way.

'I think we have a potential specimen.'

Melisa sighed, 'This will be the last one, the last one in this way.'

'You sound like you have made up your mind?' said the voice, the tone barely changing, but Melisa noticed slight annoyance.

'There are other ways.'

'Other ways have been tried, and failed. Fyre and Stone are not here by coincidence, I assure you. Time is against us. We're close, Melisa. Close to making the world a better place.'

'I'm not interested in making the world a better place. I only want what was taken from me to be returned.'

There was another soft click of a door closing. Melisa stood at the window for several minutes. She noticed Sean come back out and sit in the trap, his head held in his hands. Deep pangs of regret surfaced in her mind. She pushed them away, and tore her gaze from the boy. On an empty desk in the room, a thin paper file was sitting. It had not been there before. She opened it. It was a police file. George Shields, no known address, London. Wanted for extortion, theft, assault, and murder. There were few other details, except a poorly developed photograph, with a man's face that appeared sunken, soulless, with the eyes of a dead fish on a monger's slab.

Melisa folded the file in half and crammed it into her bag. The specimen selected was perfect. It was unfortunate that the best minds to test her work on, were minds broken by trauma or fear. She steadied herself, and tried to forget the young man outside, holding his head in his hands in grief.

'I didn't mean to be harsh just now,' Barry said as the three of them walked along the corridors to his office, 'I've ordered your prisoner sedated and we've placed him under watch in our secure wing. The chaplain sends his apologies, but he has business to attend to before my father's latest party. You're coming, I take it?'

'Yes, we were invited,' replied Fyre.

They reached Barry's office door, which was wide open. He stood to one side and gestured for them to enter.

'I believe my cousin was rather rude to you yesterday.' Barry gave out a small laugh of self-deprecation, 'and now I today. You must think awful things of the Barry family.'

'Nothing of the kind,' said Fyre, as he walked into the lushly decorated office and sat on a finely carved chair.

Stone followed Fyre into the room, but instead of sitting, he paced around, taking in the books, the ornaments and various medical apparatus encased in glass boxes. His eyes were drawn to a small silver pistol mounted on a stand.

'Medical device?' he asked.

'A silly ornament.'

'You seem to do well for yourself here,' said Stone harshly.

'Do not be fooled by the opulence of this building, or its rooms. This a place of work,' Barry said, his tone one of thinly disguising annoyance.

'Is there much money in madness?' asked Stone, his tone bordering on aggression.

Fyre could sense that his friend was on edge. Whatever

had overcome him in the entrance hall was still raw in his mind. He tried to diffuse the tension. The last thing he wanted was for Lord Barry's invitation to be withdrawn. 'I believe what my colleague is trying to ask, is that we are impressed by this institution, but are wondering how it had come to be so impressive?'

Barry rounded the large table and sat down. He seemed to take a deep breath, then answered in a calmer voice, as if he were regaining control of his emotions.

'There has been much speculation about what we do here, our successes, our failures and of course who is paying for all of it. The answers to all those questions are complicated. But, if you wish me to resort to gross generalisations, I can.'

'Please do,' said Stone flatly, as he gazed into a case containing a helmet with wires and probes covering its surface, making it look like some medieval apparatus of torture.

The doctor smiled at Fyre, who reciprocated and made a gesture with his hands as if to say, 'why not'. 'Very well,' he began, 'This institution was founded for one reason only, to find cures for illnesses of the mind. Unlike our predecessors, we are not here to lock away from society those who suffer from madness. Or, those who are deemed too different.' He threw a glance at Fyre, who didn't react to this comment, his face remaining stoic and unreadable.

Barry continued, 'We have, using methods derived from both chemistry and alienation, managed to classify several dozen illnesses, some completely new to science. We have ascertained their causes and their effects.'

'And what about curing them?' asked Fyre.

'Our successes have so far been limited, but there have been a few breakthroughs, I myself have several papers published on such successes. I will be quite happy to lend them to you.'

'It would be an honour to read them,' replied Fyre.

Barry appeared very pleased at Fyre's interest. He stood up and rooted out several printed journals and a dozen bundles of papers, carefully tied with ribbon. Fyre accepted the papers. Meanwhile Stone's attention had been drawn to a gold-plated set of dissecting tools, which were on display in a case behind the desk.

'Who pays for all this?' asked Stone. 'The fancy rooms, the great arches and towers and doorways, the gardens, the golden knives,' he pointed to the display case and then added again, 'You?'

'You mean, who pays for me, or do I pay for this institution?' asked Barry.

'Either?'

Barry's tone changed again. This time he could not hide his annoyance and Fyre and Stone both felt a chill in the conversation.

'Gentlemen, it is not my way, nor my nature to make threats or to make idle conversation.'

Barry paused, as if choosing his words carefully. 'I do however have to tell you that our family business is also complicated and can draw a man into it like quicksand. I took this position at my father's behest. You see, my late mother was a quite brilliant scientist. Father only took interest in her work after her death, he paid for and built this place as a tribute to her. So you see, my family, and myself are intertwined in what happens here.'

'And about it not being your nature to make threats, Doctor Barry?' asked Fyre. The question was loaded with intent.

'Of course, if you wish to stay as guests of my father, you are entitled to do so. By all means, do attend his party. My father is quite a pleasant man, if a little direct. But if I were you, gentlemen, I would return to Dublin tomorrow. I believe my cousin paid you in full for services that are no longer required?'

'He did,' replied Fyre.

'I am quite willing to double that fee, as compensation for any inconvenience caused to you.'

Stone wasn't going to let this offer go without comment, 'There are two dead bodies in your morgue, both murdered. We were asked to find a murderer; it seems this is the place to look for one.'

Fyre's eyes never left the doctor's. He could see a strange mix of intelligence, bitterness, and fear in those eyes. He wondered what Barry was thinking of him, or of Stone.

A knock on the open door of the office broke the moment at its most tense.

'Charles,' said Melisa from the doorway.

Fyre stood and gave a small bow to the young, beautiful woman standing in the doorway. She was dressed in the modern style, which was now beginning to replace the drab blacks and greys that had dominated women's apparel through the century. Her hair was tied back from her face, but not contained, as Irish women tended to do in public. Instead, a long ponytail of lush hair rolled down her shoulder and across her chest.

'Hello, my dear, I wasn't expecting you,' said Barry, quickly.

'Did you forget about another party?' she smiled, and took in the two men in her husband's office.

'No, my dear. Forgive me, this is Lord Fyre and Mr Stone.'

Fyre was wearing a bright suit, the kind Paris socialites wore, and Stone was dressed in a plainer one, which bulged were his barrel chest and knotted arm muscles stood out. The suit was clearly not tailored for him.

'A pleasure to meet you, gentlemen.'

'Gentlemen, my wife, Melisa.'

'The honour is all ours,' said Fyre. He took a few steps forward and kissed her hand, in a fashion that she had become accustomed to in Ireland. Men in England, even those in great households, had refrained from these gestures decades ago.

'I didn't forget about father's party; in fact, Lord Fyre and Mr Stone here are guests.'

'You're the men who caught those vile murderers in Dublin?' Melisa said with a great deal of sudden excitement.

'They almost caught us,' said Stone, from the corner of

the room.

'It was a close-run thing, actually,' Fyre jumped in, 'but in the end we managed to prevail.'

'I'd love to hear all about it,' said Melisa, her enthusiasm clear in her voice.

'Now, my dear, I don't want you hearing anything that will give you nightmares again,' Barry said.

Melisa gave a giggle, 'You'll have to forgive my husband; he can be very old fashioned when it comes to the sensibilities of women.'

Barry let out a sigh and quickly replied, 'You know that's not true, my dear.'

'No,' said Melisa, her face lighting up with a mischievous grin. 'Not always true. It's only here in Ireland; something in him changes when he sets foot on Irish soil. In England he was quite the liberal, would you believe. It's almost as if he were another man.'

'I am still the man you married,' Barry said. His whole demeanour seemed to soften when speaking to Melisa.

'Yes, you are, and you are going to be late to the party.'

'How did you know that?' he asked.

'Because I am your wife, and I know you better than you know yourself. You're still in your work suit, you have a pile of unread correspondence on the writing desk behind you, And, this is where my own detective genius comes, in …' she gave an extra grin to Fyre, '… you are always late to the party, since the day I met you. Since the day I met you in Cambridge, I bumped into you as you ran for a lecture.'

Barry allowed himself a smirk and said, 'You see gentlemen, for all the work we do studying the human mind, no man can hide himself or his secrets from his wife.'

'If only that were true, Charles.'

'And what about wives hiding secrets from men?' asked Stone, his voice almost a mumble.

All eyes fell on him. Stone instantly noted in his mind that Charles Barry's eyes were quizzical, Fyre's were exasperated, and Melisa's were sharp, darting to him in a serious way.

'Just a thought,' added Stone.

Melisa lifted her bag and placed it over her shoulder.

'If you are going to be late, then Lord Fyre and Mr Stone can escort me to the party, I'm sure they won't mind?'

'Of course not,' said Fyre, 'but I do have to confess we travelled here in the chaplain's trap.'

'That won't be a problem, I drove myself here, I have a trap outside, and the journey is only a mile,' said Melisa, with an air of authority in her voice.

Barry clearly knew better than to argue with his wife. Despite a momentary pause he replied, 'Very well. But no ghost stories; in spite of my wife's bravado, she does have nightmares.'

As Fyre walked and talked down the corridor with Melisa, Stone ambled past Barry in the doorway.

'What about the man we brought in?' he asked flatly.

'He'll still be here tomorrow. I would guess he is suffering from a great shock. Perhaps he witnessed the murders. Which would make it police business,' Barry said in an equally flat tone.

Stone threw him his most annoying smile, a sort of toothy, arrogant grin.

'I do know a lot of ghost stories, they make for interesting party conversations,' he said and without waiting for a reply he walked after the others.

CHAPTER 15

The afternoon sun was now at its zenith in the sky. As Fyre, Stone and Melisa trotted along in Melisa's trap, now driven by Sean, the landscape seemed to find a timeless beauty around them. The rough and rocky outcrops surrounded by heather shone like mirrors in a sea of wild grasses. Cattle and sheep dotted the hillsides. As they passed over the ridge on which the asylum stood, just before they dropped down into the valley, with the dark blue sea beyond, the sight of Castle Barry rising from the trees was breathtaking.

Fyre's ability for summing up small talk rose to the fore yet again. He and Melisa sat in the back of the small trap, so close that their legs touched, but this didn't seem to bother Melisa. He let Melisa to question him on the Spectre case, and even on cases which had nothing to do with him or Stone, but had made the papers over the last year. Fyre's replies were evasive but friendly and this seemed to please her.

Stone sat on the front plate with Sean, listening expertly to what was said behind him. He wanted to question Melisa, about the asylum, the Barrys and, most of all, her

husband.

Sean didn't speak at all. They passed the gate lodge for Castle Barry and Stone asked him a question. 'I thought we were going to a party in the castle?'

'Oh, it's not in the castle, sir, they never have the parties in the castle now. It's in one of the other houses owned by his lordship, just down the coast.'

'Past the house where Mr Egan was killed?'

'Just in the next cove, sir. We don't have to pass Mr Egan's house, that's a dead end anyway.'

'Interesting choice of words, Sean,' mumbled Stone.

'Sir?'

'It doesn't matter. When we stop, before you go to your other duties, I want to have a word with you,' said Stone softly; then in a whisper he added, 'privately.'

Stone gestured with his eyes toward the back of the trap. Sean nodded to show he understood.

It only took him fifteen minutes to drive the trap along the coast road to Garryhinch House. On the way they passed the turn which earlier had led them to Garretstown House. Fyre noticed that a sudden silence came over Melisa as they passed the turn.

'Terrible, whatever happened to Mr Egan; he seemed such a nice man,' Melisa said, as the trap trundled along.

'You knew him?' Fyre asked. So far on their journey he had resisted the temptation to quiz her. He had gauged that she was a complex and very intelligent woman. He could sense that she had secrets and knew how to keep them.

'Only briefly, I met him at one of his Lordship's parties, just three weeks ago, and then the following Sunday at a funeral, for his late aunt.'

'Have there been a lot of deaths around here lately?' asked Fyre, trying to ask without alerting her to his probing intent.

'I don't know what you mean,' she said. Fyre noted that, if she was aware of the reason for his line of questioning, she was hiding it skilfully.

The trap trotted on down the road. The scenery

became even more spectacular, with jagged black rock rising from the low coastline like broken obsidian daggers. Spurs of headlands drove out into the sea, on each stood a huddle of small buildings, low cottages with slate roofs, surrounded by whitewashed outbuildings.

'There can't be much of a living out there,' commented Fyre as they passed one of the headlands. In the distance, there were bent figures of farmers tending crops of beet and potatoes.

'No, I suppose not. I grew up in London. I'm not really used to the countryside. When I came to study in Cambridge, that was the closest I came to country living. Rather naively I thought all country living was lying about on the riverside, having luncheon, and watching the spring sun arc across the sky.'

'It sounds idyllic,' said Fyre.

'It was,' Melisa's tone sounded melancholic.

'You're not enjoying your time in Ireland?' Fyre asked.

Melisa threw him a smile, 'I thought Mr Stone was the detective and you were the ghost hunter, Lord Fyre?'

Fyre returned her warm smile, and replied, 'We're both detectives. As for ghosts, that is a complex matter. Oh, and do call me Sebastian.'

'We're here,' Melisa suddenly announced, and she pointed to a large gothic-style gate that stood a few feet back from the dirt road.

Fyre looked up at it. It wasn't as large and impressive as the gatehouse at Castle Barry, but, in the warm sunlight, it seemed more welcoming. The gate stood open and a well-used road lead upward steeply through neat, landscaped gardens, carved into the side of a rolling hill. Fyre could not see any house, just a wall of black and dark green trees that arced around the hill and dropped back down to the sea.

'The house is actually quite small, far too small for the gardens and the outbuilding,' Melisa explained, 'Charles told me about it, the family that lived here before the Barrys took over went bankrupt. They invested all their money in canals, just as the Great Western arrived in Ireland. So only one wing of the house was ever built. Where the main house would have been is now a farmyard.'

'How unfortunate for them,' commented Fyre.

'And how fortunate for the Barrys. They bought the estate for a very small sum. I'm not sure why, no one actually lives here. Although, I would prefer this house to the one his Lordship has given us.'

'Not suitable for your work?' asked Fyre.

Melisa threw him the warm smile again, 'Not suitable for anything, not even the work of a female chemist. Come on, let's get to the party, we're late as it is.'

Sean geed the horse up the steep road. Melisa and Fyre had to hold onto the side of the trap as they ascended. After a hundred yards climbing, they crested the hill. The house was, as Melisa had said, smaller than expected, given the grand entrance and grounds around it. It was made of black granite stone, punctured with deep-set square windows, just two storeys high. To Fyre, it did look like one wing of much larger Georgian mansion, that was missing from the landscape. The sounds of chatting voices were drifting in the air, and Melisa was eager for Fyre and Stone to follow her, past the coach house and into the pleasure gardens beyond.

'I've got duties to attend to,' Sean told Stone.

'Just show me around before you go, Sean,' replied Stone softly. He called to Fyre, who was following Melisa around the yellow brick garden wall, toward the sounds of the party.

'I'll catch up.'

Fyre nodded, knowing that Stone was better employed as an investigator than a socialite.

'Shouldn't you go to the party too, sir?' Sean asked.

'Parties aren't really for me. So, the lady said no one lives here.'

'No, sir, just the head gardener in a cottage. I come out every day to lend a hand, and some summer help with the fruit picking, but other than that, the only life this place sees is his Lordship's parties.'

Fyre & Stone: The Resurrection Men

'Have you got the key to the house?'

'The front door is kept locked. I was told never to go in the old house, sir.'

Stone gave him a knowing look. Sean smiled and sighed, 'The back door lock is broken, you can push it with your shoulder, I've never gone further than the kitchen. There's not much in there.'

'Let's take a look anyway.'

Fyre was surprised to see a large gathering of people, dressed in bright clothes, and enjoying food from a series of long tables, ladened with sandwiches and nibbles.

'Quite the party,' he said.

This was not the dour social gatherings that he remembered in his youth; Ireland had always been behind the times when it came to socialising, particularly among the upper classes.

'When his Lordship sends out invitations every family in the district comes, whether they have an invitation or not,' Melisa whispered the last bit.

'Only the well-to-do ones, I presume?' asked Fyre, rhetorically.

Melisa didn't answer. Her smile seemed permanent now. It was as if the party brought her back from a deep depression, and she appeared bubbly and full of energy.

'Come on, I'll introduce you to everyone worth talking to, and a few that aren't.' Again she whispered the last part.

Fyre took a deep breath and followed her into the garden proper.

Sean, as instructed by Stone, stayed in the kitchen. It was, as Sean had said, sparsely furnished, and clearly had not been used in years. As Stone walked through the darkened corridors into rooms more brightly lit from the large windows, a sense of familiarity came over him. Every room, every doorway, even the smell of damp plasterwork and long extinguished peat fires, seemed somehow recognisable. He reached a living room, the chalk blue paint on the walls was peeling and the floor was gritty from an accumulation of dirt. Stone noticed that there were large square patches of brighter paint, where paintings had once hung. He also noticed that each room was devoid of furniture. What must have once been a lushly decorated and comfortable home, was now a damp shell.

He entered the living room, something niggling in the back of his mind, something he couldn't quite get to come to the front. He stood at the fireplace, a was a grand sandstone affair, with fine carvings and a wide mantel that may have once held an array of ornaments. He touched it with his fingertips, his mind still swirling and sense of disorientation coming over him. A sudden realisation that he had been here before, hit him like a lump hammer. He had been in this house, this room; he had touched this sandstone fireplace. A flash of memory ran across his mind. A woman sitting by a roaring fire. A child playing on a thick rug. Heat turning to cold. Light turning to darkness.

'Hello .... Ahhhh!!!!"

Stone punched before he looked. The man beside him reeled backwards, holding his nose. He saw a large man at the doorway, holding a bundle of sticks wrapped with twine.

He reached for the gun inside his jacket, but stopped himself immediately. The large man cried out.

'What's you hit 'em for?'

Stone looked at the man he'd just struck. He was lanky, dressed in workman's clothes and clutching his long nose with both his hands.

'Yeah, what's your game?' said the lanky man in a higher-than-normal voice.

Stone realised quickly that this was not an attack. 'I'm really sorry, you surprised me,' he rushed over to the stricken man and helped him away from the far wall.

'Who are you?' demanded the large man.

'I'm a guest of his lordship,' replied Stone. He was hoping that that fact he was wearing one of Fyre's spare suits would negate his clear working-class Dublin accent.

'Oh,' said the large man, his attitude changing

instantly, 'Very sorry we startled you then sir, aren't we Mr Potts?'

Potts, still holding his nose, replied, 'Yes, sir, very sorry, sir.'

'The house isn't open to guests, actually, sir,' added the large man.

'Oh yes, I gathered, I wandered in by mistake. I'm very sorry about your nose.'

'It's alright, sir,' replied that large man, 'He's been hit on the hooter many times, he'll shake it off, won't you, Mr Potts?'

Potts looked to his colleague in confusion then to Stone, he gave a false smile and a thumbs up sign.

'I'll be fine, sir, just a bump.'

Stone continued to apologise as he walked from the living room to the now open front door of the house. There was no sign of Sean outside, and he hoped the boy had the good sense to leave the kitchen when he heard a commotion.

'It's alright, sir, no harm done,' said the large man.

'That's right, sir,' added Potts, his hand away from his nose now, Stone could see a red mark across his face, where the punch had caught him flatly, 'Me and Mr Grey here are just gonna get back to work.'

'You work for his Lordship then?' asked Stone.

The front door of the house slammed shut, and his question remined unanswered.

Stone was going to walk around the house and find Sean, but he saw the two men watching him from inside the large windows. He had no choice now but to join Fyre and the party. He could still hear the sounds of chatting and laughter beyond the brick wall that separated the empty house from the formal garden. He leaned up against the wall, out of sight of the house and just able to peer into the garden itself. He had had no time alone since they left the asylum. He checked his outside pocket. Inside his pocket were the items he had lifted from the man they had brought in. There wasn't much to speak of. A small amount of money, a key with a number of it, a luggage receipt and a note, a yellow page, folded so tightly that he had to carefully open it up to read it.

Stone read the words twice.

'Bugger,' he said to himself, 'Fyre's not going to like this.'

Mr Grey and Mr Potts watched Stone round the corner walking towards the party.

'Is he one of them two men that was described to you, Mr Potts?'

'Yes, Mr Grey, that's him alright. Why didn't you give him one when he punched me like that?'

'All in good time,' replied Grey.

A noise made them spin around from the window. Sean, the gardener's helper, was standing in the doorway, a look of fear on his face.

'Come here, boy,' said Grey.

Sean's instincts kicked in. He ran.

'After him, Mr Potts!'

CHAPTER 16

Melisa was charming everyone as she introduced Fyre to them. Fyre noted her skill at complimenting each person or grouping in turn, changing her demeanour as required.

He had, in his youth, seen many society women pull off this trick. Manipulation could be a powerful tool for women in the upper echelons of society. Finally, at the end of the garden, standing in front of a large three walled building, which Fyre recognised as an orangery, Melisa moved through the crowd toward the gathered Barry family.

'Are you ready for this?' she whispered to him.

'No, but I'll meet them anyway. Were you ready to meet them; the first time, I mean?'

'Also no. But, like you, I met them anyway. Some of them are very nice.'

'And the others?' asked Fyre, his voice a whisper, even thought there was no need, the din of the party would have drowned out anything they said.

'Some of them …,' she hesitated before continuing, 'some of them wish I would just go away. Come on, there's no time like the present.'

Melisa waved to the members of the family and moved towards them.

'I'm sure they will wish me away too,' mumbled Fyre to himself. He quickly wondered what had happened to Stone, and hoped he hadn't found too much trouble.

He took a deep breath and marched forward, his best socialite face on. Melisa introduced each of the Barry family in turn. Fyre committed each name and face to his memory as he shook hands or gave a slight bow to nieces, nephews, cousins, and other extended members of the family. Finally, standing on a small hillock that overlooked the slopes of the vast garden, Fyre was brought into the presence of Lord Barry himself.

'Your Lordship,' said Melisa, 'this is Lord Fyre, our famous ghost hunter.' She gave Fyre a cheeky grin at the last words.

Lord Barry gave the slightest bow of his head and extended his hand. Fyre reciprocated and took in the man in an instant. Lord Barry was tall and elegant. In appearance, he looked very much like his son, Charles, although he was greying at the temples and his hair thinning on top. He wore a suit of dark greens and black tweed, which was common among the Irish aristocracy. Lord Barry had a fattened face, but his thin lips and sharp nose negated that. His eyes struck Fyre immediately. They were emerald-green, and shone with an intelligence and fierceness, something which was also common among Ireland's highest grandees.

Before Melisa could speak again, and before Fyre could offer any pleasantries, Lord Barry began introducing those around him. The inner circle of the Barry stood on the hillock, almost as a parody of Irish upper-class society. They were separated by height from all the other party goers, even members of their own family, and they stood alone, a sombre grouping, compared with the revellers around them.

As Lord Barry spoke, and called each of his family forward to shake Fyre's hand, Fyre wondered why the old man threw these expensive parties if he got no pleasure from them.

'These are my sisters, Catharina and Francine.' As Lord Barry spoke, two plump, middle-aged women bustled forward. They grinned manically at Fyre as he kissed their hands. His mind was abruptly cast back to flashes of childhood at such parties. Many similar women had visited his father's grand house in the summer, following the schedule of balls and parties which seemed endlessly to dominate his early memories.

'My First cousin, Thomas,' said Lord Barry.

Thomas was another tall man, his face similar to Lord Barry's, but lacking plumpness and emotion. Fyre noticed that the man's skin was pale, almost translucent, and his handshake was stone cold to the touch. Thomas didn't speak a word, but instead formed his mouth into the shape of 'how do you do?' without actually making a sound. His eyes too caught Fyre's attention; they were small, beady, and dead like a fish on a market slab.

'My nephew, Matthew, who I believe you have met?' said Lord Barry.

The familiar frame of Matthew Barry stood out from behind his aunts, and he grinned an embarrassed grin. 'So sorry about yesterday, old chap. A terrible bish on my part. My uncle gave me a real dressing down.'

Fyre shook his hand, 'Think nothing of it.'

'You've met the charming Melisa of course, my daughter-in-law. Where is Charles, my dear?'

'Detained at the asylum once again,' replied Melisa.

'That boy will work himself into an early grave,' Lord Barry said to Fyre.

Fyre gave a polite laugh, but Melisa interjected with, 'It was you who put him in charge of the whole project, your Lordship.'

If Lord Barry was put out by this comment, he hid it well, 'Yes, I did. Don't worry, Melisa dear, it was only a figure of speech. Ah! My daughters are here.'

Lord Barry's daughters arrived on the hillock, accompanied, as Fyre found out, by their husbands. The daughters, Victoria and Elizabeth were much younger than their brother Charles, barely out of their teens. They were very pretty and wearing their latest colourful summer dresses. Fyre exchanged greetings with each of the four of them in turn. Their husband, William married to Victoria and Xander married to Elizabeth, were older men. They must both have been in the forties.

After their initial introductions, there was the usual small talk. Fyre had become adept at engaging in small talk with the front of his mind, while the rest of his brainpower worked on other matters. He took in the two husbands of the younger Barry sisters. They were not what he had been expecting.

Stone was largely ignored as he walked through the party. There were long tables laid out with food of every kind. He noticed Max the butler from Castle Barry, with two other men, dressed at servants, pouring champagne at a table full of glasses.

Although he was hungry, he couldn't resist walking over to the champagne table. With his most annoying grin across his face, he lifted an empty glass and held it toward Max. The butler paused, just enough for Stone to notice, then he gave the lightest of nods and a pained smile.

'This is a Jacquesson and Fils ... Superior, sir. All the way from the Champagne region,' Max tried to pronounced the French name in a French accent, but his Afrikaans drawl overpowered it and made it sound comical.

'Well, beggars can't be choosers, eh Max,' replied Stone, his grin wider than ever.

'I suppose not, sir,' replied Max, clearly irritated. A young couple of men approached the table and Max immediately tended to them. Stone drank the champagne in two gulps; he didn't like it. He saw Fyre, standing outside a glass fronted building, overlooking the rest of the garden. He was surrounded by a small group of finely dressed people, and given that Matthew Barry was there, Stone guessed that Fyre had fitted in with the Barry family.

Before deciding what to do next, he took a moment to

observe and listen to party around him. He was listening to chattering voices. They were a mix of southern Irish, that strong Cork accent that seemed harsh and confrontational, and a more familiar Anglo-Irish, the educated tone of wealth, in a country he knew as desperately poor. For just a moment Stone's usually rock-solid concentration wavered. The vision, or whatever it was, in the asylum, added to the sense that he had been in that ruin of house before it was a ruin, was shaking him. He had secretly wanted to believe in Fyre's claims of supernatural powers, but his character, set firmly in the here and now of reality, was steadfast and overwhelmingly against the idea. Not much frightened John Stone, but now, standing here, among the dainties and well-to-do's, he felt a pang of fear rising in his soul.

Fyre spotted Stone standing alone in a crowd of people, who were grouped into circles, of chatting and laughing. Despite the expense of his borrowed suit, Stone stood out like a sore thumb.

'... and tell me, Lord Fyre, did the ghosts of any of the murderers ever come back to haunt you?'

Fyre had briefly lost concentration, while watching Stone in the garden. He was concerned for his friend, and quietly convinced that their friendship was part of some greater universal plan.

'Oh, forgive me, Lady Catharina, what did you ask?'

Catharina and her sister Francine had cornered Fyre away from the rest of the family. They seemed obsessed with his 'adventures' as they called them. But it was clear to Fyre why they had singled him out for conversation. Both women were clearly unmarried, and, despite being twenty or more years older than him, he was a suitable target.

Fyre tried to let his ability to use social niceties overpower his desire to be rid of these two fawning women.

'No, no ghosts. Ghosts is a misnomer anyway. Those who contact us from beyond life, are spirits, lost on their way to the next world.'

'Oh, very interesting,' said Catharina, 'I read in one of the pamphlets that you can talk to your dead pets. I wonder,

Lord Fyre, could you contact my cat for me?'

Fyre had to control both the temptation to laugh in the woman's face, and the temptation to tell her to go away, in the sort of way that Stone would find easy.

Luckily for him, Fyre was saved by Stone. He took Fyre by the arm and said to the two women, who were standing so close to him that Stone had to almost barge them out of the way, 'If you will excuse Lord Fyre, ladies, there is an urgent message for him.'

'Oh, from whom?' asked Francine.

'Julius Caesar.'

Stone led Fyre into the orangery, and both of them stood behind the gnarled trucks of the trees, so as not to be seen by the Barry family, just feet away.

'Julius Caesar?' asked Fyre with a smile.

'Could be another old woman's cat,' replied Stone, but he had no smile. Fyre could tell something was wrong.

'Found something in the house?'

'Yes and no. Sort of.'

'John, are you alright?'

Stone didn't want to tell Fyre about the vision in the asylum, or the sensation in the house, not yet anyway.

'I found this in the pocket of the man we brought in this morning.'

Stone handed Fyre two sheets of paper.

Fyre read them carefully.

'Are they real?'

'I don't see why not. A postal receipt for the letter from Matthew Barry to you, and a bank receipt for the draft for our payment. All paid and send by one Daimen Holt.'

'So the letter came from London, not from Cork.'

'Seems so. He was clever about it too; he sent the letter to Cork first and gave instructions to the postmaster to re-post it to Dublin. All paid for, of course.'

'So that mean, that Matthew Barry is …'

'Yes, the Matthew Barry out there, is Matthew Barry, stands to reason. He didn't send the letter, he didn't pay us, and when he didn't know anything about it …'

'It's because he really didn't know anything about it.'

'Insane theory number one, out the window, I think,' said Stone with a laboured grin.

'So it would seem, but it does leave several unanswered questions,' stated Fyre.

Stone had already formed a list of questions before he called Fyre into the orangery, 'Yes, one, why did Matthew Barry bother to pretend he sent the letter and the money?'

'Two,' added Fyre, 'who is Holt and why did he send a letter from Matthew Barry?'

'Three, who killed William Egan and his valet?'

'Four, who attacked us at Sean's cottage last night, and why?'

'Five, who killed Sean's sister?'

'Was she murdered?' asked Fyre, genuinely.

'I …' Stone hesitated, 'I think so.'

'What do we do now?'

'You stay with Matthew Barry. If the man they arrested and are keeping in the asylum is Daimen Holt, then I need to talk to him.'

'Be careful John, they've attacked us once already.'

'I think that was a warning.'

'Charles Barry gave us a warning, in a roundabout way.'

'I'd guessed. Then he's our first suspect.'

Steve Downes

142

CHAPTER 17

Melisa stepped out from behind a knotted branch of an orange tree. She had a charming smile across her lips and inquisitive eyes.

'Are you two hunting murderers? … ghosts?' she asked, whimsically.

'We're more concerned about not making a spectacle of ourselves at this party,' replied Fyre.

'It's too late for that, your names have circulated around the garden, much thanks to his Lordship's sisters. I was trying to rescue you, but I was receiving a grilling of my own from Matthew.'

'Really?' asked Stone, 'Is that normal?'

Melisa laughed, 'You don't know Irish socialites very well, Mr Stone.'

'I know one,' he nodded toward Fyre, 'but he's not very social.'

'I beg to differ,' said Melisa, 'he's been nothing but fascinating so far. His Lordship is very impressed, and there are two ladies out there who have taken quite the fancy to him.'

Stone let out a snort of laughter, then coughed to try

and hid it. Fyre just smiled at him with his eyes.

'Come on you two, enough with your secrets and your ghosts, it's kite time, the highlight of any Barry party.'

Melisa rushed from the orangery, Fyre and Stone walking behind her, unsure what she meant by 'kite time'.

A few miles away, high on the ridge overlooking the jagged coast, the sun was baking the walls of the asylum.

Holt sat calmly in the cell. He was a man who liked to take risks, and he had taken a big one by allowing himself to be imprisoned. So many dead ends had presented themselves over the years of his obsessive investigation. When a series of murders in Dublin seemed to come out the blue, it was too good an opportunity to miss. If he was ever going to find those he so desperately sought, it would have to be now. He was running out of friends, money and hiding places.

Long ago Holt had managed to gain control of his temper and his nerves. As he sat on the thin mattress of the small bed, he noticed his left leg was slightly trembling. It would be imperceptible to anyone else, but to him it was evidence of his dire situation. So many things had to go right.

He could hear a commotion echoing down the corridor outside his cell. A familiar voice reached his ears, and his heart sank.

Perhaps, this time, he had risked too much.

'Will you be able to slip out?' whispered Fyre to Stone as they exited the orangery and stepped into the bright light of the garden terrace.

'No one here is really interested in me, despite the nice suit. You can dress a beggar as a prince, but he'll still look hungry.'

'There are plenty of hungry princes and princesses here, let me tell you.'

Stone looked at Fyre quizzically. He explained, 'Not all is as it seems. I'll take a wager with you that a lot of these landowning families are living hand-to-mouth. Times are tough and the gentry in Ireland isn't what it was. Take the two younger Barry sisters. Over there.'

Stone scanned the terrace and spotted two young women, who looked very alike. Everyone except Fyre and himself were busy staring out over the garden, it was clear some spectacle was about to take place.

'Very pretty,' said Stone, 'what about them?'

'They've married beneath themselves and their family. One such marriage could be explained away, but two.'

'Maybe they fell in love?' Stone asked, but he knew what Fyre was alluding too.

'No, they married local farmers, new money, hard workers, and older men. I'd take a second wager they were forced to marry by their father.'

'For once I wouldn't take that bet. But what does it mean to us?'

There was a loud cry from the gathered crowd and several large kites rose into the air, rising on the breeze coming off the nearby sea.

'I don't know. But I'm sure it has some significance. You'd better go now, John, I'll see you back at the cottage just before sunset, if the older Barry sisters haven't made an honest man of me.'

'That will take them longer than a day,' joked Stone. Without another word he darted to his left and disappeared behind the garden wall.

Melisa came running back from the front of the terrace and took Fyre by the hand.

'Where is Mr Stone?'

'He's gone to check for ghosts,' replied Fyre, 'and he doesn't like kite flying very much.'

'He's missing out, come on, you'll like this; his Lordship is an expert.'

He followed Melisa to the front of the terrace. The Barry family had assembled in a long line, all of the women standing beside each other to the left, and to the right, all of the men, rather awkwardly lined up, as if they didn't know, or like, each other. Only Fyre and Melisa mixed.

Below them, in the sweeping extent of the garden, over

a hundred guests craned their necks upwards as six large kites began to sweep across the clear blue sky.

'I've seen kites like these before,' Fyre said. 'In China, they can fly hundreds of them at a time.'

'I've love to see that, this is the most I've ever seen,' replied Melisa.

The six large kites swooped across the bright blue sky, accompanied by the sounds of amazement from the gathered crowd.

As Melisa had said, Lord Barry was quite an expert at controlling his kite. He was able to manoeuvre it in dazzling circles and figure-eights, far exceeding the skill of the other flyers. Fyre stood behind Melisa, watching the show. There was something about her that he couldn't quite get fathom. On the face of it, she seemed like a bright, intelligent, modern women; not the sort of woman who ended up in rural Ireland, married into an old family. He wanted to get closer to Matthew Barry. He wanted to put him under pressure about the letter and its contents. Even if it was true that the man, currently locked up in the asylum, accused of murder, had written the letter, there still must be some connection between Matthew Barry and this detective Holt. He edged across the terrace. Matthew Barry had placed himself at the far end of the rising ground. Fyre lacked Stone's seemingly natural skill of moving unseen. Matthew Barry looked over at him. It was a withering glance. Then, without a word to his family, he marched off in the opposite direction.

'Come on, let's get some wine before it's all gone,' Melisa seemed to come out of nowhere and gripped Fyre's arm, 'we've got dinner with his Lordship and his sisters; you'll need a few glasses to hold your resolve.'

'I don't drink alcohol,' stated Fyre, 'tell me, will Matthew be there?'

'I wouldn't think so, he's not in favour with his Lordship, I think he's been sent on some errand first thing in the morning.'

'Has he?' Fyre mused for a moment, then hatched an idea, 'Why don't you have that glass of wine and you and I have a chat. Get to know each other. Let's go and sit somewhere quiet.'

'Lord Fyre!' exclaimed Melisa with a girlish grin, 'tongues will wag, you know.'

'That, my dear lady, is nothing new around me,' he reciprocated with a grin.

Stone was very good at sneaking around. He moved stealthily around the old house. The front door was locked and the back door, where he and Sean had entered the house, had been wedged shut from the inside. He was concerned for Sean, but thought it probable that the boy had returned to his duties when he and Fyre had gone into the garden party. He couldn't see any sign of the two men he had encountered in the house. His instincts told him that they were trouble. They were certainly not local to the area, and had the look of the type of thugs he had known all his life.

As he pondered how he was going to get quickly back to the asylum, a trap pulled up the hill and turned into the yard. He recognised it, and both of its occupants. The chaplain was in the driving seat. He was chatting loudly to his passenger, who was sitting stoically, staring into the distance.

'What I don't understand, Charles, is why we have to have such a large morgue in the building at all. It can't be good for the mental health of the patients,' the chaplain said as he set about securing the horse.

Stone was able to watch them both from behind the corner of the old house.

'I told you, dear Chaplain, I didn't design the building. You will have to speak to father about it.'

'When I ask your father, he says to speak to you, when I ask you, you say to speak to him. It seems we are an endless circle.'

Charles Barry got from the trap and straightened his jacket.

'And where would you have the surgeon do his work?'

'Why do we need a surgeon? If the patient is already passed on?'

'Then what you're suggesting, Chaplain, is all we need for our deceased patients is a prayer book and some holy water.'

'Don't be glib, Charles.'

They began to walk towards the garden, and Stone could only catch the first words of Barry's next statement.

'I told you before, Chaplain, our work is to do with the mind and the body, we must investigate both in order ……'

Stone stood out from behind the masonry and scanned the long line of carriages and traps. He could hear several servants, chatting loudly in an outbuilding, close by.

'He's a man of God,' said Stone to himself, 'I'm sure he'll forgive me.' He unhooked the horse, patted it on the flank.

'Sorry to interrupt your rest dear boy, but my need is great.'

Fyre and Melisa sat on a bench, overlooking the flower garden, where dozens of guests were busy socialising.

Nervously, Fyre noticed the two older Barry sisters seemingly scanning the crowd for someone. He suspected that someone was him. But he and Melisa were shielded by a large rhododendron.

'You are hunting ghosts?' said Melisa as she carefully sipped her wine.

'What makes you say that?'

'You're about to attempt to glean information from me.' She gave him a knowing look.

'Perhaps about Charles, His Lordship, the wayward Matthew, or the married off girls you told John Stone about earlier?'

'You heard that?'

'Accidently, I assure you.'

Fyre felt he needed to get back on the front foot. 'Actually, I wanted to know more about you.'

'Am I a suspect in William Egan's murder?'

Fyre didn't reply to that question, instead he kept his focus. 'We all have our secrets, of course. You don't have to tell me yours.'

'What makes you think I have any secrets, I'm a scientist, despite what society thinks of women with minds of their own. And I'm married to Charles, who is a brilliant doctor of alienation.'

'Yes, I gathered all of that. But, who are you really?'

'I don't understand.'

Fyre considered his next words carefully. 'If I were my colleague, John Stone, sitting here, talking to you now, I would be quite blunt in my observations.'

Melisa sighed and pretended to take another sip of her wine.

'Very well, I'll play along. Be John Stone. Be brutal,' she gave a derogatory laugh.

'As you wish. We were not born into high society. You do a very good impression that you were.'

Melisa didn't reply immediately. Fyre was looking away from her face, but with his peripheral vision he could see concern cross her features.

'What tells you that, may I ask?'

'Only the very slightest of things. An over emphasis on certain words when you battle against whatever access you grew up with. The way you hold that glass of wine. Your unreserved nature toward men that are not your husband. But mostly it is the joy you take in the trappings of wealth. That is something I found to be joyless among those who grew up in it.'

Again Melisa left a long pause before she spoke. 'All of those things could be explained away,' she said, her voice becoming serious for the first time.

'Of course.'

Again a pause, this time Fyre could feel something about to break. He could sense her anger and her attempt to control it. 'Is it a crime for a woman to want to better herself?' she asked, her accent slipped, and Fyre could detect the harsh tone of a common London drawl.

'No, of course not.'

Melisa almost immediately regained her composure,

her voice returning to the educated sound that all Oxbridge students seemed to adopt.

'If I were a man would you point these things out?'

'I don't wish to attack you, Melisa, or expose anything of your past, unless it has something to do with the strange deaths that have taken place here in recent days.'

Melisa put her half-filled glass of wine down on the bench and stood up.

'You know, Lord Fyre, it is difficult for you to understand the true nature of class prejudice. Perhaps your colleague would have done a better job of questioning me.'

'I think undoubtedly he would. Please accept my apologies, Melisa, I did not mean to insult you.'

'You have not insulted me. I can't help you with the deaths you speak about, I can't even help you with the Barry family. For the reasons you have pointed out, and many more, I'm not really one of them. I will be leaving here soon, and Charles will be coming with me, and I hope we can leave this conversation behind.'

Fyre understood what she meant. 'Of course, dear lady.'

'I think I see Charles now. I'm going to join him. I'll see you for dinner tonight. It's quite late, his Lordship dines at strange hours. If you're lucky, his sisters will get drunk at this party and won't be there.'

'I will pray for small mercies,' Fyre threw her a smile.

'Until then.'

Fyre watched Melisa join her husband on the terrace. The kites had come down and Lord Barry was enjoying the adulation of his guests.

Fyre felt a deep sense of something being wrong with Melisa. It was not that she was hiding her past. He felt she was hiding something more dangerous.

As he sat there, isolated from the crowd, he saw a figure moving among the tall garden reeds.

It was not a living person.

Fyre watched as the barely shaped figure moved across the garden, dissolving as it moved from shadow to light. It seemed to suddenly reach out. To grab at Melisa.

For a moment Melisa turned and looked out into the nothingness. The figure melted away.

'I'm not the one hunting ghosts, Melisa,' mumbled Fyre to himself.

CHAPTER 18

Stone found it easy to pass through the security of the asylum. The building was so massive and staffed so sparely, he was able to move from room to room without being seen. As he crept along a wide corridor, the sound of approaching shoes clicking on the floor made him dart into a room to his right. He closed the door, but left it slightly ajar. He saw out of the gap in the door a constabulary officer pass by. He appeared to pause for the briefest of moment, just beyond the doorway Stone was hiding in, but he moved off again toward the main entrance. Breathing a sigh of relief, Stone continued to move down the corridor. He had passed a sign for the secure wing of the building earlier that morning, and felt sure that if this Holt man was still in the building, he would be held there.

It wasn't difficult for Fyre to slip away from the party. Lord Barry was delighting his guests with the latest invention to reach this part of Ireland. Music from the gramophone he was working himself, rang out thinly across the garden, and the crowd herded close together to get a better look at this marvellous machine.

Fyre could feel a heavy mix of sensations in his mind. The spirits that had appeared to him over the last few weeks seemed to have disappeared, and his, often debilitating, self-doubt was returning in their place. There was no doubt in his mind that Melisa was hiding something from her past, and that Matthew Barry was hiding something in the present. Equally he felt that Stone was getting caught up in the whole strangeness of the situation. Perhaps all of this was in their heads. High society families always had secrets. There were plenty of skeletons in his own family's closets, some of which he wanted to deny.

He walked into the courtyard of the abandoned house. A scream seemed to ring out across the courtyard. Fyre's eyes darted left and right, looking for the source. He knew almost immediately that the scream was only in his head. The gathered horses from the carriages and traps of the guests didn't move from their half-sleep. He could feel a spirit reaching out. This was not one of the weak voices that had invaded his consciousness in the last few weeks. This was more familiar, this was the scream of a disturbed soul. This was a victim. Dead, but not yet gone from this world. He gripped his swagger stick tightly, and followed the scream. He walked slowly, the world of reality swirling around him, so that his peripheral vision blurred into an ever-moving mirror of colours and shapes. As he got closer to the house, he could feel the presence of several souls, each one making a low wailing noise. Together, these voices formed the screaming sound he had heard. Now, as he got right up to the wall of the house, the scream had ceased and only the sickening sensation of trapped spirits enveloped him.

'What happened to you?' he asked.

He subconsciously pushed at the door of the house, which gave way easily. He was inside before he even realised. An unnatural darkness seemed to consume the summer light outside the doorway.

'What happened to you? Your voices are filled with fear.'

He walked through the rubble filled hallway and

turned into a large room. To Fyre's eyes the room was lavishly furnished. It was night-time, and a large, roaring fire was flickering in the hearth.

He could make out the figures of two women. They were sitting close to each other, almost huddled in fear. He could see their eyes, wide with terror, but nothing else was clear.

Just as he made out two more figures, small, children, hiding under the swirling shades of the women, a new presence entered the room.

Fyre reeled. A black, dense malevolent creature burst into his vision. The screams echoed and Fyre watched in horror as the formless black mass engulfed and destroyed the others. It seemed to stab at them, slashing, tearing, utterly obliterating their forms. For a moment, Fyre reached out, lashing with his stick, but there was nothing to hit. This was the past; it was a whisper of what had been.

When the moment of destruction had passed, Fyre watched the black formless figure begin to ebb away.

'Who are you? …. Why did you do this?'

The figure, just for the briefest second, solidified into the shape of a tall man. His face a blank, smooth oval of nothingness. His arm reached up, an ill-formed hand stretched out smoke-like fingers and pulled the black face away as if it were a mask.

Fyre caught a glimpse of a face.

A face he knew.

Stone watched the corridor with the locked cells for a long minute. There were no guards now, and no noise whatsoever from the cells themselves. There were two cells on each side of the corridor. The doors were elaborate ironwork made to look like the heavy wooden doors of a grand estate house, but they had solid locks on one side. The cells on the left-hand side appeared to be empty. Stone peeped through the spy hole and looked into a space filled with light from a large, barred window. The bed was large too, much more like a hotel bed. It looked quite comfortable. Stone had been in many prison cells over the years, none of them looked as clean and inviting as this.

Cautiously watching for guards, he crossed the corridor and peeped into the third cell. It was occupied. At first Stone thought that the room he was seeing through the peephole had been left in a ransacked state. The sheets of the bed and the mattress were strewn across the floor. He could make out stains on the walls, dark symbol-like scrawling that covered the entire surface. It was only at the last second that he spied the figure of a woman huddled among the debris.

He couldn't make out any of the woman's features, her long unkept hair had fallen over her face. She sat on the floor, her legs extended and under the bare bed. Stone could make out long lines on her skin, like thin scars that were still bleeding.

He jerked back from the peephole, and subconsciously checked the corridor for guards. He was still alone. He wondered to himself if this poor wretch of a woman was crazy, perhaps in this cell for her own protection. He moved the cover of the peephole once again and rested his eye against it. There was flash of movement. The woman's eye appeared right before him. It was bloodshot, wide, and wild. A sapphire blue pupil flared as their two eyes met for a split second.

Stone almost let out a scream. He pulled away from the door, letting the little metal flap fall back across the peephole. Gathering his breath, and checking the corridor again, he approached the last cell.

'I do appreciate this, sir,' said Fyre and he and the chaplain walked back from the party towards the yard.

'No problem, but I know that his Lordship is very keen that you come to dinner tonight. Are you sure this investigation of yours is worthwhile? The police have a man in custody. And that chap you brought in this morning seemed to be quite mad.'

'I have found that madness is a relative term; it all depends on where your own mind is.'

'My mind is firmly on serving my flock, even if they are mad.'

'And are they mad?' Fyre asked in a serious tone, 'Those people in the asylum, are they mad or misunderstood?'

'I'm afraid I can't answer that, that would be a question for Doctor Charles. I only see them all as God's creatures. Mad or not, I am here to save their souls.'

'What happens to the ones you can't save?' Fyre muttered under his breath.

'Ah!' exclaimed the chaplain, as they rounded the garden wall, 'Looks like you won't be joining Mr Stone just now.'

'What's the matter?'

'Someone appears to have taken my horse.'

'I think I know who that might have been.'

The chaplain laughed a genuine laugh.

'I can only apologise for my friend's behaviour.'

'Oh don't old boy, this is the most excitement we've had in these parts for years. No doubt Mr Stone is chasing ghosts and murderers as we speak.'

Fyre's mind was spurred by this statement, and he asked the next question without really thinking about it.

'What happened to the family in this house?'

The chaplain's smile disappeared, and he took on a stoic demeanour. 'Shall we walk into the village? It's not far really and it's a nice afternoon.'

'Yes, a walk will do me good.'

They walked down the hill and joined the road. In the distance, Fyre could see the steeple of the village church above a sea of bright green trees. The road stood back from the rocky coast to their right. The sea seemed clam, but below them, Fyre could make out breaking waves battering themselves against the jagged granite outcrops.

As the chaplain told him a long and sometimes winding story of the fate of the family who had lived in the house, Fyre began to piece together a tragic event.

'They said he lost all his money gambling,' the

chaplain said, 'something I myself abhor. I suppose he just snapped.'

'So the father killed his own wife and children?'

'Yes, that's the crux of it.'

'I suppose it was quite a scandal at the time?'

'Yes, I suppose it was. I wasn't here of course. I was studying in Trinity at the time. But I believe his Lordship kept the worst of the story away from the press.'

'He can do that?'

The chaplain snorted a laugh, 'Surely, Lord Fyre, you know who really runs this country.'

Fyre knew exactly what the chaplain meant by that remark. Despite all the talk of unions, and home rule and power to the masses, it was still a select group of rich and powerful men who ran Ireland as a largely private concern.

'Tell me, sir, where was Charles Barry, during all of this?'

'Oh,' the chaplain seemed to think hard about the question as they walked along the road, 'you must remember this is second hand information. I wasn't even in Ireland at the time. In fact, I had never dreamt of coming here, that is before his Lordship offered me the position. Let me think, young Charles would have been in Cambridge. No! wait, he wouldn't, he was too young, he was still at school. About sixteen or seventeen years old. Why do you ask?'

'He's a man who interests me. Have you gotta to know him well?'

The chaplain gave another laugh of derision, 'No, unlike his eccentric father, Charles is very insular. More like his mother.'

'Tell me about his mother,' asked Fyre, his mind storing every word the chaplain said.

'Seen enough?' asked Holt.

The eye watching him for a long minute didn't blink. Holt had been aware of his observer, the tell-tale slide of metal on metal as the peephole cover opening alerted him. He didn't have to look, he kept his eyes focused on the sun's shadow crawling across the far wall of his cell.

'Why did you fake a letter to me and Fyre?' asked Stone's voice.

Holt immediately leapt up from the bed and ran to the door. 'Detective John Stone?'

'Ex-detective, as are you, Mr Holt. Answer my question.'

'There will be time enough for answers later. You've got to get me out of here.'

Stone tried to read Holt's eyes. They were concerned, but not panicked. They had intelligence. The man was not insane, but there was a wildness in his eyes that Stone had seen before in obsessives and zealots.

'I don't think so. They say you killed two men.'

'One of those was in self-defence.'

'And the other one?'

Holt grinned. It wasn't a manic grin, but there was malice in it.

'You and I are on the same side, Stone. Help me out of here and you can have your answers.'

'I prefer my answers from this side of the locked door,' Stone replied.

Holt took in a lungful of air. 'Then we are at an impasse.'

Stone didn't see it that way. He checked the corridor again. He was still alone. 'Why did you get us to come here? Was it the dead girl?'

Holt had sauntered over the small bed and sat back down. 'Dead girl?'

'The one in the morgue, the one I believe was murdered.'

Holt looked over at Stone's eyes once more. 'You've seen one, haven't you?'

'One what?'

'Don't play dumb, Stone. Fyre can see them, they can see them too. And now you.'

'You're mad,' spat Stone.

'Maybe. But you won't find any answers unless you

free me. Perhaps you should examine this dead girl of yours more closely, and while you're at it, check the bodies of one Mr Egan and Miss French.'

'What does that even mean?'

'Goodbye, Mr Stone, the next time you come here I might be dead. So I'd hurry if I were you.'

Stone heard the footsteps echo down the corridor before anyone appeared. He was moving in the opposite direction at speed.

CHAPTER 19

The chaplain had been very chatty, but his mind seemed never to focus on one subject. He went off on asides and Fyre found it difficult to bring him back naturally to the subject at hand.

He stopped at Sean's cottage, on the outskirts of the village. A feeling of dread came over him at he said goodbye to the chaplain, but kept his eyes on the small, thatched cottage.

'I suspect your friend has taken my horse to the asylum,' the chaplain said.

'I suppose he has. Once again I can only apologise for his behaviour. I'm sure he had a good reason for his actions.'

'I'm sure he had. Never mind, I enjoyed our walk and our chat. And I will see you both at his Lordship's dinner tonight at ten?'

'Of course.'

Fyre watched the chaplain walk up the hill and

disappear around the corner of the wooded road. He could sense that something was wrong in Sean's house. Cautiously he stepped inside the door. The living space was just as they had left it earlier in the morning.

'Hello,' Fyre called out. He walked through the house. Nothing seemed out of place, and yet he got the distinct impression there was something here; something he couldn't quite place. It felt like it was neither living, nor dead. This was a presence that terrified him. It was the same presence he had felt when the letter, supposedly from Matthew Barry, had arrived.

'You're trying to reach me but I can't contact you,' he said to the spirit he was sure was there in some sense, 'I wonder why. Is it John Stone you want to contact? Are you Sean's sister?'

He hesitated, A thought occurred to him. 'Where are you? Where are you that you are neither dead nor alive?'

The chaplain walked along the road that led past the junction for Charles and Melisa Barry's house. On the hill above he could see the dark frame of the asylum looming into the late afternoon blue sky. His eyes caught a familiar shape up ahead. On the side of the road, with the reins carefully tied around a low tree branch, his horse stood calmly. The chaplain quickened his pace and joined his horse, undid the reins, and patted the animal on the flank.

'You've had a long day, old fellow. Now, where is the wayward Mr Stone?'

Stone watched from the thicket of trees as, after a long look around, the chaplain mounted his horse and rode it back up the hill toward the asylum. He had always had a paranoid mindset. Much of his youth had been spent dodging police, gangs, and child abductors on the back streets of Dublin; it had left his trust in humanity very low. He needed to talk to Fyre. He didn't want to believe the sensations and thoughts that were invading his mind, nor did he want to believe that Holt was ensnaring him in some conspiracy, but this unquenchable curiosity had now got the better of him.

Holt heard the door bolt being undone. He steadied himself, but feared the worst. He had hoped and gambled that Stone would act on his words without needing solid proof. He had also hoped that it was Lord Fyre who came to his rescue rather than Stone. Fyre would be easier to manipulate. Although there was something about Stone, something more than he was expecting.

The door swung outwards and standing there was a man in a long coat.

Holt made the slightest movement, as if he were about to leap up and challenge the man physically. Before he could do so, the man in the long coat raised his index finger and two men dressed in uniforms appeared, their heads covered with cage-like helmets, their hands gripping vicious looking batons.

'You're a very dangerous man, I believe,' said the chief surgeon.

'A rat is always dangerous when he is cornered,' replied Holt.

He had looked around his cell, when they first put him in it, for anything that could be fashioned into a weapon. His own hands could be deadly, as he had trained himself to fight at close quarters from an early age.

The chief surgeon slid his right hand into his white overall and carefully took out a pistol.

'This is yours, I believe,' he aimed the weapon at Holt.

'Yes.'

'I was issued one of these when I was in the army. I never used it in combat of course, being a man of medicine, you understand?'

'Of course.'

'I did become quite a good shot at the range,' spoke the chief surgeon in a whisper, then he added in a sudden harsh tone, 'I don't want to shoot you, Mr Holt, but I have been asked to examine you. I would prefer if you complied. But if not, I have drugs that will make you comply.'

'I see. Well I don't want to be shot, or drugged.'

'Very good, then we have an understanding.'

The chief surgeon gestured, and the guards entered the cell, one of them taking the pistol from his hand and holding it toward Holt.

'Now, shall we begin?'

The cell door slammed shut.

The evening was drawing in fast, and although there was plenty of light left in the western sun, the tree shadows were drawing long silhouettes across the fields. Fyre had looked around Sean's cottage, to see if anything would spring a vision or offer a clue. He found nothing of note. Sean had few possessions, outside of domestic cookware and old clothes. Fyre felt a pang of guilt at having snooped around the boy's home.

He entered Roisin's room. From his experience, those who took their own lives were often temporarily trapped as spirits in this world. In his early days of enlightenment in India, he had been haunted by such spirits. He ran his bare hand across the bedsheets of her small bed. There were no immediate sensations in his mind. If this were under different circumstances, he would not find it strange. The spirits chose when to speak to him, not the other way around. Fyre was sure that this unfortunate girl would speak to him here. But there was nothing, just an empty bed. Nervous while waiting for either Stone or Sean to return, Fyre hit on the idea of examining the garden where he had been attacked last night. In the evening light, with the purple hills of gorse behind and the blanket of trees around it, the garden at the back of the house seemed just as sinister as it had the night before.

He held his swagger stick tightly in his hand as he walked around. There seemed to be nothing unusual in the garden space. Beds of root vegetables were laid out neatly; beyond them several sheds were in various states of collapse. Fyre supposed that small animals may have been kept there at some point. A rhubarb patch had been left to go wild, the plants were now shoulder high. He noticed that several of the plants had been cut down at an angle. As he looked closer, he could see the fresh sap from the cuts across the rhubarb stems. They had been made sharply from right to left, going downwards. He followed the line of the cuts to a disturbed piece of ground nearby, the exact spot where he had been attacked last night.

'No spirit did this,' he whispered to himself.

'Then what did?' Stone's unexpected voice made Fyre jump and spin his stick around.

'Careful now,' said Stone, 'you could have someone's eyes out with that.'

'John! I wish you wouldn't keep doing that.'

'I have to do something,' said Stone.

'Me too,' said Fyre.

They both spoke at once, 'I have to dig a grave.'

They both looked at each other.

'I wasn't expecting you to say that,' said Stone.

'Nor I you.'

'Which one?'

'Miss French. I believe William Egan may have been drawn here by her death, which makes her death suspicious. I had a vision of Egan back in Dublin, only to find his name, and dead body here, connected to our suspects.'

'Good enough reason, I guess,' said Stone, 'Better than mine.'

'And yours is?'

Stone hesitated. He tried to find the right words to express what he was feeling, but somehow no sentence in his mind could make it to his mouth. Fyre came to his aid.

'You think Rosin was murdered, and that her spirit has tried to contact you.'

'The first part, yes.'

'And the second?'

'Can we not talk about that now?'

'As you wish. There are shovels in the hallway.'

'We'd better change into something more suitable for grave digging,' said Stone, looking at his own clothes that he had barrowed form Fyre, 'This looks ridiculous even without digging up a dead body.'

'It's too bright now for such a thing,' Fyre had his reservations. He had secretly hoped Stone would have disagreed with the plan and convinced him to do something else.

'We'll go down to the catholic graveyard at sundown, by the time we get to the one in the village it will be dark enough to hide us.'

'We'll miss his lordship's dinner,' Fyre pointed out.

'We'll be fashionably late.'

Sean woke up, not from sleep, but from a waking nightmare that physically seemed to distress him.

'Welcome back, young man,' said a soft voice.

'Where am I,' Sean asked; his eyesight was blurred, and his senses dulled.

'You've returned from the grave, if only for a short while, in the body of this unwitting young man.'

Sean struggled, but he was restrained in a metal chair by tightly bound leather straps.

'Yes, I see and feel your rage. Listen to my voice and that anger will be your energy.'

'Who am I?' screamed Sean, 'Who am I?'

There was a slow, dreary laughter, followed by the words, 'You are a murderer.'

With each passing hour, Fyre and Stone grew more concerned about Sean's welfare.

'He could be working late, summer hours and all that,' said Stone unconvincingly.

'Perhaps,' replied Fyre, scribbling on a piece of paper.

'What are you doing?'

'Leaving a note for him.'

'Don't say anything about the graves.'

'Of course not.'

'Or my suspicions.'

'No.'

'Or about my conversation with Holt.'

'I'm not an idiot, Stone!'

Stone giggled, 'Sorry. Come on, it's getting dark.'

They went to the door, but the trot of a horse on the road above the cottage made them slip back inside.

'What is it?' asked Stone.

'Lord Barry must have sent a trap for us.'

'Bugger! Come on then, out the back, we'll rough it across country.'

Stone struggled through the scrubland, but not as badly as Fyre, who found it difficult to keep his balance and snagged himself on every thornbush and low hanging branch.

'Keep up,' whispered Stone.

'Don't wait for me.'

They emerged on the roadside near the Protestant church. The nearby houses had a few lamps lit inside their windows, but otherwise there was no one about. As Stone had suggested they followed the lane, as they had done for the funeral, to the circular graveyard that stood alone, surrounded only by fields of bleating sheep.

'Ready to do this?' asked Stone.

'No,' said Fyre, honestly, 'are you sure about this, John?'

'It's the only way we'll know, I don't trust anyone around here, this whole place is rotten to the core. Can't you feel it?'

Fyre pressed his friend, 'Tell me what it is you feel?'

Stone thought about this for a moment, as he stood over the fresh cut grave of the young woman he was about to exhume.

'It feels like I've been here before, as if something or someone has drawn me here and is in control of everything that's happening.'

'Interesting.'

'You think I'm irrational?'

'Yes, but not about this.'

Stone didn't reply. His mind was now set on the task in hand. He lit a hooded lantern to its lowest setting and drove his shovel into the still loose soil of the grave. They made quick work on removing the soil, and Stone, without hesitancy, lowered himself into the grave cut and was able to pry open the cheap coffin. Fyre moved the lantern closer to the cut and saw the hollow face of a young woman looking up at him. He had seen many dead bodies in his time, but somehow her pale skin and closed eyes seemed to stab at his courage. He leaned back as Stone took the lantern down into the grave.

After a few moments, Fyre asked, 'Anything?'

'Yes,' replied Stone, his voice steady as a rock, 'her neck is badly bruised.'

'If she did hang herself, that would be the case, wouldn't it?'

'Yes, it would, but this is different, the bruising goes down her arms, her chest, one side of her face. This was no suicide.'

'If anyone at Castle Barry is involved in this, they know we're up to something now,' said Fyre as they made their way back down the laneway.

'For sure,' replied Stone.

They had filled in the grave and Stone had been silent since they left it. Fyre had noticed that he had even stood for a moment at the graveside, as if in prayer or respect for the dead.

'If she did try to speak to you,' said Fyre as they reached the gates of church, 'then at least she got her message across and is at peace now.'

Stone carefully opened the gate. A chain was sitting across the rungs on one side, but it was unlocked.

'That's the thing, Fyre, I don't think she is at rest. That was her body, but it didn't feel like she was there. It was like an empty grave.'

Fyre had a sudden feeling of dread come over him. He had read ancient texts on such things, but they were too nightmarish even to contemplate.

'Now,' said Stone, as he made his way across the grave, 'let's see what's in grave number two.'

Fyre stood behind Stone as he made the first cut into

the soil of Miss French's grave.
He feared for his friend, and he feared what they may find.

CHAPTER 20

'The soil shouldn't be this loose,' said Stone as he shovelled further downwards into the grave.

'She was only buried a few weeks ago,' Fyre had stopped digging after they breached the first few feet of the grave. He was now holding the lantern above Stone.

'It should have settled by now; this has been dug up in the last few days.'

Just as Stone spoke, Fyre felt the familiar sensation of a vision coming over him. His mind was elevated from his body. He felt his consciousness moving across time and space as if some celestial storms were blowing it toward its destination. Once again, he was looking at the Dublin townhouse of William Egan, a man he knew to be lying dead on a cold slab in the nearby asylum. Egan was again trying to reach his front door, but some invisible force was preventing him.

'What does it mean?' said Fyre aloud.

'What?' called Stone from the grave cut.

Fyre snapped from his trance. 'William Egan, he's trapped somewhere, trying to escape. It is as if his spirit was unwillingly being held in this world.'

'I'm not sure about spirits, but I have found a body,' said Stone.

Stone reached up from the grave and took the lantern from Fyre. He held it close to what he had found in the hole.

The soil strewn face of a dead middle-aged man looked up at Fyre with eyes wide open.

'He's not been dead long,' said Stone.

'It's William Egan,' said Fyre, his mind drawing up a face from his memory. A meeting in Dublin Castle two years ago, a handshake and an exchange of pleasantries.

'Are you sure?'

'Yes, I'm sure.'

Stone took a closer look. He could see no injuries on the man's upper body or face.

'He does look uncannily like the man we saw in the mortuary yesterday, same clothes, same haircut, even the same facial features.'

'This is certainly Mr Egan, I met him once.'

'Then who are the two dead men in the asylum?'

Before Fyre could answer, a sensation of being watched made the hairs on the back of his neck stand up. He spun on his heels to see a figure standing close by, covered by the dark shadow of the church steeple, and standing on a raised tabletop grave, the figure was cloaked from head to below the knees. Fyre didn't move as the figure moved, leaping from the grave top, and racing for the gate. Stone had to scramble from the hole he had dug, but he was running at full pace within a few seconds. Fyre followed the pursuit.

The cloaked figure moved at great speed, expertly dodging the crooked gravestones, and leaping over the sunken beds. Stone was able to keep pace but could not close in. Once the figure reached the road, they began to run at full pelt upward toward the hills and woods beyond. Here, on even ground, Stone was able to close in on it. He was within yards of the cloaked figure when it ripped the cloak off and flung it backwards into his path. Fyre was tens of yards behind. Although he was wiry and fit, he lacked the dexterity and initial pace of Stone.

The cloak hit Stone across his upper body, slowing him just for a split second, but it was enough for the figure to dart from the road into a field. An abrupt yellow light flashed into Stone's eyes, and a loud, demanding voice called out.

Stone skidded to a halt, the light now temporarily blinding in his eyes. He shielded them with his hand and caught a momentary glimpse of the figure racing across the open field. It looked back, a mistake if you're trying to hide your features, Stone was able to make out, just for fleeting second, the face of Melisa Barry.

'I said hold it there!' roared the demanding voice.

The uniform of a policemen came close to Stone. He was holding a bright lantern and a pistol, outstretched in one hand.

'Hands up; I won't warn you again.'

Stone complied. He looked over his shoulder into the field, Melisa Barry was a dark speck in the distance. Fyre arrived on the scene just as a second policemen did the same. He too was holding a pistol in his hand.

'Stop. Hands up where I can see them.'

'Constable,' panted Fyre. 'We can explain.'

Murphy put the lantern on the wall and reached into Stone's coat, he retrieved the pistol from the holster inside.

'Can you explain this?' asked Murphy.

'Yes,' said Stone, 'well, maybe no, but we were chasing someone.'

'I bet you were,' said Murphy, 'we've had two murders here already this weekend. You two are under arrest.'

'On what charge?' asked Fyre.

Murphy looked them up and down, they were in work clothes, borrowed from Sean's cottage, and covered in muck.

'That depends on what you have been doing.'

The watcher on the church tower could see the policemen handcuffing Fyre and Stone.

They were led to a waiting carriage and secured inside, while one of the policemen retraced their steps back to the graveyard. For a country copper, this man is smarter than most, thought the watcher as they watched Cieran Murphy moving through the graveyard methodically. He would find the open grave with the body of William Egan very shortly. That was unfortunate. But the arrest of Fyre and Stone was worth the risk.

The watcher silently went down the spiral stairs of the tower, waited for the policeman to move back up the road and trot the carriage away.

There was a moment of doubt, but it passed. The lips smiled wickedly, and a small light flashed across the field. Within a second, a light in the distance responded.

Fyre opened his eyes, the morning sunlight woke him, although he had only slept for a single hour, worry and Stone's snoring had kept him conscious.

'Morning, sweetheart,' said Stone sarcastically, 'breakfast will be served from seven 'til nine, kippers, followed by wholemeal bread and French paté, we have a choice of wines …'

'That'll do, Stone. What do you think is going to happen?'

'Well, let's sum up. No, actually, let me rant at you for getting me into this situation.'

'Sounds fair.'

'We are under arrest, imprisoned in the asylum, with one or more people who have committed a murder. There are two disturbed graves in the village, both of which we are responsible for. There are two William Egans, both dead. And a young woman married into a rich family, who you think is an imposter, was spying on us gravedigging. Have I got everything?'

'Not quite, there's still the case of Holt, Matthew Barry and strong conviction that something sinister is taking place in this building.'

'I didn't need to be a ghost whisperer to tell you that,' said Stone. He was still lying on the bare bed, staring up at the ceiling.

'I take it you considered all the possibilities of

escaping?'

'Considered, planned, and doomed to fail. Whoever built this place made sure no one was leaving without their permission. It's more like a fortress than a hospital.'

Just as Stone spoke, the metal peephole on the door slid noisily across.

'Ah, that'll be the bacon and eggs I ordered,' Stone sat up and grinned at the eyeball in the door.

Charles Barry opened it. Behind him stood several guards. Stone noted their presence and Barry saw him do so.

'If you're thinking of making a run for it, there are also two armed policemen in the corridor, they arrived in the early hours with a very nervous sergeant,' Barry said.

'I'm quite happy here, thank you,' smiled Stone and he lay his head back down.

'Your absence was noted at dinner last night, by my father, my cousin and by my aunts, who seemed particularly keen to meet Lord Fyre again.'

'I bet they are not so keen now,' said Fyre, honestly.

'You would be surprised,' Barry said, with a hint of regret in his voice.

'And what about your good lady wife?' said Stone in his plain manner. 'Did she note our absence?'

'I don't know what you're getting at.'

'I think my colleague is asking, was your wife at dinner last night?' Fyre said in a friendlier tone.

Barry's defensive mannerism remained, 'Yes, she was, she didn't stay late. She said the day's activities had worn her out.'

'Not quite worn out,' said Stone.

Charles Barry's face turned to a scowl.

'You gentlemen are in serious trouble. When I told you to go back to Dublin and keep out of my family's affairs, it was not a suggestion, it was a warning. One I thought you would listen to. But instead, you are under arrest on suspicion of murder, grave robbery, and the defilement of a corpse. I have to say, gentlemen, you surprised even me. I've dealt with some disturbed people in my professional time, but you seem to be a case study in insanity.'

'We were asked here to investigate a murder,' said Fyre.

'I was told. A murder of a man who is still alive.'

'There are several dead people in this village in the last forty-eight hours. Don't you think it worth investigating?' Stone asked.

'I think it worth my time to help those whose minds are driven to criminality out of madness. But not those who do it out of delusion,' Barry said. He composed himself, pulling down his waistcoat.

'I doubt I will be able to help you. The police have informed my father of the events of last night, and the matter is now in their hands. One of our local constables is coming to take your statements, and tomorrow detectives from Dublin Castle will take you into their custody. I only hope, gentlemen, that you give reason enough to a judge to avoid the hangman's noose.'

'Perhaps we're both insane,' said Stone, his sarcasm not escaping Barry.

'I don't think so,' Barry said and he walked out of the cell, the heavy metal door slamming behind him.

'Well,' said Fyre, lying back down on the hard bed, 'That couldn't have gone any worse.'

Murphy walked through the asylum garden. He watched the inmates being filed out of the doors and marched over the greenery by the guards. The group of men, dressed in the same clothes, lumbered across the green in a wayward line. As they drew toward Murphy, he felt a sickening in his stomach. They didn't seem human to him. These unfortunate souls, with their long-drawn faces and dead eyes looked more like rag doll toys that had horribly come to life. Murphy stood still as two of the inmates hobbled past him. Their gaze never fell on him, it was as if he wasn't in their world.

'Constable,' Bary said.

Murphy kept his eyes on the men, aimlessly walking around on the grass. The two guards had abandoned their duties and were smoking in one corner of the garden.

'Doctor Barry, good morning,' he didn't wait for him to reply. 'Why do they look like that?'

'Like what?'

'Like … like they're not with us?'

Barry drew up beside him.

'Are you familiar with the medical world?'

'No.'

'Few are. These men have been introduced to new drugs that will alter the chemicals in their brains, and ultimately cure them of their insanity.'

'They don't look like they're getting better,' commented Murphy, as much to himself as anyone.

Barry changed the subject abruptly, 'Are you here to interview the suspects?'

'Yes, Lord Fyre and John Stone, the men who tracked down a coven of habitual homicides.'

'That's them.'

'Hard to believe they would kill anyone … under the circumstances.'

'Didn't you yourself catch them in the act?'

Murphy broke his gaze from the inmates for the first time and looked at Charles Barry.

'I caught them doing something they shouldn't have been doing; murder is a tall order from that.'

'They're in the cell next to Holt; he's been very quiet.'

'Good, he definitely killed someone, but I don't know why.'

Melisa was panicking. She had made it back to the house just before Charles had arrived back from Castle Barry. She had become an expert at hiding her other life from Charles, although, since they had come back to Ireland, she suspected that he had his suspicions. Charles had become distant, his tone hard, his mannerisms bordering on unkind. She had put this down to his love/hate relationship with his father and his family. Melisa had spent months perfecting her serum. If it worked, it would change the world, and prove that everything she had sacrificed was worthwhile. The man in the chair on the other side of the room was barely conscious. She needed to take him to the brink of his fear, to the point where his mind became susceptible to suggestion. Only then would the serum work.

Her mother-in-law's notes made clear references to experiments carried out in other, unnamed institutions. The subjects in Lady Barry's notes had all been women. Somehow they had been more receptive to the fear factor of the process. Melisa hated this part. She jabbed a needle into the man's arm and began to speak to him.

CHAPTER 21

Cieran Murphy opened the door of the cell without bothering to look inside first.

'Morning, gentlemen.'

'Constable,' began Fyre, ' we can explain the events of last night.'

'Explaining it to me is pointless,' replied Murphy, 'it's out of my hands, Dublin Castle are sending down detectives and they have warrants to bring you back with them.'

'That was quick,' commented Stone.

'Yeah, I think celebrities like you get special treatment.'

'I bet we will,' Stone sat up. At the back of his mind was still contemplating an escape, even though he knew it was near impossible.

'What if I were to tell you that Roisin Black was murdered?' Fyre said.

'I knew her, I knew the family well. After Miss French died, Roisin was found in the woods, babbling, screaming, looking like a crazy person. I'm the one who brought her here.'

'She was strangled, possibly beaten to death,' said

Stone coldly.

'Doctor Barry told me she killed herself with a bedsheet hung around the bars of the window.'

'He's lying,' replied Stone.

'You'll forgive me if I take everything you say with a pinch of salt. After all you two are in here, having been caught grave digging in the middle of the night.'

'And who was in that grave?' asked Fyre.

Murphy seemed to think about the question, but didn't answer.

'Where is the body of the man we found?' asked Stone.

'In the morgue with the other two. I read the stories about your escapades in Dublin, it seems wherever you go there are dead bodies.'

'Why don't you check which one of the dead bodies is the real William Egan? I think whoever the other one is will give us all some answers,' said Fyre.

Once again Murphy thought about what Fyre had said.

'Tomorrow morning, you and the English man in the other cell will be out of my village, and we can bury our dead in peace. That's all I know, gentlemen. I'll make my report and hope that's the end of the matter.'

Just as Murphy walked out of the door, Fyre spoke to him in a serious tone, 'They won't rest in peace, not tomorrow, not any day, not until whoever really killed them is found. You still have a murderer on the loose, Constable.'

Murphy looked into Fyre's eyes; he could see the sincerity in both their faces.

'And you know it, don't you?' asked Stone, but Murphy didn't reply. He closed the cell door.

'What did they say?' asked Owens, who had been standing against the far wall of the brightly lit corridor.

Murphy leaned against the door of the cell.

'Do you remember Roisin Black?'

'Yeah, I knew her, her brother works up at the castle.'

'She seemed normal, didn't she? I mean up until we found her that time.'

'Yeah, I guess so. What's the matter?'

'Probably nothing, I'm going to go have a chat with the surgeon and take a look at our two William Egans again.'

'Rather you than me.'

'I know,' said Murphy honestly, 'you stay here, don't let anyone in to see them or Holt.'

'Not even the doctor?'

'No one!'

As much as Melisa hated Castle Barry, there were moments of peace she could find in its vast landscaped gardens. For several years now, his Lordship had kept a small staff at the castle. Immediately after the death of his wife, just as Charles was leaving for Cambridge, Lord Barry had become somewhat of a recluse. Over the course of the following decade he had opened up a little, his lavish parties had made him the darling of his social circle. His willingness to spend vast amounts of money on entertainment and philanthropy was very unlike anything the Barry family had done in the past. They were known in previous generations as dour protestant landlords. They were serious people, who put money and position above the happiness of others, and even themselves.

Melisa was glad to feel the heat of the morning sun on her pale skin. At Cambridge she had worked long hard hours in libraries and laboratories, but she had always found time for the river walks and parks that surrounded the colleges of the university.

Castle Barry's gardens were kept in a state constantly bordering on going wild. The box hedges of the formal garden, just beyond the castle yard, were uneven and perforated with wild weeds and thorn bushes. She noted that, among the flowerbeds, even the nettles and dandelions were in full bloom and looked as pretty as any well-gardened plot.

She saw Lord Barry walking toward her for some distance. It was time enough for her to stop daydreaming, to hide her real self and put on the mask she had to constantly wear around him and the family. 'Good morning, your

Lordship.'

Lord Barry was a master at keeping his face unreadable. 'Melisa, my dear. I've just heard what happened to young Lord Fyre and Mr Stone last night.'

'Something happened to them?' she asked genuinely. Melisa had left her home just after dawn, and just after her husband travelled the short distance to the asylum. She had been occupied all morning with administering the formula to their new subject. The work was clandestine, but she had become used to that.

'They've been arrested.'

'Oh.'

'You don't sound very concerned about them. I thought you had made a friend of that young Lord?'

'Em, no, not really, I was just being social. They do seem very odd, coming down here to chase ghosts and murderers.'

'To be fair there has been a murder, or two. And we have plenty of ghosts.'

'I don't believe in ghosts, your Lordship. Dead is dead.'

'My wife would have disagreed with you.'

'I'm sorry!'

'Don't be,' his Lordship looked over at the castle looming nearby, 'I have to talk with my nephew, matters of business.'

'I hope you have a good day, your Lordship,' said Melisa, her mind replaying the events of last night. She had hoped no one would ever find out about her failures, but Fyre and Stone seemed to have stumbled on them. She couldn't decide if their arrest was good news or bad.

Lord Barry walked up a few steps, through the hedgerow and toward the castle, then he turned and said, 'Everything I've done I have done in her memory.'

There was an awkward pause between them.

'You remind me of her. Intelligent, single-minded, and beautiful.'

'Thank you,' was all Melisa could manage to say. This

was the first time she felt he was speaking to her as a real person and not just the wife of his son.

When he had disappeared into the castle, Melisa lifted her dress from the ground and began to run. She needed to know what Fyre was doing, what he knew about her and, crucially, what he was going to tell the authorities.

Murphy had been indifferent to the massive pile of stone that was the asylum. When it was first put up, he felt that it was a boon for the local community. That proved not to be the case. Those employed in the asylum had all come from mainland Britain. The guards, the nurses, even the administrators were all strangers and remained strangers. With increasing republican tensions across the whole country, Murphy felt that the asylum was driving a wedge between the Barry family and the local community. Previously the Barrys had been held in high regard, but in recent years their good name had come under question.

Murphy knocked on the door of the mortuary. After a few moments of silence, he looked around the corridor to see if anyone was about. Despite the number of inmates and staff, the building was so vast it was easy to think it was abandoned. He stepped inside the large room. As he looked over to where three bodies were covered by snow white sheets. Fyre's words echoed in his head. Who were these men, and why were they killed here?

Murphy had a feeling that this situation was spinning out of his control. His sergeant had refused to leave the barracks in Kinsale, citing that Dublin Castle was running the show now, and that he and Murphy should keep their mouths firmly shut.

He cautiously walked over to the tables, and, as if trying not to wake anyone, slipped the sheets down on the first dead man. It was the body that Fyre and Stone had dug up in a grave that should have only contained the corpse of a woman. The face was contorted, the eyes rolled backward to leave only blood-black holes. Murphy had a strong stomach, but even he could feel a shake in his body as he looked down on the dead man.

Under the second sheet was the man they had found dead in Garretstown House. The one shot by the mysterious and clearly dangerous Detective Holt. Murphy took a closer look at the dead man. He wasn't sure what he was looking for. The two men did look somewhat similar, roughly the same height, same build, their faces the same sharp, their suits cut to the same length. But the second man's skin was slightly darker, as if exposed to sunlight for long periods.

Murphy undid the buttons on the dead man's coat, the dried blood peeled apart and flaked as he eased back one side of his jacket. He could see nothing else unusual, but then he saw a blue stain just on the exposed right shoulder. He forcefully pulled the sleeve of the jacket down and could now make out the blue-black of a tattoo. He'd seen this and similar ones in his youth growing up in the slums of Cork city's docklands. This man had served in the British navy.

'One thing is for sure, you're not William Egan. But who the hell are you?'

Lord Barry watched Melisa leave in a hurry from his office window. He smiled as he watched her trap become a speck down the long driveway of his castle. She was very much like his wife. The same drive, character, the same ability to wrap men around her finger with her beauty and charm.

There was a sharp knock at the door. Barry knew whose hand it was, just by the forceful sound.

'Come in, Max.'

Max's giant frame strode into the room. He was carrying a large bundle of letters.

'You got them?' asked Barry.

'Yes, your Lordship, she hadn't even bothered to hide them.'

Barry smiled again, 'Of course not,' he said to himself. 'Leave them on my desk, I wish to show them to young Lord Fyre.'

'Lord Fyre is being held in the asylum, they are sending men down from Dublin in the morning to bring him to the Castle,' Max told him.

'That will be time enough,' Lord Barry went back to gazing out of the window overlooking his estate. 'That will be all, for now, Max. But do stay close, I have a feeling that events are about to take a sudden turn.'

'As you wish, my Lord,' Max gave a bow to Lord Barry's turned back and walked out of the room, clicking the door softly closed behind him.

Barry waited a few minutes before he sat at his desk. He could feel a heavy tremble coming in his left hand and left leg. Almost in panic he unlocked and rooted through the bottom draw of his desk. Inside he found a small glass vial, half-filled with a brownish liquid. It took him several attempts to fill a brass syringe with the liquid, and he had to steady himself with deep breaths before he could inject the substance into his arm.

The hours passed by painfully slowly. As morning turned to afternoon, the sunlight in the cell window faded and Stone began to feel the cold air.

'What did they make this building out of, ice?' Stone asked of no one in particular.

Fyre was sitting with his legs crossed, under the window, his eyes were closed, and he was clearing his mind of doubts trying to find the truths in a sea of confusion.

'I like the cold; bracing, good for the soul.'

'My soul doesn't feel the cold, but my feet, they are frozen.'

Before Fyre could answer, the slip of metal on metal alerted them to someone watching them through the peephole in the door.

Fyre opened his eyes and said, 'Hello Melisa.'

'How did you know it was me?' she asked softly.

'None of the guards, so far, has been wearing rouge,' said Fyre.

'Clever. You two are in trouble.'

'So are you, my dear girl, why don't you let us help you?' asked Fyre, his voice calm and certain.

'I'm not the one in a cell,' Melisa replied.

'Are you sure?' asked Fyre; the question was loaded.

Melisa's eye disappeared from the door, then reappeared.

'The guard is coming back. I'm going to have a word with this Mr Holt.'

'That is really unadvisable,' Stone said.

'If you want advice, from someone who is on this side of the locked door, then you will both appeal to Lord Barry to have you released.' '

'And we all go home and forget about the dead bodies,' said Stone.

Melisa once again moved her eye from the peephole. She could be heard talking to a guard outside, it was too muffled for Fyre or Stone to make out the conversation.

A few moments later, a single key slid under the door and into the cell.

CHAPTER 22

Melisa watched as the guard walked along the corridor and reached the corner. He seemed to hesitate but then turned and disappeared. She had a way of convincing people to help her, it was a talent she had discovered in her youth. The guard was on his way to find the chaplain, Melisa had told him that she had wanted to give the three incarcerated men a prayer book, so that they may ask for forgiveness in their darkest hours. It was a nice piece of improvisation.

She had, some time ago, had copies of her husband's master keys made, so that she could move around the building freely, to conduct her clandestine business.

She slid one of the keys under the cell door for Fyre and Stone. It was an insurance policy.

Melisa quickly opened the cell containing Holt. He was standing close to the door and his eyes widened when he saw Melisa.

'You!" exclaimed Holt, 'I thought you were dead.'

'If you know what's good for you, you'll get out of here,' said Melisa, her accent slipped from an educated one to an aggressive East London twang, but only temporarily.

'I've come too far and risked too much to turn back now,' Holt said. He took a deliberate step toward her.

Melisa drew a small pistol from inside her shawl and aimed it squarely at Holt.

'I know how to use this.'

Holt stopped. He could tell she wasn't bluffing. Stone appeared out of the neighbouring cell door. He looked at Melisa, holding a gun, standing in the other doorway.

'Well, this is a turn up for the books. Why don't we put the pistol down and talk?'

Fyre cautiously walked out of the cell behind Stone. 'Melisa, or whatever your real name is, whatever is hanging over you, whoever is using you, we can help.'

Melisa kept her educated accent this time. She answered with a tone of hostility in her voice, 'I assure you, Lord Fyre, no one is using me. And you cannot help me, I am here to help you. An offer open only for the next ten seconds; run. Now! Get out of this village and this country and don't come back. Or,....' She waved the gun from side to side, person to person, '... go back in your cell and see how many offers the authorities hand you. You have seconds to decide, that stupid policemen will be back in a moment from his fool's errand.'

There was an exchange of glances between the three men.

Holt broke the tension, 'You're a dead woman walking if you think they will let you live after helping us to escape.'

'Who are they?' asked Stone.

'Isn't that what we're all here to find out?' replied Holt.

'We're here to find a murderer,' stated Fyre.

'You've found two,' said Holt, his eyes falling on Melisa.

A shot rang out. The loud metallic sound of a bullet ricocheting off the marble walls was temporarily deafening. Holt and Stone were the first to react. Holt made a grab for Melisa's pistol. The struggle was brief; Melisa had dropped to the ground as if hit by something. Stone dashed to the far wall and upturned a large table for cover. Fyre momentarily froze, then ducked back into the cell as a second shot was fired. He had enough time to see the oncoming man, running toward them with his right arm held out, a pistol aimed in their direction.

It was Sean.

The second shot flashed over their heads. Before Sean could fire a third shot, Holt took aim at him with Melisa's gun. With his left hand he was holding Melisa to the ground. As he fired, she struggled and connected a palm to his jaw with expert precision.

Holt's shot was wayward, and he forced to let Melisa go.

Sean was close now. He fired a third shot toward Melisa, as she lay on her side on the ground, she was able to roll just enough for the bullet to ping off the marble floor. It was now that Stone leapt from behind the table. He was able to gain enough momentum and height that he landed on Sean's right shoulder, dislodging the gun, which slid down the corridor. Stone knocked the boy firmly into the wall.

On the other side of the corridor, a policeman was running toward them, yelling, his pistol drawn.

Some distance behind him, the chaplain was running toward them too.

Holt made a grab for Melisa, but failed to catch hold of her. As he rose from the ground, he let off a single shot in the direction of the oncoming policeman.

This time there was no sound of metal on marble. Holt didn't wait to see the result of his shot. He grabbed Stone by the collar, poked the gun into his back and yelled, 'Come on, run or die here.'

As the noise of Holt's and Stone's shoes faded away in the direction Sean had come. Fyre dashed out of the cell and pulled Melisa inside, grabbing her roughly by her clothes. She protested, but the sight of blood on the white sleeve of her arm made her stop. Her face went immediately pale. Fyre peered out of the door. Holt and Stone were gone.

Sean was lying up against the wall, semi-conscious. Fyre leaned down and checked that he was alive.

Yards away, the chaplain called out for help. Fyre could see that he was leaning over a stricken policeman, a large pool of claret-red blood forming on the cream floor tiles.

A second policeman was running at full pelt toward them.

Michael's hands shook as he carried the tray of food toward the room at the top of one of the corner towers of the asylum. Doctor Barry had told him to bring the tray to the man at this time.

'It's quite alright, Michael, he's under a mild sedation.'

Michael had heard, from the chaplain, that the man had been found wandering in the woods near the coast, babbling, tearing at his clothes.

There were stories, old stories, and newer ones, about those found in the wild places, their minds driven mad by ancient and malicious spirits.

Michael was a fearful man, God and pagan spirits were as one in his mind. He had been raised that way as a child. After his grandmother died and his father disappeared, he had been placed in the care of this institution. The chaplain had instilled in him the belief that God was as real as any physical object he could touch. Yet, there was a pagan fear inside him. Just as the Bible was read to him as a child, so the stories of the older beliefs, the old fears, were as real as those sacred words.

Out of habit, Michael knocked on the door. It was bolted from the outside, and he had to put the tray on the ground to undo the lock. The heavy door opened to reveal a room he had been in many times over the last few years.

It was here that he had brought food and water to the young girl, Roisin. She too had been found in a state of anguish, and rumours in the village had reached Michael's ears through visitors and delivery men. The old stories were coming back, the old spirits were still alive in the darker parts of the country. The room inside was square and well lit, with tall windows on three sides, offering spectacular views right over the valley and sea beyond. Michael had always thought that this room would have felt like a room at the top of Castle Barry, were it not for the iron bars that crisscrossed the windows. The man inside was not asleep, as Michael was expecting, he was standing at one of the windows with his back to the door.

'Hello,' muttered Michael.

'Good afternoon,' said the man, without turning around. He had a strong English accent, which Michael didn't recognise as being from any region he knew of. The only English men he knew were the chaplain and the chief surgeon.

'I brought your lunch, the doctor said you might be awake.'

'I'm more than awake, I have been renewed.'

Michael's nervous voice stuttered even more, and he considered running down the five flights of stairs to fetch a member of staff.

'Do you know what fear is?' asked the man, his voice filled with menace.

'Yes, sort of, I do,' Michael said in quick succession.

'I've seen oblivion and I have returned from the gates of Hades.'

'Where?'

The man laughed. It was an ice-cold cackle, as if he were drawing it from his throat with a metal implement.

'I've been given a new life, but in order to keep it, I must kill a man.'

'Oh, God!' cried Michael and he turned and ran.

Michael was down two flights of stairs, his weak legs buckling under him, before he realised he had left the door unlocked. Looking up into the dizzying spiral above, he could see the shadow of the man from the room moving downward.

Michael screamed and ran.

Murphy cradled his dying colleague and friend. The chaplain had run for help, and Fyre was binding the wound on Melisa's arm with a strip of bed linen. Murphy opened his friend's tunic.

'Easy, Frank,' he whispered. He could see the wound was bad, very bad. The bullet had hit Frank just under the right ribcage, the blood was dark, almost black, his liver had been punctured and the exit wound in his back was gaping.

He tried to stem the flood of blood with his own tunic, but it was pointless. Murphy had seen gunshot wounds before. He knew this one was fatal, and even if a doctor could arrive in moments, there was nothing anyone could do.

'You should have run,' whispered Melisa to Fyre.

'You need to tell me everything, Melisa. The policemen Holt shot is going to die, and so will others.'

'It would take a long time to tell you everything. Some secrets I have to keep.'

Fyre could tell by her eyes that she was being genuine, and he felt that this as a rare moment for her. Before he could ask another question a terrible wail came from the mouth of the policeman holding his colleague.

'I'll see what I can do for him,' said Fyre, 'your arm should be alright, the bullet just nicked you.'

'He was trying to kill me.'

'I don't think so,' replied Fyre, 'he was shooting at random.'

Fyre stood up and walked toward the two policemen.

Murphy was holding his bloodied friend close to him. It was clear the man was dead.

'He's gone,' said Fyre, his voice a whisper, but the echo of the hall made it cut through the air.

Murphy raised his gun and pointed it squarely at Fyre.

'Stay away from him!' he yelled.

'He's gone, Constable, there's nothing we can do for him now.'

'Stay away!'

'I didn't shoot him.'

Murphy's eyes were wide and filled with an angry madness.

'Who did?' he demanded.

Fyre held out his hand, Murphy's gun was just inches away from his fingers.

'Let's have no more blood here today.'

'Who … Shot … Him?' screamed Murphy.

'Holt,' shouted Melisa, 'It was that man, Holt. He ran off. He kidnapped Mr Stone, and he knocked out the young gardener.'

Fyre let this mistelling of the truth go. There was a loaded gun pointed at him.

'Put the gun down, we're not your enemy,' said Fyre. He reached out his hand and touched the barrel of pistol, lowering it to the ground.

With tears in his eyes, Murphy dropped the weapon to the ground.

Further along the long corridor, several members of staff, including Charles Barry, were racing to the scene.

CHAPTER 23

They were still within sight of the monstrous asylum when Holt called a halt to their escape.

'What now?' panted Stone, as he leaned up against a tree trunk.

'We need to find my driver, I have all the evidence I need to prove to you that I'm on your side,' replied Holt. He still had the pistol aimed at Stone.

'If you were on my side then that gun wouldn't be pointing at me.'

Holt let out a derogatory laugh, 'Don't take me for a fool, Stone. Me and you come from the same streets, different cities, but the same streets.'

'What side, exactly, do you think I'm on? Because right now we're on the run for killing a copper, and you killed at least two other men.'

'You hunted down the Spectres in Dublin, I have to say it was impressive.'

'It didn't feel like it,' spat Stone.

'Nevertheless, you started a chain of events that has led us both here. You hunted them for one winter, I've been hunting them all my life.'

'You're mad!'

'You think so? Do you think Fyre is mad? Do you think he can speak to the dead, that he can see the future, see across time?'

'No.'

'That's a lie. You've seen it yourself. You saw the girl, she called to you. Listen to me, Stone, I've traced the Spectres across all of Europe, but whatever they are planning it's centred here in Ireland, in this place.'

'You *are* mad,' said Stone dismissively.

A bell sounded. The evening sun was just beginning to dip below the canopies of the treetops.

'Mad or not, I have proof. We have to get back to William Egan's house, my driver was once a lacky for one of the Spectres, an English Lord with a taste for young ladies. He'd hidden a box in the grounds. Its contents will show you who is mad and who is sane.'

Holt gestured to Stone by waving the barrel at him.

'Both of us are going to swing for this,' commented Stone, as he stood away from the tree and began to move further into the rough undergrowth.

'I don't think so, Stone, we're survivors.'

Further up the hill, two sets of eyes watched them battle their way through the tall grasses and scrubland that divided the coast from the rocky hills above.

'Should we follow them, Mr Potts?' asked one.

'No need to scramble through the bushes today, Mr Grey, we know exactly where they are going.'

Charles Barry sent all but two of the eight guards on duty to search the grounds of the asylum.

'Chances of finding them are limited, sir,' said one of the guards, his English West Country accent seeming out of place to Barry.

'It's a police matter now. Let us just make sure that our institution is safe, and everyone in it. Have you issued all of your men with firearms as I ordered?'

'Yes, sir, and I told them your instructions, not to shoot

Mr Stone, unless he shoots at them.'

'Excellent.'

Along the corridor Barry could see a stumbling figure racing toward them. The guard beside him immediately raised his rifle. Barry put his hand on the barrel and lowered it.

'It's Michael,' he said.

'Oh that idiot.'

Barry threw the guard a withering look.

The guard duly withered under his stare and put the gun down by his side, 'Sorry, sir, slip of the tongue.'

Michael half-ran half-fell toward Barry and came skidding to a halt in front of him.

'He got out!' he yelled.

'Calm yourself, Michael, we are aware that Mr Holt and Mr Stone are …' Barry struggled to find the right words, '… on the run.'

'No, Doctor, not them, the man they found in the woods, the man that was driven mad, the one you put in the tower.'

'What do you mean he got out?'

'He talked to me and then he just walked out, Doctor, just walked down the stairs and out the door.'

'Impossible, he was heavily sedated, he shouldn't have been barely able to sit up, never mind walk out!'

'He's gone, Doctor.'

Barry looked at his pocket watch. It would be dark soon, and he was concerned for the safety of his wife. He had left her, under guard, with Lord Fyre in his office. Although he had wanted to lock Fyre back up in the cell, Melisa had been insistent that he was no danger and should be allowed to remain out.

Murphy was in no condition to disagree.

'You stay here, Michael,' Barry said, his mind trying to piece together a logical course of action. 'You come with me,' he said to the guard.

'Stay here,' complained Michael in a stutter, 'on my own.'

Barry didn't answer; he and guard marched off toward the staircase at the far end of the building.

Murphy pulled the sheet over the face of his dead friend.

The chief surgeon walked over from the other side of the mortuary; he was carrying a metal bowl of surgical instruments.

'Don't touch his body, I don't want him cut up like you do with these poor wretches locked in here,' said Murphy with great menace.

The surgeon looked at him with wide-eyed surprise. 'I'm not a monster, you know,' he said coldly, 'I was going to clean up his wound.' He put down the metal bowl and walked away again.

Murphy left the mortuary and once outside he fell back on the heavy wooden door. His tears, his shock, his grief, all seemed to go numb inside him. He raised his right hand to see if it were shaking. It was steady as a rock. He checked his sidearm, six bullets.

Murphy marched along the corridor, just in time to meet Doctor Barry and the guard coming the other way.

'Constable Murphy, you should go home,' said Barry.

'No thank you, Doctor, there's work to be done,' replied Murphy, his voice was rasping and low.

'Very well. I have sent the messages you asked to be telegraphed to Kinsale. There was a reply, your sergeant is on his way here with a troop of men.'

'Very good.'

'And the farm boy Sean has been treated and locked up in a room.'

'You think he's dangerous?'

'It's a matter of precaution, he was half-sensible, so I gave him a sleeping draft and put him in a room.'

'Very good,' said Murphy; his mind was on Holt and Stone.

'It seems that our peaceful existence has been shattered by the arrival of these ghost hunters,' stated Charles.

'In my experience,' replied Murphy, 'there is no such

thing as ghost, I don't fear the dead, I fear the living. And, as for our peaceful existence, that was shattered when your father built this horrible place.'

'My father funded this hospital to help heal the sick, officer,' Barry answered, with a genuine sense of displeasure.

'In seven years, I've never seen anyone walk out of here cured of anything.' Murphy's eyes met Charles's for the first time. They were filled with anger, and Charles not wishing to risk angering the constable more, decided to change the conversation.

'We have another problem; a third patient has escaped, it would seem.'

'Who?'

'The man who Fyre and Stone found wandering the woods near William Egan's house.'

'He was with Holt; they must have been in on this together.'

'The thing is, Murphy, he shouldn't have been able to leave at all, follow me.'

Barry led Murphy and the guard up one of the winding staircases that ran through the building at either end. At the top, there was the room, where Barry and the guard had deposited the man found in the woods.

'I administered the sedative myself, enough to keep him disabled and barely conscious for the rest of the day and night.'

'And you say he just walked out?' Murphy asked.

'Our trustee, Michael, said that the man even spoke to him, clear as day, which should have been impossible.'

'A lot of impossible things have been happening around here,' Murphy said drily.

As Murphy was looking around the largely empty room, Barry noticed something catching a sparkle from the evening light. When Murphy's back was turned, he leaned down and scooped the small object into his hand.

Murphy spun around. 'Find something?' he asked.

'There's nothing to find, there was nothing in here and no one except me is allowed in.'

'You and the trustee, Michael?'

Barry smiled, 'That was under my orders.'

'I have to go back to the station house.' Murphy stopped at the door, 'How's your wife's arm?'

'She'll recover, thank you.'

'Oh, and by the way, don't let Fyre leave the building; he's still under arrest.'

As Murphy noisily walked down the stairs, Barry mumbled to himself, 'Don't worry, he's going nowhere.'

Fyre and Melisa sat in silence, in Barry's office. The armed guard stood outside the open door, close enough to hear anything they said. Fyre leaned forward and took a writing pad and fountain pen from the desk. He began to scribble.

Melisa, who had been placed on the couch by her husband felt uncomfortable lying down, so she drew up a chair and sat just feet away from Fyre. He glanced at the door where the guard was scratching himself and sighing a lot.

He slipped the pad over to Melisa. 'My offer to help you was genuine, but we need to be away from this building and the Barry family, including your husband. My friend's life is in danger. Help me to help you. … Whoever you are.'

Melisa read the note twice. She then, very carefully with her left hand, tore away the single page from the pad and slipped it inside her pocket. She scribbled her own words and, glancing again to see the guard not paying attention, she passed the pad back.

Before Fyre could read her note, they both heard the approaching footsteps. Fyre tore the page off the pad and pocketed it. He stood up, keeping his back to the door and replaced the pad and pen where they had been. Barry marched into the room.

'How are you, my dear?' he asked in his most commanding voice.

She winced at the thought of her bandaged arm. 'Some discomfort, but it's bearable.'

'I'll inject you with a mild pain killer,' her husband said.

Melisa's protest was loud and swift, 'No! … sorry, I hate injections.'

'You're a chemist,' commented Fyre.

'That doesn't mean I like putting chemicals into my body,' she scowled him.

'I have some pills somewhere, that will do the same job. I actually think they are at home. We should go, the constabulary are sending men. They'll soon sort all of this out.'

'What about Mr Fyre, I mean Lord Fyre?' Melisa asked.

'Sebastian,' whispered Fyre.

'I have been informed that he is still under arrest, so must remain here,' Barry replied.

'There have been crimes committed in this place,' stated Fyre, 'but not by me.'

Barry didn't let any emotion across his face, 'That may be the case, but I am not your judge nor your jury.'

'And what about my executioner?' asked Fyre with his most annoying smile on.

'I'm a doctor, not a hangman. I've been asked to keep you here, Lord Fyre. I would prefer it if you would stay in my office. There is a small bedchamber and lavatory through that door. I'm afraid there are no windows, it was very much an afterthought by the architect, at my insistence. There will be guards at the door, of course …'

'Of course,' agreed Fyre.

'If you prefer I can have them return you to the secure wing. But I was hoping we would be a little more civilised than that.'

'I will gratefully accept the offer of your office, Doctor Barry.'

'When all of this is over,' said Barry, as he helped Melisa to her feet, 'those responsible for these events will be held to account.'

'Goodbye, Lord Fyre, I hope you don't have nightmares,' Melisa said as they left the office.

'You too, my dear lady,' mumbled Fyre.

Holt seemed at ease picking his way through the undergrowth. Stone, on the other hand, seemed to stubble on every sharp rock and tear his skin on every bramble. Holt called a halt to their progress in the woods overlooking the late William Egan's house. He slid down the trunk of a tree, keeping the gun on Stone.

Stone licked his fingers where a thorn had got deep into his skin.

'The countryside is not so good for a city boy.'

Stone looked over at Holt from where he was sitting, the twilight made his features indistinct.

'I hate the countryside, there's nowhere to put your elbows.'

Holt laughed, a real hearty laugh.

'So you're chasing Spectres?' asked Stone.

'Fifteen years, yes, chasing them. Every time I get close they melt away, or kill everyone who had contacted with them.'

'Is that it?' asked Stone, 'Did they kill your family, murder your wife, bury your children in a shallow grave?'

'Don't worry, Stone, I have my sad tale too, but you'll never know it.'

'Why did you kill Egan?'

'I didn't, I killed his replacement. I've killed a few of them now. Wealthy, powerful men, who weren't who they claimed to be.'

'And you're telling me you're not mad?'

'Not as mad as you think. I met Charles Barry before, when I was a real copper. Interviewed him about a murder in Cambridge.'

'You think Doctor Barry is a murderer?'

'I think everyone is a suspect. No one is who they seem, John Stone of Dublin.'

'I'm definitely me,' Stone said.

'Are you sure?' Holt gave a cackle, then added, 'We'll wait until it's fully dark, then go down to the house. Be on your guard.' Holt fished inside his jacket and ripped away some of the lining, revealing a string of pistol bullets. He pushed the extra ammunition into his pocket.

'Why?'

'Because, if I'm right, they'll be waiting for us and will try to kill us.'

'Sounds about right,' said Stone, he leaned his head back on the tree and closed his eyes, his keen mind doing calculations all the time.

CHAPTER 24

Fyre found the bed in Charles Barry's office. It was little more than a long cupboard with a mattress laid on plain wooden boards, but it proved quite comfortable. As Barry had said, two guards were posted outside the door, sitting on chairs, Fyre could hear them muttering to each other. He lit a small oil lamp and lay back on the pillow. He held a book he had taken from the many hundreds that lined the walls of Charles Barry's office. The book was a thesis on psychotic tendencies in the children of the uneducated classes. Fyre snorted a derisive laugh at the title. He wasn't really reading the book. The guards were keeping a close eye on him, so he had secreted Melisa's note in the open page of the book.

He read her scribbled words.

'Meet me at Castle Barry at midnight, in the stable courtyard. There is a red door with no marking, just under a square tower. If you cannot or will not be there, I have plans to leave Ireland, I will not be here tomorrow. Do not blame Charles for all of this madness. He isn't the man you think he is.'

Fyre folded the page into his pocket again, and

checked his watch. He had just over an hour to get out and make his way the mile or so to the castle.

Stone couldn't understand why Holt wanted to convince him that the Spectres, or some similar shadowy group of rich and powerful men, were behind the killing of a maid and several other people in this backwater part of rural Ireland.

He had figured out that Holt was mad, but clever, and certainly not mad enough to drop his guard around Stone. They followed a game trail down through the long grasses and onto the unkempt lawn of Garretstown House.

'Why was Sean trying to kill you?' asked Stone as the last red remnant of sunlight dropped behind the square frame of the house.

'Who said he was trying to kill me?'

'You think he was after Fyre? Or Me?'

'Or the girl.'

'Why would Sean try to kill Melisa Barry?'

'Because she's not Melisa Barry.'

Holt's darting eyes caught a flash of twilight as he looked over at Stone. The pistol in his hand was still aimed at Stone's midriff.

'Fyre thinks she's an imposter too.'

'He has a talent, Lord Fyre, but let me tell you, it's not a unique one. You're the smart one, John Stone, you can work it all out. Now, let's get over to the house.'

Holt followed Stone across the lawn, keeping his distance, making sure not to give Stone any opportunities to go the for gun or make a break for it.

'You think Melisa Barry could have killed Sean's sister?' asked Stone as they approached the outbuildings of the house.

'Keep your voice down, this place is being watched,' replied Holt in a whisper.

'I thought you wanted them to find you?'

'Only on my terms and when you see that I'm right.'

'On the same side as me,' said Stone in a mocking tone.

Stone heard the mechanism of the pistol click.

'I can do this without you, Stone, but it would be easier for both of us if you were onboard,' Holt's voice was filled with a threatening tone, one that Stone knew couldn't be faked.

'I'd prefer not to be shot in the back.'

'Good, then keep walking and keep quiet. Just at the back of the stable, where it meets the garden, stop there.'

Stone followed the instructions.

'Just here,' said Holt, 'dig under that water box.'

'For what?' snapped Stone.

'I told my man to leave something there.'

Stone pulled the empty water box to one side. He could see that the ground underneath had been recently disturbed. Just an inch under the topsoil, his finger hit something metallic.

'In that is all the evidence you'll need to believe me, Stone. This goes right to the top. The Barrys are only a cog in a very big wheel. You think murdering a few whores in Dublin, or London or Birmingham is what they're after, think again.'

Stone stood up, holding the long metal box in his arms. There was no lock, just three catches fastened along its length. He flicked them open and lifted the lid.

Holt had a near manic grin on his face.

'Now you'll see,' he said.

Stone turned the box, so its interior was visible in the twilight to Holt. It was empty. Completely empty.

'Bastards!' exclaimed Holt, his eyes widening with genuine surprise.

Stone dropped the box on the cobbled surface of the yard. It made a loud ringing that echoed across the bowl-shaped hollow that Gerretstown House sat in. Holt's eyes followed the box down to the ground. That was a mistake, and all the opportunity Stone needed. Stone's kick caught Holt in the side of the head. It wasn't enough contact to knock him to the ground, or dislodge the gun from his hand, but it was enough for Stone to make a break for the stable doors.

Holt didn't fire.

'Stone, wait!' he called out, but it was too late. Stone was already under cover, through the building and running into the darkness of the back garden before Holt could get moving.

High above the garden of Garretstown, two swooping figures dropped out of the still night sky. They came at great speed, making a sound like a bird of prey's wings cutting the air as it fell on a small creature.

Fyre checked his watch again. He was running out of time. Even if he could get out of this office right now, he would have to find a horse. On foot it would take all his speed and stamina to run to the castle. He wasn't sure he could do that, even in daylight. He found himself wishing Stone would make one of his timely appearances. If he were here, in this situation, he would have some cunning plan, some way of distracting the guards or breaking through the wall. Idly, Fyre tested the wall of the small bedchamber. It was, disappointingly, solid masonry. Footsteps made the guards stand up, and made Fyre's eyes widen in the dim light of the room. A man, in a staff uniform, approached the guards. He was holding a tray, with tea mugs and plate on it.

'Doctor Barry said I was to bring you up tea before I turned in for the night,' said the bearer.

Fyre recognised the voice. He smiled to himself.

The guards drank their tea, nosily, and munched on the biscuits. The staff member who brought the tray, sauntered off back down the corridor.

Fyre wasn't sure what was going to happen next. He was tempted to try something. Maybe if he asked the guards could he have tea …

While he was thinking there was a loud slump just outside the office. Fyre sat up and saw one of the guards prone on the marble floor. The other man was snoring loudly, his head propped up against the doorframe.

The staff member returned. Fyre, cautiously, walked

across the room to meet him.

'Hello Bertie,' he said with great relief, as Bertie lit a hooded lantern and smiled at him.

'I got the sleeping drug from the medicine office downstairs, I wasn't sure how much was too much or too little,' said Bertie in his usual cheerful Dublin accent.

'It seems to have worked, Bertie.'

'No surprise really, I used the whole bottle in the end.'

Fyre pushed at the seated guard, who fell lifeless-like to the ground.

'Will he be alright, sir?'

'Oh, yes, I think so, come on, we'd better get out of here, Stone's in trouble.'

'Isn't he always, sir?' grinned Bertie.

'How did you get here?' asked Fyre, his delight at seeing his driver and friend, tempered only by his curiosity.

'Mr Stone, sir, he sent me a telegram just before you boarded the train, and some monies, sir. I was to follow you down here on the evening train and …' Bertie hesitated.

'Go on, Bertie.'

'Well, sir, this is Mr Stone's words, not mine, you understand?'

'Of course,' said Fyre, rolling his eyes.

'I was to follow you, at a distance, because you were too stupid not to get yourself killed … sir. His words, as I said.'

Fyre laughed. He had to put his hand over his mouth to stop the echo going through the vast building.

'John Stone to the rescue,' he giggled, 'Come on Bertie, we're got to get to Castle Barry before the hour is out, but first we have to find someone.'

Stone didn't have a plan. But he didn't need one. So long as he was away from Holt and not in a prison cell, he felt he was master of his own destiny. Fyre and Sean's welfare did flash across his mind as he bolted along the gardens of Garretstown. He had to let those thoughts go immediately when a shot rang out behind him.

If Holt did want his help, he had a funny way of going about it. Stone dived for the damp grass, and lay flat on a hillock just a hundred yards from the back of the house. Holt fired a second shot. This time Stone could see the flash of the pistol, and in the dim moonlight, he could just make out Holt's figure flailing about.

He wasn't firing at Stone. It was something else. Holt let out a yelp of pain. He followed this by firing three more shots, before a second yelp and his figure fell to the ground.

Stone had little sympathy in his mind for Holt. But he could use that pistol, and he could use some answers. If he left Holt to die most of those answers would go with him.

'Bugger it!' Stone grunted.

He stood up and looked around. There were two ways he could play this. He chose the second one, not because it made sense, but because it didn't. That might give him an advantage.

'Alright,' he yelled into the darkness of the night, 'It's me, John Stone, I'm here and I want to talk.'

Stone held his hands up and started to walk toward the stricken Holt.

'Let's put our guns down and talk this out,' yelled Stone.

He was getting closer to Holt. Now that he was just a few yards away, he could see Holt's body crumpled in the grass. Holt's head moved. He was alive anyway, maybe shot and badly wounded, but alive.

Holt called out, 'Get down, you fool!!'
The first attack caught Stone across side of his neck, up as far as his ear. He felt the stinging, as if a razor blade were drawn across exposed skin. He headed for the ground, just as Holt fired one last round into the air.

Stone felt the trickle of blood on his skin. He raised his head from the grass, as he did so, something fast dropped on him, he felt like the claws of an animal ripping at his jacket. He struggled, he lashed out with his arms, but another thin razor cut appeared out of nowhere on his wrist. He made a dash for Holt. He reached him, just as a second creature ripped at his back. He yelled out. A pointed dagger felt like it was jammed into his shoulder. He dropped to the ground once more.

'Save yourself,' spat Holt, blood pouring from him mouth.

Stone didn't need a second invitation for that. Answers were no good if he was dead. Whatever was attacking him, he couldn't outrun it. The house was still fifty yards away. He saw a movement in the sky above his head. Followed by a second figure, high above him, circling like monstrous eagle, trails of dark, mist-like material in its wake.

A thought occurred to him. He dropped to the ground again and pulled the empty revolver from Holt's hands. Holt was barely conscious.

Stone rummaged in Holt's jacket, he had several paper strings of bullets secreted about him. With the gun loaded, Stone knelt up. He fired all six shots in quick succession, not upwards as Holt had done, but horizontally out into the darkness. He dropped again and reloaded. When he sat up a second time, he fired another volley, this time in a different direction. For a third time, Stone reloaded and kneel up. He paused and looked up into the darkened sky.

Nothing.

He waved the gun around, looking for a target.

Still nothing.

Trying to catch his breath, Stone looked down at Holt. Holt's face was criss-crossed with long thin cuts of fresh blood. A large hole was gouged out of his breast. He was alive, but for how long?

It proved more difficult to find where Doctor Barry had put Sean than Fyre had hoped. Eventually they found the boy. He was unconscious and could not be woken. Bertie, without questioning Fyre's motives, lifted the boy in his strong arms and carried him down the stairs to the front door.

A guard was sitting there. He rose to feet when he saw Fyre coming, and Bertie behind carrying Sean.

'Emergency withdrawal,' said Fyre, as he breezed past

the guard.

'What? I didn't hear about this!' protested the guard. He ran behind Fyre and blocked Bertie's path to the main door.

'The thing about that, is this …' said Fyre and he whacked the man square in the jaw.

The guard fell to the ground. Fyre grabbed his knuckles and winced.

'How does Stone do that all the time.'

'Come on, sir, I have a trap outside.'

They rushed out into the night.

CHAPTER 25

The short journey from the asylum to their house was made in almost complete silence. Melisa could feel her husband's tension. His breathing was heavy and deliberate. He stared out of the window of the carriage at the passing landscape, as if trying to find something in the distance that would distract him from her. Charles curtly refused her offer of dinner. He told her, in no uncertain terms, to stay in the house for the remainder of the evening, and that she was never again to contact the troublesome Lord Fyre.

'We cannot get our family's name involved with these men. All of this will blow over and the Barry family will outlast Sebastian Fyre and John Stone.'

'Isn't that what the Barry family do,' mumbled Melisa, 'outlast everyone else, until the family name is all that is left.'

'It's worked for three-hundred years,' snapped Charles, 'I need to speak to my father, I will be back late. Don't wait up for me.'

She could tell he was uncharacteristically angry. The more time they spent in Ireland, the more Charles's character seemed to change, and not for the better.

As she sat there in the drawing room of the house, watching the evening sun dip behind the tall treeline that surrounded the nearby Castle Barry, she considered all sorts of drastic actions. The path she had put herself on was always going to lead to conflict with Charles, and his family. She needed Charles. She needed his unwitting help in completing her life's work, and she needed his money. The amounts of money she had used up over the years had never been questioned by him, she had made sure of that. But now, the Charles she had met in Cambridge, that malleable man, who seemed to love her unconditionally, was not the same.

Terrible thoughts were crossing her mind. There was always a danger she would lose him. But now, as she watched his carriage move down the drive and out onto the rough road, she felt her grip on him was so slender as to be slipping completely. She had, secretly, hoped this day would never come. At the beginning, when she first choose Charles as the man she would manipulate, it was just that, manipulation. Now, enough years had passed, that her feelings for him, faked in Cambridge, had become, somehow, real in Ireland.

Melisa ran to her laboratory, moments after Charles's carriage was out of sight. Despite her doubts, her decision was made. It was time. She had nearly perfected the serum. Working from Lady Barry's notes, it would be possible to complete the process once she was back in England. She had, using the allowances Charles had given her, secured a location on the outskirts of London. Once there, she could begin the final tests. It wasn't a nice process, but she had justified all of it in her mind. It was a means to an end. There was someone waiting for her in London, and that person was the driving force behind all of her life. She had become the woman she was now because of them. She had become Melisa, so much so, that she had almost forgotten her real name. She grabbed her travel bag. If Fyre could be there at midnight, he could be her ticket out of here; another man she could manipulate. His mind was strong, but the stronger the mind the better the serum worked. Weak minds had fallen apart, become unstable. Sebastian Fyre was just the sort of mind she needed right now.

She had prepared everything. Melisa was meticulous, like all chemists. Everything in its place, a place for everything.

She stopped, stood still, a red flush of panic rose in her face. A small glass vial was sitting on a low wash table, on its own. It was one of the vials she used to administer the drug into test subjects. She must have dropped it in her haste; a mistake that could have been covered at any other time. It shouldn't be here.

'Charles,' she said to herself.

More panic set in. It was beginning to get dark. It was time to leave the life and name of Melisa Barry behind. It was time to leave it all behind.

Stone had no choice but to leave Holt where he was, and hope he survived whatever or whoever was attacking them. He ran for the house. It was only a few yards. He dived across a privet, hit a patch of gravel pathway, and rolled until he came to an abrupt stop against the wall of the house. He rose to his feet, fresh blood trickling down his face and arm. He glared into the darkness, looking for movement. Whatever it was that had attacked him and Holt, it wasn't human. Crazy thoughts ran through his head. Stories from his childhood of dangerous spirits and undead monsters in the Irish countryside, but then Fyre words drew into his mind, 'The dead are not malicious, they cannot harm the living, only living flesh and blood will make you bleed.'

Stone rubbed his fingers on his cut forehead. Whatever had cut him was real; someone alive was out there.

The movement of a light caused him to huddle closer to the masonry of the house.

'Constabulary!' yelled a voice into the darkness.

Stone saw three more lanterns follow the first. They fanned out into the wide back garden of the house and called out for anyone who could hear them to drop their weapons and surrender. His keen eyes made out the face of Murphy, as he moved along the pathways of the garden, near to where

Stone was hiding. Murphy turned his lantern around, letting its yellow circle of light cross the walls of the house. Stone dropped to his knees, his left hand almost slipped into a sheer drop just inches away. It was the basement gulley, that allowed light into the working rooms of large houses. He slid down, without knowing what lay at the bottom. He heard footsteps approaching. The yellow light overhead grew more intense. As he looked up into the star-laden sky, the toe of a black boot poked over the edge of the gulley.

Stone held his breath.

'Over here!' yelled a voice in the distance, 'I've found someone.'

Murphy didn't rush off into the garden straight away. He paused, shinning the light from his lantern, not downward but into the ground floor window, as if he were expecting to see movement in the empty house.

'He's still alive!' yelled the panicky voice.

'I'll be there now,' Murphy cried out in his distinctive accent.

Stone let out his breath. The light and the footsteps faded. Voices exchanged words, but he couldn't make out what they were saying.

Holt was still alive, for now, and that was a relief. The man might be mad, but he clearly had information that would shed light on whatever was happening here. Stone's mind turned to his own situation. Then briefly he thought about Fyre, Sean and the girl, Melisa. He knew Bertie should have arrived by now. What help he could offer was a different matter. He checked his wounds. In the darkness of the gulley it was impossible to tell if they were serious or not. There was the cold sensation of blood and stings across his face and arms. He moved, as silently as he could, along the weed infested gulley, feeling for the windows as he did.

Luck was on his side. A window was unlocked. He couldn't risk putting pressure on it to slide down until the policemen above began yelling once more. There seemed to be a panicked confusion. Stone took his chance. The window was stiff and made a brief loud squeak, but he hoped it was drowned out by the voices in the garden. He dropped into a long disused kitchen. He found himself scrambling out of a massive sink and finding his feet on a brick surface. He knew he wasn't safe. A smart policeman would light the lamps in the house and search it. He had to get away from here. Despite the near darkness, Stone was able to find the stairs. He got to the ground floor. Starlight streaming through the large windows aided him through the rooms. Outside he could see several lights flittering around.

A voice calmly spoke behind him. 'We arranged a little distraction for them, just enough for us to get away,' the voice said in a heavy English accent.

Stone raised his pistol to his chest. He was about to spin around and take a shot when the voice added, 'I wouldn't bother, Mr Stone, your gun is empty and I doubt you had time to reload, the last shot you took was a lucky one, it hit Mr Potts right in the elbow. Just a nick, mind. He didn't even yell out.'

Stone spun around and aimed the gun at a large, barrel-chest man blocking the hallway behind him.

The man was aiming his own gun, he pointed the thin barrel straight at Stone.

'Come quietly now.'

Stone pulled the trigger. There was no shot.

'Bloody hell!' exclaimed the man, but still in a whispered tone, 'you are a killer.'

Stone was hit in the crown of the head, hard. He fell unconscious to the ground.

'That's for me arm,' said Mr Potts, as he emerged from a doorway.

'Now, now, Mr Potts, Mr Stone is going to be our friend. Come on, gather him up, we've only got moments before those coppers outside come back this way.'

Murphy ducked as something moved in the air over his head. It felt like the swooping a large bird of prey.

To his right, two of his colleagues, who had just come down from Kinsale, were carrying the stricken man they had found in the long grass.

To his left, the district sergeant had pulled out his sidearm and was waving it around manically.

'Don't waste your time,' shouted Murphy, 'whatever it is, it's not going to be taken down by a bullet.'

'It's a spirit!' yelled one of the policemen to his right. He crossed himself and let go of the stricken man's legs.

'Pick him back up!' barked Murphy, 'there's no spirits here, just murderers. Come on, get him back to the carriage. He needs a doctor.'

Reluctantly the three nervous policemen lifted the man and made their way around the side of the house, into the front drive. They were just in time to see a trap race away down the road. It was too dark and too far away to make out any details.

'We'll never catch them, they're too light and too fast,' said the sergeant.

'I know,' replied Murphy, as he watched the trap vanish behind a wall of black trees, 'I told you there were no spirits, just murderers.'

'This fellas in bits,' said one of the Kinsale policemen.

Murphy walked back to where they were loading him into the carriage.

'Him again!' exclaimed the Sergeant.

'Yeah, him,' Murphy recalled the shot in the corridor earlier that killed his friend. 'He'll hang for what he's done.'

Murphy could feel a deep, almost uncontrollable anger beating inside his chest. He could sense his hand dropping to find the cold steel of his pistol.

He just about managed to restraint himself, and said, 'Let's get him to the asylum, and hope he lives long enough to hang.'

Sean woke up with a start. Above him, Lord Fyre, and a large, older man were standing. Fyre checked his watch.

'Just ten minutes to make my rendezvous with the lady Melisa.'

'Are you sure you want to go alone, sir?' asked Bertie.

'I don't think Melisa will trust me otherwise, and I

believe she is caught up in some web of deceit and criminality.'

'He's come round, sir, he can hear us,' said Bertie, as he looked down on Sean's blinking eyes.

Sean knew he was in his own cottage, but he was tied fast by his hands and feet, and a large leather horse strap was wrapped around his body, holding him to his bed.

'Let me loose.'

'We can't do that, Sean, there's something not right about you. You're not yourself.'

'I want to kill him!' Sean snapped.

Fyre leaned down and looked into the boy's eyes. They were filled with manic rage. He had seen this look before.

'Someone has tried to control you, Sean.'

'He killed my sister!' snapped the boy, as he fought, pointlessly against his restraints.

'Who killed your sister?'

'The man in the cell, the English man.'

'That's impossible, he wasn't even here,' Fyre placed his hand on Sean's forehead and tried to feel his emotions. After a moment he whispered, 'You believe he killed her, you believe it so much that it's your only thought. This rage is hiding your true self. You're still in there, Sean; this will pass. Whatever method they had used to make a killer out of a boy will fade, I promise I will get you back.'

Sean tried to lash out at him in a vicious, animalistic way.

'Are you sure about that, sir?' asked Bertie, as he stood back a step. Fyre didn't reply, he wasn't sure. Right now, if he wanted answers, he had to find Melisa, and he had to find Stone.

'I'll be back by morning, and if I'm not …'

'Yes?' asked Bertie, with a seriousness in his voice.

'Take him to the police in Kinsale and explain everything you have seen.'

'Everything?'

'As best you can, Bertie. I have to go. I have to find who did this to him and why.'

CHAPTER 26

Melisa changed into clothes she had especially put aside for her clandestine work. She worn men's trousers, a thick shirt covered by a leather waistcoat, and tied her hair up so it fit under a workman's cap. In her younger days, before she had managed to lie her way into Cambridge, she had found moving around the dangerous streets of London was much safer if she were dressed as a boy. She had everything she needed packed in a single bag. A large amount of money was thrown into the bag on top of several bottles of her serum. Hard to believe, she thought to herself, that this bag and its contents represented her entire life's work. She was leaving Charles, her comfortable position, and her name behind. There was only one thing she needed to do now.

Melisa rushed around the laboratory. Her notes were precisely written in three ledgers. They were the culmination of ten years' secret labour. Something that would change the world forever, something that would give her back the only thing she had ever really wanted.

She checked the clock. She had left herself just enough time to meet Fyre and show him the truth about the asylum.

She couldn't risk giving him the ledgers, they were too precious to her, but there was other evidence she could part with. She opened the drawer where Lady Barry's letters and notes were kept. The notes were there, untidy folders of papers, just as they had been given to Melisa. A sense of anxiety rose once more. The letters were missing. The one thing that would convince Sebastian Fyre that dark forces were at work. Forces she had used, but now feared more than anything.

Pointlessly she rummaged through the drawer and papers. The letters were gone.

Did Charles take them? She supposed it didn't matter now. She was back on the run. She would still meet Fyre, in just thirty minutes, and hope he would listen to her explanation.

She hoped even more he would not try to stop her from leaving. Melisa was willing to sacrifice anything to achieve her goal. Lives had been lost already; one more wouldn't matter.

Holt was barely sensible in the back of the carriage.

'You killed my friend,' whispered Murphy to him, his voice just audible enough over the boneshaking rattle of the carriage making its way through the village and toward the main road. He turned his head toward Murphy, the dried blood on his face forming a crisscross of scars.

'Sorry about your mate. A lot of good people have died,' he muttered.

Murphy had to lean down to heard him. The anger inside him was just under control. He could reach out his hands and strangle the man, choke the life right out of him. The other policemen were at the plate, picking their way through the rough roads.

'Why?' asked Murphy, his hands twitching.

Holt formed a smile on his lips and replied, 'You want to kill me?'

'Yes.'

'Good. Do it, be the angel of mercy. I've chased them

so long and lost so much, it's not worth living on.'

'Who the hell are 'them'!' demanded Murphy, his voice rising without him realising.

'The resurrection men,' said Holt, 'ghosts made flesh. Stone … find Stone, he knows more than anyone. He'll be drawn to the castle, they all will.'

Holt passed out. Murphy checked that he was still alive. He was. Again the anger rose in him, he had his hand around Holt's neck without thinking about it.

Something in Murphy's mind was whirling, putting impossible sums together. He took his hands away from Holt.

'Stop the carriage!' he yelled to the driver, 'I'm going back.'

Fyre rode the horse through the darkness to the gothic gate of Castle Barry. He it with just a few minutes to spare. The massive wooden gate stood slightly open, and immediately Fyre sensed death was close by. He tied the horse to a branch and looked around to see if anything could be used as a weapon. He should have asked Bertie for a pistol, but he hated guns so much, and hated violence in general. He touched the black stonework of the gatehouse with his hand. He could feel a spirit, a screaming, fearful essence. It was not strong enough to speak to him, but it was there, swirling around like smoke. He could feel that whoever the essence had been was dissipating, drifting away from this world to another. His thoughts turned to his friend, but he felt sure that if John Stone were a spirit, he would be a stronger presence than this. This was a weak mind, fading fast.

Fyre slid inside the gate as quietly as he could. Somehow it seemed darker on this side; the trees seemed to loom in from either side of the long driveway to form a black, jagged sky. It was colder too, as if the sun had never warmed this side of the gate.

Fyre could see a small flickering orange glow to his right. The gatekeeper's door was also open, letting in the cold night air. He could sense the presence of death here. Without thinking about it, he walked to the door and looked into the small living space. The gatekeeper's body lay slumped in his chair, his mouth hanging open in an unnatural position. His neck had been viciously ripped apart, fleshly congealed blood sat in fist-size blobs across his jaw and shoulder. Fyre stepped into the room, the tiny amount of warmth from the stove hitting his exposed skin like pinpricks.

The gatekeeper showed signs of other injuries. He had been savagely beaten, and may even have been dead before his throat was ripped open.

'I found him like this, a few minutes before you arrived.'

Fyre's mind registered Melisa's voice, but his eyes stayed firmly fixed on the dead man.

'It looks like a senseless killing. What could any of this have to do with him?'

'It's a side effect of the treatment,' Melisa said. She was standing at the door, 'the mind can revert to its most base forms, animalistic instincts. Fear, violence, and …' she hesitated.

'The base needs, to survive, to eat?' asked Fyre.

'Yes, in extreme cases.'

'Is this what you and your husband were working on? What that monstrosity of a building was created for?'

'Not my husband; he is innocent in all of this.'

Fyre took his eyes off the desecrated corpse of the gatekeeper and looked over to Melisa.

She was cowering at the door, dressed in men's clothes, with a workman's backpack across her shoulder.

'Who are you?' asked Fyre, his voice direct and threatening, something which did not come naturally to him.

'No one,' Melisa said, 'I came from nothing, from the streets.' She let her face come into the light a little.

Fyre could see her features differently now. Without the adornment of makeup and the garments of wealth, she looked like any working girl would look. Her face, now that he could see it like this, seemed angular, and lacked the plump softness that aristocratic women had.

'Who did this?' asked Fyre, pointing to the dead man

in the chair.

Melisa gulped, she couldn't look at the horrible wounds of the gatekeeper.

'I administered treatment to a new patient. Over time, with careful manipulation the treatment can alter the mind for good, restore personalities to their former state. But it requires bringing that mind to the very brink of its baseness. Only then does it work.'

'I think we can safely say, Melisa, or whatever your real name is, that this is the brink of baseness. Who was it?'

'I don't know their names,' Melisa looked into Fyre's eyes for the first time in the conversation. He could see that desperation in them, there was honesty too.

'They bring them here from other places, different parts of Ireland, Britain, God knows where. People with no names, criminals, the insane. People that no one will miss.'

'So all those poor souls up in the alyssum, they're being used for experiments?'

'Some of them, yes. You're judging me.'

'Yes, yes I am. And rightly so, why would you do such a thing? How could you create an animal that could do this?' Fyre raised his voice and pointed to the dead man again.

Melisa turned her head.

'I want to save someone, I want to save them from the living death of madness. Restore their mind, bring them back.'

'This sounds like witchcraft.'

'That's what they said about all medicine!' Melisa snapped back at him.

'Melisa, what have you done here?' exclaimed Fyre in horror. This was far worse than anything he could have imagined. 'Who are these people who are helping you?'

Melisa hesitated, then, looking straight at him again, he could see an almost manic determination in her stare.

'I made a deal with the devil, Sebastian. I'm sorry, but in order to get away from here, to save someone I love, I gave them you.'

Fyre's skin suddenly paled with fear. Melisa stepped

back into the darkness and was replaced by the large frame of Max the butler.

'There's no way out of that room,' said Lord Barry's distinctive voice from somewhere in the darkness, 'we have a killer on the loose, I'd think both of you would be better off in the safety of the castle.'

'Both of us!' exclaimed Melisa, 'you said I could go, if I brought you Fyre and half the serum.'

'Oh, my dear daughter-in-law, I do this for your own protection.'

Fyre stepped into the doorframe. Max was standing like a statue beside him. Lord Barry, dressed in a long riding cloak, was close to Melisa, holding a small silver pistol to her chest.

'Wait,' said Fyre.

'Oh don't worry, old boy, I don't want to hurt dear … Melisa, she is and will be the love of my boy's life. With careful treatment, her own ingenious creation will ensure that.'

Melisa's eyes darted around for something to help her.

'I'll take the bag, it contains several lifetime's work, and we wouldn't want anything to happen to it.'

Fyre moved before Melisa could reply and think of anything. His arm reached out and knocked into Barry's hand. The pistol clicked but didn't fire.

Max was quick to react, he grabbed Fyre in a vice-like grip. Melisa too reacted quickly; she tried to tug the bag away from Barry, but his grip reminded firm. All she could do was dart off into the darkness of the trees.

Lord Barry dropped the gun and held onto the bag with both arms. 'You're insane,' snapped Fyre. Max was holding him so tight that his joints protested.

'I assure you, my dear boy, that I am not. Now, Melisa will be back. The contents of this bag are far too important to her. Let us get back to the castle, there is a real madman on the loose and we don't want to run into him.'

Fyre pulled his arms against the strength of Max, but clearly in vain.

'I wouldn't bother, Max worked in a circus when I met him, as a strongman. He could, with a word from me, dislocated both your arms at the shoulder. Or, if you prefer, you can come with us without such violence?'

Fyre relaxed his body.

'Do we have an agreement?' asked Barry quietly.

'Yes,' replied Fyre, 'what about Stone, where is he?'

'I have no idea. But, for now, I need your help. If you want to help my daughter-in-law too, then you will listen to me very carefully.'

Stone opened his eyes, the room he was in was brightly lit.

'He's back with us, Mr Potts,' said a harsh voice.

Stone could feel the throbbing lump on the side of his head giving him a blinding headache. He was tied to a metal chair, which itself was bolted directed into the ground.

'Good evening, Mr Stone, famous detective and ghost hunter,' said a second voice.

'He'll see plenty of ghosts tonight, won't he, Mr Potts?'

Mr Potts appeared in Stone's eyeline. 'Oh yes, we've got lots of them here.'

Stone's eyes had still not adjusted to his new surroundings, but his brain was telling him he was in trouble. He was looking for solutions to problems he couldn't yet understand. When in doubt, he thought, stall for time.

'And where is here, exactly?' spluttered Stone.

'Deep in our lair,' said Mr Grey with an attempt at an evil laugh.

Stone's eyes were beginning to pick out details, 'It looks like the mortuary of asylum.'

'Yeah,' Mr Gray's voice mumbled, 'that can be our lair.'

'Who are you two idiots?'

Mr Potts leaned down so he could look into Stone's face directly, 'We work for the Barry family. We were once patients in this place, but now we is cured.'

'I don't think so,' said Stone flatly.

Mr Potts raised his hand to smack Stone, but a direct

voice of authority stopped him.

'That will be enough of that.'

Stone caught a glimpse of a well-dressed man in the corner of the room.

'Matthew Barry, or do you have another name?' asked Stone.

'No other name, I am Matthew Barry, at your service.'

Barry stepped forward and gestured to Potts and Grey. The two lackies shuffled off to the other side of the room.

'If only you hadn't answered that stupid letter. Holt has been a thorn in our side for some time now. We even moved our operations to this backwater to get away from him and others like him. We should have killed him years ago.'

'Why didn't you?'

Barry laughed, 'Like you, Mr Stone, Holt is a survivor, the cockroach of truth-seekers. When we all know that the truth is sometimes best left unfound.'

'You do talk a lot of balls, even for a posh idiot.'

'Charming to the last,' replied Barry, 'I wanted to get rid of you and Fyre, when you first arrived. I mean, who in Irish society would mourn your loss?'

'Are you going to kill me now?' asked Stone. He was tugging and pulling at his bonds, but they were not giving way.

'Not at all, we're going to cure you.'

Just as Barry spoke, Potts and Grey wheeled a trolly across the marble floor, with a man strapped tightly to it.

'Say goodbye to your mind, Mr Stone.'

CHAPTER 27

Bertie watched over the young man who lay restrained on the bed. The fire was running low, and it had long gone past midnight. In a few hours the early June sun would creep up in the eastern sky. Bertie had had little sleep since arriving in southern Ireland; he could feel the heaviness of his eyes beginning to take hold.

He wasn't sure if he had fallen asleep for any length of time, or if he had just closed his eyes, but a cry for help from Sean made him jump to his feet.

'What's happening?' asked Sean, his eyes desperately looking around in the darkened room.

'Relax son, I'll get a light going,' Bertie looked over to where the fire was a pile of smouldering ash. He had been asleep longer than a few moments.

He managed to light a small lamp and held it close to Sean's face.

'Who are you?' Sean asked, desperately.

'I'm Bertie, Lord Fyre's driver and sort of bodyguard.'

'How did I get here? Last thing I remember was being at the garden party.'

'Really,' said Bertie. He took a close look at Sean's

face. His eyes were wide with fear and confusion, but there was an honesty there. The twisted anger that seemed to turn him from a boy into a snarling man, appeared to be completely gone.

'Lord Fyre told me to keep you here, to mind you, you were mad like a bull with a sore head. You shot a gun at someone.'

'What!'

'Don't you remember?'

Sean shook his head. 'Please, sir, let me go.'

'I can't do that, son, I have me orders from Lord Fyre. Although I'll admit I'd rather have spoken to Mr Stone. Young Mr Fyre can be a bit … strange. Why don't I get you some tea?'

Before Bertie could rise from the chair beside Sean's bed, a loud crashing noise from the other room of the cottage made him freeze for a moment. A split second was all it took for the intruder to smash his way through the back door of the house. Bertie was on his feet, his hands wrapped around a fireiron, ready to defend himself. Sean frantically struggled with the bonds holding him down, but to no avail. Bertie and the intruder stood just feet apart. The man was wide-eyed, his mouth held open and his hands clinging to two serrated daggers, that looked like they could tear through flesh easily.

'You wanna a fight I'll give you one,' screamed Bertie, as his brandished the fireiron at the man. There was a moment's pause, the intruder's wild eyes scanning the room.

'You're not him,' he spat out, 'you're not Fyre.'

Bertie was about to make a lunge forward when the man dashed for the front door and was gone through it before another word could be said.

Bertie let out a breath, but still clung to the iron.

'That was the man from the woods,' said Sean, his voice breaking with fear.

'Who?'

'The man Mr Stone and Mr Fyre found in the woods near Garretstown House, they brought him into the asylum. He was like a madman.'

'You're tell'n me,' commented Bertie to himself, 'sounds like he's going after Lord Fyre.'

'We've got to warm them. Will you please let me out?' pleaded Sean.

Bertie had a think about the situation.

'Bugger it, Lord Fyre gave me orders, but Mr Stone gave them first. Come on, kid, you and me and going for a bit of a walk.'

Fyre didn't bother putting up any further resistance. Once inside the walls of Castle Barry, Max firmly locked the massive front door. The sound of the gun-barrel-sized bolts sliding into place echoed through the halls of the great building. Fyre had been in many of Ireland's grand houses. He expected Castle Barry to be no different from any other, but he was surprised. The interior was sparsely decorated. A black and white chequerboard floor stretched into the darkness, uncluttered by the usual collections of furniture and oddities that other stately home had accumulated, including his own.

Lord Barry could see Fyre looking around. He walked to a small table by the door and lit a lamp. Raising it over his head, he allowed the light to creep across the walls of the grand entrance hall. The architecture was impressive, thought Fyre, but something was missing. All of the large painting that would normally adorn such walls were missing. Some of the painting had left dust and water marks, shadows of where they once hung. The hall was more than sparse on furniture, it was completely devoid of it.

'The other rooms, apart from my office, are the same,' Barry said as the light continued its journey around the great space, 'we never have guests here, even Melisa is a rare visitor.'

'Why are you showing me this?' asked Fyre.

'So you understand the sacrifices I have made. Our estates, our accounts, our family treasures are all depleted.'

'You paid for the asylum?' asked Fyre.

'Yes, that was the paintings, sold in Berlin and Paris,

anywhere they could be sold.'

'That's why you've been acquiring other houses and estates around you. Selling off their assets and making sure their rightful owners are no longer in the picture.'

Lord Barry gestured for Fyre to follow him through the hall and toward a large doorway that was already glowing with the tell-tale red of a dying fire in the hearth.

'If you are inferring that I gained those properties by dispatching their owners, then you are wrong.'

'What about William Egan. He was dispatched?' asked Fyre. The terrified face of William Egan flash across his mind.

'A charming man.'

'I'm sure he was, until someone buried him alive in a shallow grave.'

'Let's speak no more about these matters, I have something to show you, young Lord Fyre.'

Behind Fyre, Max pushed his huge frame into Fyre's back for force him to follow Barry. Fyre sat down inside Barry's office. Max locked the only door and then stoked the fire, adding fuel so that it gave a roar up the chimney. Fyre checked his pocket watch, it was approaching two in the morning. He wondered to himself how far Melisa had managed to get, where Stone was, and how safe were Bertie and Sean? Trapped here, he was of no use to them.

'You have a unique gift, young Fyre,' said Lord Barry as he sat down, 'my wife was a believer in such things. Strange, for a woman who could outdo any man in the sciences, she believed she could speak to the ghosts in the very castle. None of them have ever spoken to me.'

Fyre could feel his skin going as cold as ice. Behind Barry a figure had appeared. It was just a wisp of smoke, as if some breeze had blown down the chimney. Within a frozen moment, before Barry could speak again, Fyre perceived the essence that had been visiting him since Matthew Barry's letter arrived. Fyre understood now the nature of this vision. It was gone as quickly as it came. His skin seemed to thaw, but for another fleeting glimpse of the spirit world. He could see Lord Barry's aura, that light that all creatures shone into the normally imperceptible world. It was a dark light, like the fire in the room when they first arrived. It was dying; Lord Barry's time in this world was near an end. Fyre could see a violent black hanging over the man, like the Sword of Damocles, ready to fall.

'Perhaps,' said Fyre, 'those spirits who have moved on are speaking to you, your Lordship, but you are unwilling to hear them.'

Barry smirked, 'Perhaps,' he said, 'my wife believed that chemicals in the human brain could be altered to perceive and even interact with such spirits. Perhaps even more.'

'It sounds like the work of alchemists,' replied Fyre, dismissively.

Barry grinned, 'I agree, it does. However, you have seen the results yourself, have you not?'

Fyre's mind was still processing the vision that had assailed him. Lord Barry answered for him.

'The so-called Spectres of Dublin, those vile men praying on women, using mind-control chemicals to make killers out of factory girls? You have seen these results.'

Fyre suddenly did see. A horrible thought, that had been an inkling in the back of his mind, came forward and shook his entire body.

'Are you saying your wife was involved in creating such chemicals?'

'Not directly,' Lord Barry sat back and nodded to Max.

Max took a bundle of letters from a side-table and dropped them, unceremoniously, on Fyre's lap.

'I don't expect you to read them all, of course. But just take a glance, and careful note of their author.'

Fyre read the first few lines of the top letter. It appeared to be a detailed academic correspondence from one scientist to another. He flicked through the pages and found the signature and return address.

'Oh,' was all he said.

'Doctor Keogh, Portraine Hospital,' said Lord Barry,

'implicated in the Spectre case, and committed suicide, which I believe you witnessed, before he could face trail.'

'It's more likely he was pushed,' said Fyre.

'Perhaps, but it's of no matter. He was working closely with my wife, many years ago. I only recently found the letters, too late to take him to task.'

'Why would you do that?'

'My wife was trying to make something that would make the world better, she was trying to help ...' Lord Barry hesitated, '..others,' he finally said.

'And Keogh stole her work?'

'So it would seem.'

'This drug, this chemical you speak of, Melisa was using it. It was used on Sean, the gardener's helper, and others. It's being used in the asylum?'

'Yes, Melisa has being using it, developing it, perfecting it. And I believe she is close to a breakthrough. Imagine it, Fyre, a way of bringing people back from the little death that is madness. No more prisons, no more asylums, no more suffering ... no more violent madness.'

'It sounds ideal,' said Fyre flatly, 'A pity so many had to die to achieve it ... if it can indeed be achieved.'

'Oh it can, and I told you, I have made many sacrifices to complete my wife's work.'

'It sounds to me like others have made those sacrifices,' Fyre commented.

Barry flashed with anger and slammed his fist into his desk.

'You have no idea!' he yelled, his voice rebounding from the bookshelves that enveloped the room.

Barry straightened himself up, 'You think I enjoyed watching those poor people die? In Dublin, or here? You're wrong about me, Fyre, I'm not your enemy.'

'Then why do I feel like a prisoner?'

'You won't feel that way for very long.'

Fyre grasped the meaning of this threat. 'What about Melisa? She's one of those poor girls, she's from the streets, a con artist, who ensnared your son.'

Barry laughed a real laugh. 'My dear boy, I handpicked her from those streets. I made sure she attended Cambridge, I funded her studies, I ensured her meeting with Charles.'

'All so she could finish your wife's experiment?'

Lord Barry stood up and walked to the fireplace.

'Melisa is a remarkable woman, filled with all the knowledge that my wife had, all of it. Even down to her tenacious personality. The Spectres were not the only ones who could change people's characters. The only difference between them and me, is that I do it for the greater good.'

'You experimented on Melisa?'

Barry threw him a grin, 'My dear boy, Melisa *is* the experiment, she *is* its success.'

'I don't believe you.'

'You will.'

Max produced a gun and poked it into Fyre's back, pulled him up by the collar and pushed him toward the door of the study.

'If you made a deal with the type of people who called themselves Spectres, then they will betray you,' he said.

'I have nothing to fear; wheels are in motion. They will get what they want, and I will get what I have always wanted.'

'This is madness, Lord Barry, see reason.'

'You are the one who will see reason. You will be the receptacle for this new serum. You will become my ally, marry into my family, and help me rebuild this family's name and fortune. Future generations will thank us. Your portrait will hang on these walls for centuries. Who knows, perhaps your ghost will be here too.'

'Just one more thing, Lord Barry,' Fyre said as Max pushed him forward.

'Yes? My son.'

'Where is your wife, Lord Barry?' he said in flat, deliberate tone.

Barry's eyes enlarged, and the flames from the fire seemed to flicker in them for a moment.

'She died, a long time ago, when my boy and girls were just children.'

'No,' said Fyre plainly, 'You're lying.'

CHAPTER 28

olt was barely conscious. He knew his wounds were serious, and he may not make it to end of the journey. The sergeant ordered the carriage to stop. Holt could just about hear his gruff Irish voice, telling his constables to go for a smoke.

'So, this is it,' he mumbled to himself.

A few moments later the carriage door opened, and the sergeant clamoured in. He sat bolt upright at Holt's side, looking down at the blood-soaked clothes of his prisoner.

Holt's mind was fading, low on blood and short on breath, he struggled to spit out his words.

'What are you waiting for, get on with it, you Irish bastard!'

The sergeant dithered, his hands came up from his side and dropped again.

'You think they've won?' asked Holt in a stutter, blood spewing from his lips.

'You don't understand,' said the sergeant, his own voice a shaky rattle.

'I know more than you, I know I've set a fire going that will burn all of them,' the struggle of those last words made

Holt pass out.

Nervously the sergeant put his hand out and checked Holt. He gently nudged him, then more violently shook him.

There was no reaction.

The sergeant looked around, checked out of the carriage's barred window, then picked up a heavy night coat that was balled up in the corner of the cab.

'I'm sorry, but they have my boy, you see, they said they could bring him back, make him better,' whispered the sergeant. He placed the heavy coat over Holt's face, then leaned all his strength on it, making sure to cover Holt's mouth and nose. A frenzy came over him, an angry, separated rage. He squeezed and he squeezed. Only the sound of his returning constables made him stop. He could hear them loudly talking as they walked along the coast road.

The sergeant quickly pulled the coat away. He looked at Holt, his eyes rolled back into his head, his mouth hanging loose. He could only presume he was dead. If he wasn't dead, he would have to find another way of dispatching him later.

'Sarge, you there?'

'Yeah,' replied the sergeant, 'Just making sure he's gripped up.'

He hopped out of the carriage, 'Come on then lads, we can make it back just in time for breakfast.'

Max locked Fyre into a room deep below the castle. It was a wine cellar that had once held a vast store of bottles. Now it was empty, except for damp shelves and shattered bits of furniture. The cellar was lit by three oil lamps, that gave out a yellow, sickly light. The smell of sulphur invaded Fyre's nostrils, and he could feel the burning sensation of the gas in the back of his throat. He leaned against a massive stone pillar in the centre of the room, it was so large it must have been supporting the entire kitchen above. He closed his mind off, and allowed his mind to wander. He was not alone. He could feel Lord Barry's unique aura. But there were other things here, whispers of minds that had gone before.

Lady Barry had been right to believe in ghosts. These,

however, were not ghosts of long dead ancestors, they were more recent, and they were fearful things. Quaking spirits clinging to the stones of the castle. Something flew by him. Something small and silent, it caught a glancing blow on his neck. Fyre put his gloved hand to the spot, a tell-tale trace of blood was on the tip of his finger when he took his hand away again. Desperately he tried to squeeze out the wound.

'It works instantly, Lord Fyre,' echoed the disembodied voice of Lord Barry. 'There's no point in fighting it.'

Nevertheless, Fyre did try to fight it. He clawed at the tiny slit in his skin, hoping to stop the serum before it could fully enter his system. A noise made him stop. A horrible squeaking came from multiple creatures somewhere close by. The gas lights lowered, until they were just a flicker, like dying candles. Fyre felt the first rat before he saw it. Dozens of them, large brown rodents, scurried around his feet. They were hungry, and made a noise that offended the ears as they rushed around Fyre, looking for anything to eat. One rat landed on his boot. He idly kicked it away.

Fyre had spent much of his youth in India. He had given himself over to the teaching of Jainism. That experience had been fearful too, but he had found his spirit was stronger than he ever imagined. He leaned down and picked up one of the rats, almost cradling it in his arms. He could feel the creature's discomfort and tried to send it healing thoughts.

'I quite like rats,' he said aloud, 'a much-misunderstood animal, like myself.'

Fyre carefully put the rat back on the bare stone floor, where it raced away into the darker reaches of the cellar, joining its friends.

'You'll have to do better than that, your Lordship, you know this is a pointless waste of your time. John Stone is out there, and Melisa too. It won't take them long to work out who has been behind all of this.'

There was a long silence, only broken by the popping of gas lights on the walls.

The sensation of air moving took Fyre out of his semi-mediative state. Something black and swirling was moving across the cellar, just below the brick lined celling. He smiled.

'I presume the tricks of the circus you learned from Max have come in useful in scaring others, the kites you so enjoy in the daylight hours, were a bit of giveaway. The one you used to attack me with at Sean's cottage had strings laced with razor blades, a nice touch. The dead don't scare me, at least not in the way you want to.'

The black swirling bundle of cloth overhead disappeared as quickly as it had appeared. Fyre could feel a hot flush running down his neck. Whatever serum Melisa had perfected, it was in his blood now. He wasn't sure whether the serum or his own fear was making him feel dizzy, but he had to lean back on the large pillar to stay upright. His only chances were to reason with Lord Barry, or to play for time and hope Stone was able to help him.

'I'm not a brave man, your Lordship, but I'm not a fool. And neither, I suspect, are you. Melisa made a deal with you, you broke it, she's probably on her way to the police right now.'

Fyre waited for a reply, but none came. Behind him a sharp mechanical click made him spin on his heels. His head spun too, and he had to reach out and grip the stonework to stay standing. He wasn't sure what the serum was doing to his mind, and he wasn't sure how long he could fight its effects. A strong white light had come on in the most distant corner of the cellar. Fyre could see three coffins lined up on low stone tables. The coffins looked old, worn, as if they had been dug from the earth. He staggered over to them. His mind now beginning to fill with random images and thoughts, in an uncontrolled manner.

He reached the first coffin and looked into the sunken, decomposed face of a young woman. She was wearing an expensive dress and jewellery to match. Somehow, despite the decomposition of her features, Fyre recognised her. She looked eerily close to one of Charles Barry's sisters. Not exactly like her, but close enough. Fyre had to put his hand over his nose and mouth, as the smell of rotten flesh hit him like a hammer blow.

The second coffin had another woman in it. Dressed in a similar fashion, her features were even more decomposed. Her body had begun to fall apart, and the fluids from her organs seeped into the linin-lined casket.

Fyre felt like he was going to be sick. He spun on his feet, falling sideways, and hitting the far wall of the cellar.

'You see, Lord Fyre, I am willing to make any sacrifice,' said the disembodied voice, 'anything to achieve my vision.'

Fyre fell again, but this time he was caught. Powerful hands gripped his shoulders and pushed him forward. He had no strength to resist. Fyre fell helplessly down into the third, empty, coffin.

The lid slammed down and darkness consumed him.

Bertie and Sean reached the gatehouse of Castle Barry.

How do you know they'll be here?' whispered Sean, as they tied up the horses in a cart track near the gatehouse.

'Spooky castle, lots of dead bodies and stories of ghosts,' replied Bertie, 'this is exactly the sort of place they'll be. Come on, kid, where I go, you go.'

They approached the gate. It was closed over, but not locked.

'Long drive up to the castle?' asked Bertie in a hushed tone.

'Oh yeah, but we can take a short cut across the fields, come in by the gardens: no one will see us. Used to go that way all the time as kids.'

'Fair enough,' replied Bertie.

He had a dread feeling welling inside, something he couldn't quite put his finger on. Perhaps he'd be around Lord Fyre too long, but he felt he could sense danger coming.

'The door of the gatehouse is open, sir,' said Sean.

'Stay here,' Bertie looked over at the open door, a very dim firelight was making a moving shadow against the doorframe.

Bertie crept up to the door. His eyes took a moment to adjust, but as they did he could see the horrible scene inside.

He came back to the road where he had left Sean.

'Come on,' he said, 'let's go through the gardens.'

'Is everything alright, sir?' asked Sean.

'Let's just say I'm sure Lord Fyre and Mr Stone are around here somewhere. … and don't call me sir.'

Melisa watched the figures of two men move through the woods and into the walled gardens beyond.

As the moonlight caught their silhouettes, she recognised Sean, but the second man, much larger, was a stranger to her. She had hidden herself in the woods for an hour now, waiting to see if Fyre would come out from the castle.

All of her instincts had told her to run, to get away from this madness. She had to push those thoughts away, as she had pushed many thoughts away. Her life's work was in that castle. Without it, all of her sacrifices, all she had gained and all she was about to lose, was meaningless. Hugging the treeline, she moved around the castle, until she reached the entranceway near the stables. The very place she would go to meet Lord Barry in secret. He had been keen for her to continue his late wife's work, but determined that she kept this work from her husband. She was only too willing to comply. Lord Barry had made veiled threats, and she suspected that he knew of her dark and illicit past. It was a past that seemed dream-like now. She could only remember her pre-Cambridge days in visions, glimpses of life, just ten years ago, that appeared to be dissolving in her mind. As she stood by the doorway to the stables, terrible thoughts tried to occupy her mind, but she was determined not to let them in.

Melisa couldn't make sense of why she was drawn to Lord Fyre, but something inside her, something she had not felt before, wanted to find him safe and well. She took a step forward and stopped abruptly.

Someone was standing right behind her. So close she could feel his breath on her neck.

'My dear,' said a voice.

'Charles, I can explain.'

'No need,' he paused and walked around to her side, 'I found your little bottles of potions quite some time ago. You've been administering them to me for years.'

'Your father …' Melisa began.

'My father,' screamed Charles, 'is dead to me! Just as my mother is.'

She saw his eyes flash under the moonlight; they were not the eyes of her husband, they were the eyes of madman.

Fyre's unconscious mind was filled with demons. Screaming, crying, begging for mercy that he could not give. He struggled to find some order in the madness of his mind. There were voices from beyond the threshold of death, interspersed with living spirits, somehow trapped. Then, out of nowhere, there was a calmness. A child appeared in his vision. He knew instinctively that this was John Stone. He watched in horror as this young boy's mother, a formless figure, was wrenched away from his side, leaving him alone, afraid, and vulnerable. Fyre opened his eyes. There was complete and utter blackness. His fear began to rise, his heart pounded so loud he could hear nothing else. Desperately he scraped at the close wooden walls that surrounded him. He could feel the weight of soil piled on top of him. A claustrophobic panic set in. He screamed.

But the scream went nowhere, it dissipated into the tiny space he was trapped in. Fyre's own fear overtook his logical mind.

CHAPTER 29

Dawn spread across the landscape, a cold pale blue light woke nature and took the fear of the inky night away from Cieran Murphy as he walked along the road.

'What the hell am I doing?' he asked himself for the tenth time as he trudged the long path back to the village. 'If only you were here to talk some sense into me, Frank,' he whispered, as he watched the top of the village steeple bathe in golden sunrise.

From the cliffside road that he had followed back, he could see down on the dark expanse of woods that surrounded Castle Barry. The Castle itself only gave glimpses of its scale, black stone neogothic turrets poked out of the sea of green treetops.

Murphy felt a shiver down his back, not from the cold of the predawn walk, but a fearful sensation. As he reached the village, a new noise rang out and made his already nervous mind jump into a defensive state. A trap rounded the corner of the Protestant Church. Murphy, without realising it, had placed his hand over his pistol. He removed it when he spied the driver of the trap.

'Thank god it's you, Chaplain.'

The chaplain smiled, 'Constable Murphy, I must say I never have any of my parishioners so happy to see me.'

Murphy let out a nervous laugh, 'Maybe I'm in the wrong religion.'

'There is no wrong religion, I could tell you a good story about a man who thought he was in the wrong …'

'Sorry, Chaplain, but I need a lift, police business, very urgent.'

'It seems this whole village has become police business. Very well, where are you going to?'

Murphy had a pang of self-doubt, then announced with little confidence, 'Castle Barry.'

'Then we're both in luck; that's where I'm going anyway.'

Murphy climbed into the trap. The chaplain set off, at far too leisurely a pace, but Murphy said nothing, he was just happy not to be walking anymore.

'A bit early to be visiting his lordship, isn't it?' asked Murphy.

'Not at all, once a week, his Lordship insists I give prayers for himself and his son Charles.'

'No one else?'

'Just Max, his lordship's valet, but he generally stands at the back and says nothing. Has he ever spoken to you?'

'No, I've not met him.'

'You're not missing much. Very strange, very strange indeed.'

'There's a lot of strange people about recently.'

'That there is.'

'They should never had built that cursed asylum here, I never saw any reasoning in it.'

The chaplain threw him a friendly smile.

'No personal offence, Chaplain.'

'None taken, I tend to agree with you. Young Charles Barry's methods are very … difficult to understand, for a man of the cloth. And as for that chief surgeon, he's bordering on ungodliness.'

Murphy wasn't sure what to say; he just nodded in agreement.

Within a minute they had reached the gate of Castle Barry.

'Strange,' said the chaplain, 'I usually have to knock up the gatekeeper, it's wide open now.'

'Stop here,' said Murphy, his sense of foreboding returning, 'I'll have a look around.'

Cautiously Murphy walked through the gate and came across the torn-up body of the gatekeeper. The chaplain had followed him and let out a squeal as he saw the dark blood-stained scene. He put his own hand over his mouth to stop himself from making any more noise.

'We've got to get to the castle quickly; this isn't going to be the last death here today,' Murphy said.

'I'd better stay here with this poor soul,' spoke the chaplain in a panicked whisper, 'give him last rights.'

'Isn't that more a Catholic thing?' asked Murphy, absentmindedly, as he led the horse and trap inside the gate.

'Yes, but does that matter now?' replied the chaplain.

'I suppose not. But also, do you really want to stay out here alone? Whoever did that is still on the loose.'

The chaplain didn't answer. As Murphy sat in the plate of the trap and began to trot up the road, he rushed after him and scrambled into the passenger side.

Lord Barry sat in his office alone. This had been an unexpected and unfortunate turn of events. However, in his mind, all could be fixed. He had overcome disasters before; he was sure that he would do so again.

A creak on the floorboard just outside his door alerted him to an intruder.

'Come in, Melisa,' he cried out.

The door to the office slowly swung open. Melisa stepped through. The dawn light from the windows behind her surrounded her figure and made her appear to glow.

'You look as beautiful as ever,' commented Lord Barry. He stood up and turned off the gas lamp on his desk, with a dramatic flourish he whipped open the heavy curtains to let the blueish natural light in.

'Hardly,' replied Melisa.

She was still dressed in boys' clothes, her pants and boots caked in mud from the woods, and her hair tied back in a tight bun.

'Does she remind you of anyone?' Charles asked just before he too stepped into the room.

Lord Barry seemed to be taken aback a little.

'My son.'

'Father.'

'Here for the service?'

'I'm here for justice.'

Melisa gestured to the gun in Charles's hand.

'He knows everything, your Lordship,' she stated.

'I doubt that,' answered Lord Barry, seating himself at his desk.

'I know that my mother developed a serum to try and control my personality, I know that you employed Melisa to seduce me and administer this serum, while I was away at college.'

Lord Barry took in a deep breath. 'You told him this?' he asked Melisa.

'It's the truth, isn't it?'

'It's part of the truth. There is so much more.'

'I found out about your little potion some time ago. I was able to swap the serum for a harmless sugar solution,' Charles took a further step into the room and forcefully pushed Melisa toward the desk.

'You see, father, I have returned to being the real me. The son you never wanted.'

'I wanted you, Charles, but you were sick, disturbed, violent, even as a child your mother could see the evil in you. I was only trying to save you, just as I am trying to save her.'

'Mother is dead.'

'Not dead, not yet anyway, some semblance of her remains.'

'Your little experiment is over,' Charles spat through

his teeth. His eyes, in the dawn light, seemed to spark with white fire.

'What are you going to do?' asked Lord Barry.

'End your control over me, free myself.'

'Charles,' began Melisa, her voice soft like a lover's, 'listen to your father, we were trying to help you. You're a good man, a good man I fell in love with.'

'You lying bitch, that good man came from a bottle. And you're not in love with me, you're a whore from the streets, all your talent, all your work came from my mother's papers.'

'That's not strictly speaking, true,' said Lord Barry.

His voice was stopped by the crack of a bullet smashing through the office.

Bertie followed Sean through the maze of the walled gardens and the outbuildings that sat up against the main castle. The place was in complete darkness, and doubts were beginning to creep into Bertie's mind. Perhaps he should have just done as Lord Fyre had asked. The sun was just about to come up and a dark blue predawn light made the masonry of Castle Barry glimmer, as if it were alive.

'Do you know which part of this place is most used?' Bertie whispered to Sean.

'No, sir, I've never been inside, I've only ever been in the gardens.'

'This place is massive, and I have a gut feeling the sooner we find either Mr Stone or Lord Fyre, the better.'

'I hear something,' Sean said.

Bertie bent his ears to the windless dawn. The distinctive sound of a single horse pulling a two-wheeler echoed off the tall walls.

'That's round the front, I think,' Sean muttered.

Bertie wasn't listening. A sudden sensation came over him, a mix of fear and strength. He couldn't see anything, or hear anything, but somehow he could feel the presence of his master and friend.

'What's down there?' Bertie asked, pointing to a

doorway, half-sunk in a trench that ran around the back of the house.

'The old kitchens, sir, no one goes in there,' Sean told him.

'Then that's where he is, and he's in trouble.'

'Shouldn't I go for help of something?' asked the chaplain, his voice filled with anxiety.

'Probably,' replied Murphy, his mind focusing on the situation in hand, 'but who is close enough to help us.'

'I suppose you're right.'

'How do you usually get in?'

'Max is normally here waiting for me.'

'But not this morning?'

'No, that is odd.'

'Come on.'

Murphy led the way up the stone steps to the towering main door of the castle. Nervously he turned the ringed handle on the door and put his weight against it. The door effortlessly swung open.

'Are you sure we're allowed to go in?' asked the chaplain.

'I represent the law, and if they don't like that, you represent a higher law.'

Murphy walked inside, the chaplain following him, mumbling, 'I'm not sure Lord Barry will see it that way.'

Bertie lit a match. The rising dawn light could not yet penetrate into the half-submerged kitchens of the Castle, so he lit a lantern that sat by the door and looked around. As Sean had said, the old kitchen of the castle had not been used in years. Dust coated ever surface and a musty odour overpowered every other scent. The kitchen was vast, room after room spreading out under the main building. At one time there must have been dozens of staff working ovens, fires and boilers. Bertie flashed the lantern to an arched doorway that stood beyond a wide fireplace, big enough for several men to stand in.

'That'll be the cellar, I'd bet, he'll be down there.'

'How do you know, can you feel his spirit?' whispered Sean.

'No, I can see his footprints in the dust on the ground,' Bertie dropped the light and sure enough, several sets of prints to and from the arched door were clear.

'See those pointy toed ones there?'

'Yeah?'

'Lord Fyre's fancy Italian boots. Never cared for them meself. Come on, stay close, boy.'

Carefully they both made their way down into the wine cellar. The stairs were well-worn, bowed in the centre and slippery from centuries of use.

Bertie had been in the cellar of Drumcrow House, it seemed large and foreboding, but it was nothing compared with this space.

He flashed the lantern around, hoping to see some clue of Fyre's whereabouts, the thin light could not even illuminate the far walls of the cellar.

'There's a smell, sir,' Sean said. 'Something rotten.'

Bertie, who smoked and spend his life around horses, would be the first to admit that he had little sense of smell, but something in one corner of the cellar was definingly off. With Sean standing as close to him as he could get, so as not to step outside the light, Bertie walked across the stone flagged floor.

'Coffins.'

'Oh, sweet Jesus!' Sean said, clapping his hand over his mouth to stop himself from screaming.

Bertie looked into the first open casket.

'Whoever these poor souls are, they've been here a long time.'

He looked over at Sean, who was shaking like a leaf and close to passing out.

'Mr Fyre always said there was nothing to fear from the dead, only the living can cause us harm.' Just as he spoke a loud bump from the third, closed coffin.

'But then he talks a lot of shite,' yelled Bertie and he

began to run for it.

He only got a few steps, he reached out and gripped the fleeing Sean by the collar, stopping him in his tracks.

'Wait, I have a feeling.'

CHAPTER 30

The first ray of sunlight struck the grey walls of the asylum, but seemed to be absorbed into its massive dark bulk. The chief surgeon was frantically moving around his office in the corner of the vast mortuary chamber. He was gathering papers and stuffing them into a large brown folding leather bag.

'Sir?' a voice rang out, rebounding off the bare, whitewashed walls.

The chief surgeon leapt across the office space and grabbed a small pistol that was sitting on his desk. A face appeared out of the twilight, the high windows allowing slanted beams of the dawn to fall down into the mortuary.

'Michael,' said the chief surgeon, his breath coming hard and his eyes darting.

Michael's sluggish frame walked into one of the beams of light. He had his usually worried and innocent expression on his face.

'Is that a gun?' he asked.

'Yes, I keep it for protection,' replied the chief surgeon.

'From what?'

The chief surgeon let out a fake laugh, 'I'm not sure,

I'm not sure at all. Why are you here, Michael?'

'The whole place is in chaos,' Michael replied, his voice almost breaking into tears.

'What do you mean?'

'The guards have all gone, just gone, as if they disappeared. Doctor Barry can't be found anywhere, and the chaplain drove off before dawn to go to the castle. There's no one about.'

'No one?'

'No, well, just the patients. And they're all in their cells, making an awful racket. Howling, screaming, and shouting strange things.'

'I'll bet they are,' said the chief surgeon to himself.

'What am I going to do?' Michael's voice sounded like a child pleading for mercy.

The chief surgeon lowered the pistol, but kept his distance from Michael.

'If you know what's good for you, Michael, you'll leave this place. As for me, I have to go, I'm taking these papers and leaving, There's someone I have to see.'

'But I have nowhere to go.'

'Then stay and wait for the police to come.'

'No, please, don't leave me here.'

The chief surgeon bundled the last of the papers he wanted into his bag and slipped on his jacket, he placed the pistol in the pocket and ran for the door.

Michael followed him, just a few paces behind.

'Michael, the best thing you can do now is go and hide in your room.'

He didn't listen to Michael pleading and muttering as they ran down the long corridor. It was only when they reached the main intersection that the din of screaming voices made him stop in his tracks.

Michael skidded to a halt behind him.

'Can you hear them? I can't stay here.'

The entire main building of the Asylum reverberated with the screeches of its inmates. A symphony of terrible noises seemed to come from the walls themselves.

The chief surgeon spun on his heels, his heart beating like a badly played drum, and sweat beginning to run down his skin.

'Oh my God, what have they done here?' he muttered.

He looked over at the terrified face of Michael. 'Come on, follow me. Run now, run.'

They ran back through the west wing of the building. As they moved along they reached the secure cells that lined the corridor heading back to the mortuary, a violent impact on the inside of one of the cell doors, stopped them in their tracks again.

'What was that?' cried Michael.

'That's just a mad old woman. Leave her. There's no helping her. Let's get out of here, we need to find John Stone.'

Bertie didn't hesitate, he undid the brass screws holding down the heavy lid of the solid casket.

Sean, scared and unsure what was happening, undid the last screw.

Using his raw strength, Bertie pulled the lid across and let it fall noisily to the flagstone floor.

Fyre sat up and took in a massive gulp of air. His eyes looked around wildly in the dim lamp light, and he gripped the sides of the coffin.

'Good morning, Bertie,' he panted, 'am I glad to see you!'

'Mr Fyre, what happened to you?' Sean cried, his heart pounding in his chest and his brain trying to catch up on what he had just witnessed.

'Oh nothing much, I just took a small nap into death, … I didn't care for it. Nor did I care for having to face my own fears … but face them I did.'

'Let's get you out of there,' said Bertie, as he lifted Fyre clear of the coffin and stood him unsteadily on the floor.

'We need to find Lord Barry, and Stone, and the girl Melisa … and that policeman,' said Fyre, his breath still coming hard.

'That'll be just about everyone then,' commented Bertie. 'Come on, let's get out of here.'

'What about the two women in the coffins,' Sean asked.

'Lord Barry's daughters, I suspect they didn't want to get married to old farmers for their money, but someone else claiming to be them clearly did.'

Fyre spoke as he ran, his strength beginning to return. They were almost at the cellar stairwell when the large frame of Max stood out from behind a wooden partition. Fyre stopped and pushed Sean behind him.

'Your master is a madman, he's let his whole family suffer for a delusion. Stand aside, Max,' spoke Fyre, 'Stand aside and we can help end this madness.'

Max glowered at them, the flickering light he held in his hand making his features even more animal-like.

'I don't think that's worked,' said Bertie, 'you go and find Mr Stone, I'll deal with this one.'

'Are you sure?' asked Fyre.

'Sure,' said Bertie, plainly.

Slowly Fyre led Sean to the foot of the stair. Max watched them, but kept his eye on the approaching bulk of Bertie.

'Good luck, Bert,' said Fyre and he and Sean raced up the stair.

Cieran Murphy, followed by the chaplain, still protesting, moved through the grand entrance hall of Castle Barry. The early morning sun flooded into the vast rooms through the tall windows, making slanted columns of sparking light that appeared magical.

'Nice place,' muttered Murphy to himself.

'I always found it a little cold, even in the summer,' commented the chaplain, 'there's not much in the way of furnishing in the whole castle, only his Lordship's office and the chapel remain as they must have been years ago.'

Murphy was about to inquire as to why the house was so empty when a shot rang out. He was moving at speed up the stairs before the chaplain could say a word.

Bertie and Max circled each other closely. The only light in the wine cellar was the oil lamp resting on a barrel and a shaft of daylight that crept down the stairwell. Without any warning, the two men simultaneously grabbed each other.

Bertie struck a hammer-fist blow down on Max's left shoulder. Max countered with a powerful straight punch to Bertie's chest, momentarily sending him backwards. Bertie recovered and rushed forward. The two giants interlocked arms and began to wrestle, raw strength against strength. Max had bulging muscles, barely contained by his black jacket. Bertie was barrel-chested and his muscles hardened from years of labour. Slowly they performed a terrible dance, their feet struggling to stay still on the cobbled floor.

Max gave a loud grunt and with all his strength he was able to force Bertie against the cellar wall. Bertie tried a second hammer-fist to Max's head, but his opponent countered it with a quick shot to Bertie's ribs. This blow gave Max the advantage. Instantly Max had his iron-like hands around Bertie's throat. With nowhere to manoeuvre, Bertie tried to pull Max's hands away from his windpipe.

The grip on his throat was too strong. He could feel his lungs being deprived of air.

Fyre led Sean through the maze of Castle Barry, despite the fact he was unsure where he was going, he felt that moving upwards was the right thing to do. They found a servants' staircase close to the kitchen's main doorway. Fyre looked up into the stairwell, it appeared to lead right up through the full height of the building.

'This will do us,' he said to Sean.

The boy didn't respond immediately; his wild eyes were fixed on something behind Fyre. He raised his finger and pointed.

'It's Mr Stone.'

There was a broken glass partition, separating the stairwell from a long corridor which ran under the main block of the building. Stone was standing beyond the partition, he had been running and his breath was coming hard.

'John!' called Fyre.

What light there was, in these lower rooms of the castle, fell on Stone's face.

Fyre saw something he feared, something terrible.

'You're not John Stone,' he said quietly, his voice had a slight tremble, 'What did they do to you, John?'

Stone's eyes glinted in the twilight, like mad diamonds. He bared his teeth, like an animal threatened. A shot rang out, somewhere above them. The echo rebounded down the stairwell.

For a second, Fyre took his eyes off Stone. When he looked back, Stone had fled into the darkness.

Fyre instinctively knew he couldn't hesitate. He began to climb the stairs, Sean chasing after him.

Bertie could feel the life being choked out of him.

Max hunched his shoulders and bore his full strength down on Bertie's windpipe.

'Die an honourable death,' he muttered, as he pushed one last time to kill this man.

Bertie closed his eyes, but it was not to fall into a deathly sleep. He raised his knee sharply and connected a beautiful strike into Max's unprotected groin.

Max folded, his grip released, and Bertie continued his attack with a haymaker to the jaw.

'I'd rather live a dishonourable life, if it's all the same to you,' croaked Bertie and he looked down on the unconscious body of Max.

He too heard the shot ring through the castle. He had no time to secure Max, so he left him. He ran up the stairs of the cellar and pulled a large wooden box across the doorway, before continuing upwards into the building.

The bullet from Charles's pistol slammed into the wood panelling of Lord Barry's office.

Melisa dived for safety, but Lord Barry stood statue still.

'Tell me why I shouldn't kill you both?' asked Charles, his voice breaking as his anger grew further and further.

Lord Barry smiled a laboured smile, then said, 'Everything my wife sacrificed, was for you, Charles. She loved you far more than I. You were her greatest success. She used her own body, her own mind to create a cure for your illness.'

'Listen to him, Charles,' panted Melisa, from the other side of the room, 'Your mother's work was genius, she was in contact with some of the greatest minds in Europe, she was on the brink of curing madness, changing the human mind.'

Charles spun on his heels and pointed the gun at Melisa.

'And where and when did you come into all of this? My dear wife!'

'My own mother is institutionalised in a home in England, she suffers from the same illness as you, Charles, the same, terrible illness. The work your mother did was a cure, a real cure, a way of rebuilding a human being's personality. Making them better, making them new. ... She was recreating life itself.'

'You stole my mind,' said Charles.

He raised the gun, a point-blank shot to Melisa's head.

Murphy came through the main door of the office. Without waiting to see who it was, Melisa ran for a second door, nestled between two bookshelves. Murphy held his pistol out toward Charles Barry, who held his toward Murphy and the chaplain standing close behind him in the doorway.

Melisa slipped through the door. Lord Barry remained motionless at his desk.

'Enough of this!' shouted Lord Barry, 'It's over, Charles, whatever demons are in your head, you need to control them.'

'Put the gun down, Doctor Barry, enough people have been hurt,' spoke Murphy, slowly.

The door between the bookshelves opened and Melisa

cautiously walked back into the room. With the daylight now streaming through the windows, her mud-stained clothes were more obvious. Close behind her, the lanky figure of Fyre emerged from the servants' stairs. Sean stood behind him, like a shadow in the doorway, peeping around the corner.

'It seems, Lord Barry that we have reached endgame,' Fyre said.

After a long pause, in which Lord Barry looked from face to face in the room, he said with great resignation, 'Yes, Lord Fyre, you are right.'

With their weapons still aimed, Murphy and Charles had their eyes locked on each other.

'It's time to confess,' said Lord Barry, 'all of us have committed terrible sins.'

Fyre's eyes caught those of Melisa, who wilted under his gaze.

'Chaplain, would you hear my last confession?' Lord Barry asked.

'I'm sure,' replied the chaplain, 'we would all like to hear the truth, but is it wise now, your Lordship, with your son holding us at gunpoint?'

Lord Barry walked around his desk and held his hands out to Charles.

'My son,' he managed to say.

Two shots rang out, so close together that they sounded like one.

Fyre dived down, pulling Melisa down to the floor with him. Sean ducked behind the doorway. The chaplain too moved backwards, reeling into the corridor. Murphy stood facing Charles, his firing arm still held out fully, smoke drifting up from his discharged pistol. The body of Lord Barry was already on the floor, crumpled unnaturally, his legs folded underneath him as if they were broken twigs. Charles wavered for a moment, a round spot of blood bloomed on his jacket breast. The gun fell from his hand, and he slumped forward on his knees, then fell face down to the floorboards.

CHAPTER 31

'The bullet has missed his vital organs,' said Melisa, as she put pressure down on Charles's wound. With Bertie's help, they loaded Charles onto the back of a trap, Melisa and the chaplain joined him, taking turns to stem the flow of blood from his shoulder.

'I'm not sure who to trust here,' Murphy said to Fyre, as he led Max into the courtyard at gunpoint.

'Neither am I, but I do trust you, constable,' replied Fyre, 'so perhaps we should trust each other.'

Max's reaction when he saw the dead body of his master lying on the back of another trap in the yard, was one of total despair. He fell to his knees and began weeping like a lost child.

'We need to get Charles to the infirmary,' Melisa called out from the back of the first trap.

'She's right,' said Fyre, 'if we can save his life, he can answer a lot of questions.'

'Alright then, I'll take the girl and the chaplain and go to the asylum. Will you be able to manage this big fella until more of my men arrive back from Kinsale?'

Fyre looked down at the weeping heap of Max at the

foot of the second trap.

'I don't think he'll be any trouble from here on,' Fyre replied.

'You'd better all be here when I get back; you can consider yourselves all under arrest,' said Murphy, seriously.

'Understandable,' answered Fyre, honestly.

'What the hell has happened here?' asked Murphy in a whisper.

'Madness, in more ways than one, but there are other elements at work here too,' said Fyre.

'Hurry,' called out Melisa.

'You'd better go, we'll be here when you get back,' Fyre said.

Murphy jumped into the driver's seat of the trap, 'Chaplain, you'd better come too.'

'No, I'll stay here, Lord Barry was my patron and my friend, I'll stay with his remains.'

'Sean, you go with them,' said Fyre, as he half-pushed Sean into the trap in place of the chaplain, 'do as Melisa says, I feel she is genuinely trying to save her husband.'

Melisa looked up from her efforts to contain the wound, 'For once, Lord Fyre, understand me completely.'

'I hope so,' replied Fyre, as Murphy whipped the horse and pulled the trap away.

Fyre watched the trap round the corner of the long drive and disappear.

'Do you think he'll make it?' asked the chaplain.

'He might, he and Melisa are the only connection now to people who wish to play God, and don't care about human life.'

'People?' asked the chaplain.

'There are dark forces behind all of this, Chaplain, I have an understanding that Lord Barry and his family were only pawns in a much more expansive game.'

'Speaking of which, what are we going to do about Max?'

Fyre looked over to where Max was holding the legs of his former master, his eyes a stream of tears.

'I've never seen such loyalty in a servant, I wonder why he loved Lord Barry so?' Fyre asked.

'He was a good man, if deluded, all he ever wanted was for his wife to come back. Everything he did, he did in her memory,' said the chaplain solemnly.

'Strange,' said Fyre, to himself.

'What's strange about that?'

'I got the feeling that his wife never really left him.'

The chaplain laughed, 'We all feel like that, about the ones we love.'

'Bertie, help Max to his feet and let's get inside, we can do nothing now but wait.'

'What about Mr Stone?' asked Bertie with genuine concern.

Fyre spoke to himself again. 'I'm hoping his mind is as strong as mine was, when faced with what we fear the most.'

'Well, you can ask him,' said the chaplain.

'What?'

The chaplain pointed to the approaching John Stone, walking with purpose across the courtyard. In his hand, he held a long dagger.

The trap driven by Murphy raced through the village and reached the long winding hill that led to the asylum.

Two men were walking down the hill, blocking the road.

'Who the hell are these, now?' called Murphy.

Melisa looked up from treating the barely conscious Charles and saw Lord Barry's servants, Mr Potts and Mr Grey, standing across the narrow road.

'Drive the horse on!' she yelled.

'Why?'

'Just do it!'

Instinctively Murphy knew she was right. He gave the horse an extra crack with the whip and rattled the trap past the two men, forcing them to dive for the ditch. Melisa looked back as the trap raced up the hill. Mr Potts and Mr Grey stood back in the centre of the road, watching her intently. A third figure came out of the ditch, well dressed.

Just as the trap rounded a corner, she recognised Matthew Barry, staring at her, with a manic grin on his face. Melisa looked down at Charles, the blood flow had stemmed, and she was sure the wound, while serious, wasn't fatal. Without speaking a word she dived out of the back of the trap, made a heavy impact on the road, rolled for several yards and was on her feet running for the woods before the pain of her actions became obvious to her.

'Well, that was rude, wasn't it, Mr Potts?'

'It was indeed, Mr Grey,' replied Mr Potts, 'what shall we do now, Mr Matthew? I see they have Doctor Charles in the back of that trap, and he don't look too well to me.'

'He was never well,' muttered Matthew Barry to himself, 'we will do as we were ordered to do. You two follow them and take care of our business as planned.'

'We got everything in place over the last few days,' said Mr Grey.

'Good, I will find the girl, and take care of her.'

'What about the surgeon? Him and that idiot left in a hurry.'

Matthew Barry laughed, 'Our master has plans for him. Go, destroy all the evidence, then disappear back to the underworld of crime where I found you.'

'And our payments?' asked Mr Potts.

'When the job is done, I will meet you in Dublin and our debt to you will be paid.'

'No offence, Mr Matthew, sir, but your record in paying debt isn't great.'

Matthew Barry scowled at both of them, 'You doubt our master?'

'Not at all,' said Mr Grey.

'Then do your job, and all will be well.'

'Mr Stone, sir!' called out Bertie as Stone arrived. His face twisted, his eyes widened as to be wild, like a trapped animal.

'John,' Fyre shouted at his friend, 'You've got to fight

this, you're still in there, John, you're still you.'

'I'm not sure about that,' said Bertie as he moved backward.

Stone brandished the large dagger and began to run across the courtyard.

'Run!' yelled Fyre as Stone drew close.

Fyre wasn't sure how he was going to fight off his friend, but, in that moment, he was sure that someone had manipulated Stone into killing him. Stone didn't chase after Fyre, instead he leapt toward the chaplain, who let out a yelp of pain. Bertie and Sean had dived behind the cart containing the body of Lord Barry. Fyre ran to the aid of the chaplain. Stone had driven the tip of the blade into the chaplain's upper arm, and was throttling him with his other hand. A heavy kick from a large boot connected with Stone's head and sent him reeling across the ground, hurt but not unconscious.

Max followed up the kick with a punch aimed downwards, the force of which knocked Stone out cold. There was a long moment's silence, punctuated only by the whistling of birds in the nearby trees.

'That'll do, Max,' said Fyre as he stood over his friend.

Max, his eyes red with tears, nodded his head and returned to the side of his dead master.

'Bertie, tie John up, so as he is no further danger to us or himself.'

'Yes, sir.'

Fyre and Sean helped the chaplain to his feet.

'Why would he attack me?' cried the chaplain. There was a trickle of ruby blood running down his arm.

Fyre inspected the wound 'It's not too bad, you got lucky, it's just a cut, we'll patch you up with some handkerchiefs. But we'd better get you to the asylum. In fact, I think we'd all better go.'

'But Constable Murphy said …' began Sean.

'I think Constable Murphy is in more danger than we currently are. Come on, we're all going, including the late Lord Barry.'

Melisa could hear the horse running her down. She was tough, resourceful, and now desperate. She chose to run away from the roads and paths, across the scrubland, toward the coast. The horseman behind her was skilful and able to negotiate the rough terrain. Melisa could feel the heat of the morning sun bearing down on her exposed face, a cold layer of sweat was covering her entire body. She wished now that she had stayed with Lord Fyre, he seemed to be her only protection. Her husband was not the man she married; that man had been controlled, created, partly by her and partly by his parents.

The horseman slowed his progress. Melisa stopped too, her chest heaving for air. The sound of crashing waves hitting jagged rocks suddenly became clear to her.

'I rode this landscape all my life,' shouted Matthew Barry, 'You've run onto one of the promontories, cliff on three sides. They're all along this coast.'

Melisa frantically looked around. He was right. She had just run. Had she taken a moment to think, the woods would have provided her with a pathway inland, away from Castle Barry.

Matthew Barry steered his horse through the rocks and stopped just ten feet away from her.

'So, my dear girl, whoever you really are, what do we do now?'

Melisa looked around for anything that could be a weapon. All she had was her own wit.

'I suppose we could laugh it all off, and you could let me go?'

Matthew Barry did laugh, but it was a dark, heavy laugh.

'I could kill you now,' he said, producing a hunting gun, the type used to kill large animals at close range.

'You could, but what good would it be to you?'

'There are a lot of nasty people involved in all of this. I had some bad luck at cards against some of them. Very bad luck. You're worth more to me alive than dead … Melisa,' he stressed her name with a horrible smile.

'Why?'

'You really don't know do you. You, Melisa, are not the genius you think you are, you're not even the woman you think you are. There is no loving mother in a lunatic asylum in England, waiting to be rescued by her devoted daughter. It's all a delusion, just like the delusions you put in her husband's head.'

'You're lying,' Melisa spat out.

'No, my dear, I'm not. You were just a baby when they took you from the orphanage, Lord Barry wanted his wife back. So you have her memories, her character, her mind. You, Melisa, are Lady Barry, reborn. You're not the experimenter … you are the experiment.'

'Not possible, none of that is possible!'

'You know you've done great things here, terrible things. You know it is possible. All you wanted to do was to recreate your mother's mind, with the same desire that Lady Barry had to recreate her insane son.'

Melisa picked up a large rock and brandished it at him.

'Oh come on, child, be sensible. Come with me, arrangements have been made for us to travel to England, as husband and wife. New identities, new lives. My debts repaid and your mind … renewed.'

'So that's what you want!' she said in disgust.

'You are my reward, for my sacrifices.'

'Go to hell!'

'Don't worry my dear, you won't remember hating me, you'll love me like you did Charles.'

Melisa's anger rose up and she drew back her hand holding the rock. Knowing that a shot from the powerful gun he held would be instant and lethal at this range, she was accepting death, rather than this twisted truth he was offering.

A large explosion broke through the air like a thunderclap. Matthew Barry momentarily turned in his saddle. Beyond the treeline and the grey turrets of Castle

Barry, one tower of the vast asylum was engulfed in flames. Melisa took the opportunity and she ran further along the promontory.

'Damn it!' yelled Matthew Barry, when he turned back, he spurred his hose on.

Melisa didn't have a plan, she just ran, as before, but now her mind was awash with his words.

Matthew Barry closed on her, the sound of his horse's hooves echoing more explosions in the distance.

'There's nowhere left to go!' he called to her.

She had reached the edge. The thin grasses gave way to bare Atlantic-washed rocks.

'Yes, there is,' she replied in a low tone, and with no hesitation, Melisa jumped into the raging sea.

Matthew Barry looked down on the churning waves and jagged rocks for as long as he could spare.

His time was running out. Behind him, thick, black and grey smoke was filling the sky.

'The plan will still work, there is another one,' he muttered and turned his horse away from the cliffs.

CHAPTER 32

Bertie drove the horse hard up the hill.

'You sure about this, sir?' he asked Fyre, as the vast building came into view.

'No, but what choice do we have?'

Fyre looked down at his friend. Stone was beginning to stir, his eyes flickered open, but there was no focus in them yet.

'The policeman's trap is outside, looks like Charles Barry is still in the back of it,' called Bertie as he steered their carriage up alongside the other one.

Fyre helped Stone down from the carriage and lay him up against a hitching post in the yard.

'What happened?' muttered Stone.

'They used some of their drugs on you. My guess is that it stimulates parts of the brain that are dormant, allowing them to access your more primitive side.'

'Primitive?'

'You attacked the chaplain.'

'Is he alright?'

'Surprisingly, yes,' Fyre untied his friend, 'The drug may also allow someone to implant false memories, perhaps even false personalities into your mind. It's really quite brilliant and terrifying.'

'What's our situation now?' asked Stone as he pushed himself up the hitching post and shakily stood, he checked in his jacket pocket, and produced a small silver pistol, which had not been there before.

'This isn't mine,' he said

'No, I believe I saw that in Charles Barry's office,' replied Fyre.

'What's going on?' asked Stone.

'I believe I have some answers, but not all of them ....'

Fyre's words were drowned out by the massive explosion that engulfed one side of the building.

The chief surgeon and Michael raced through the building.

'Where are we going, sir?' yelled Michael as struggled to keep up. His twisted body frame ached as he ran. He rounded a corner and came to a sudden stop behind the chief surgeon. Who was standing under the bulk of the west tower, its stairway disappearing into the darkness above them.

A man was leaning over roughly stacked boxes. It was now that Michael noticed his feet were in a half inch of liquid that was seeping across the tiles.

'Who are you?' stuttered the chief surgeon. He clutched the leather bag, containing the papers he had gathered, to his chest.

'You don't know who I am,' said Mr Potts, a horrible gin on his face, 'But I knows you, and your nasty little letters to that detective Holt back in England. We've had our eyes on you.'

'You won't get away with this,' screamed the chief surgeon.

Mr Potts backed away, his grin still across his dirty face, he pushed open the external door with his back and reached his left hand outside.

'When a job goes wrong, get rid of all the evidence, that what Mr Barry said, so that what we're doing, all of it, including you.'

His hand came back into view, holding a lantern with no hood enclosing its naked flame.

'Butter fingers!' yelled Mr Potts and he smashed the lantern to oil-soaked floor.

The flames took immediately and spread instantly along the floor and up the walls.

Within seconds the rush of blue and orange flame had reached the store of boxes and the blast funnelled up the tower like a cannon roar.

Panic erupted.

From every doorway, from every shattered window, the inmates of the asylum spewed out into the courtyards and gardens and raced wildly away in every direct.

Murphy appeared from the main door, holding a handkerchief to his face, to stop the black smoke from getting into his lungs. Behind him, more, violent, explosions rocked other parts of the building.

Murphy tried to stop one of the inmates as he ran by, his white overalls stained with black patches from the fire that now raged across the building.

'Leave them,' shouted Fyre, 'don't waste your time, let them run.'

'What the hell has happened!' roared Murphy, the noise of the inferno forcing him to.

'I don't know. Where is Melisa?'

'Gone when I pulled up, she must have jumped off and ran for it,' replied Murphy, 'Where is Charles Barry?'

Fyre looked around to the cart. Charles Barry was gone.

'There!' said Stone, who was now on his feet, but still leaning heavily on the side of the trap.

He was pointing to a door, halfway down the west wing of the building. This side was now a fireball, and parts of the roof were imploding from the heat of the flames.

Charles Barry was staggering his way forward, he had reached the door, he momentarily looked back to the group in the courtyard, then swung the door open and disappeared in a cloud of black smoke.

'I'll get him,' said Fyre, he ripped his jacket off and placed in over his head, then ran toward the building. Bertie followed, doing the same with his jacket. Murphy's mind was dazed, but he had an overriding duty to protect lives.

'Sean, will you come with me, the East Wing isn't fully gone yet, and there might be people still trapped in there?'

'Yes, sir,' Sean replied.

'You wait here, Chaplain,' said Murphy.

'Are you sure?' stuttered the chaplain.

'Your services may be needed here more than inside.'

Murphy looked back at the cart containing the body of Lord Barry. His servant was standing over his master, as if waiting for him to wake up.

'Come on, Sean, let's see if anyone is left inside before the fire spreads any more.'

Fyre and Bertie reached the door that Charles Barry had used, but it was now impassable.

Fyre was beaten back by the intensity of flames. Bertie grabbed him by the coat tail and pulled him further away.

'You're wasting your time, if he's in there, he's dead,' screamed Bertie.

Fyre, was not willing to give up just yet. He ran further down the building, glass from the shattered windows crushing under his footfalls. He reached a window which was broken open, but, despite the smoke, flames were not yet pouring out of it.

'Boost me up to the sill, Bert.'

Bertie used his enormous strength to left Fyre by the legs up into the giant window frame.

It took a few seconds for Fyre to be able to see anything through the smoke. He could just about make out Charles Barry stumbling down the corridor. He was skirting the wall, feeling his way, until he reached a cell door, opposite the window, where Fyre had just his head and shoulders visible.

'Charles,' screamed Fyre.

Charles Barry looked over to him. A smile drew across his lips. His face was badly burnt, and blood from his gunshot wound was flowing again.

'Tell Sean I'm sorry about his sister, she was an easy victim, and I took her.'

'It doesn't have to be like this, Charles!'

'Oh, but it does, let the bad hearts burn,' he replied, his voice low but audible.

He opened the cell door. A whoosh of smoke and flame temporarily blinded Fyre.

When the smoke had cleared enough for him to see again, he could see Charles Barry being embraced by an older woman, dressed in a white gown.

Fyre eyes didn't remain on them long. The giant figure of Max was coming down the corridor. In his arms he was carrying the limp body of his master. His suit was on fire, and blisters were erupting on his exposed skin as the heat in this part of the building reached unbearable levels.

Fyre could hardly stand the heat now, he had to shield his face with his jacket. He tried to yell to Max, but the smoke choked his words. The last thing he saw before Bertie let him down and dragged him away from the fire, was Max following Charles into the cell and the door swinging shut.

Flames engulfed them all.

Unseen by anyone else, inside the cell, Charles Barry watched Max fall to his knees, overcome by the smoke. The body of his father rolled from Max's arms and landed at the feet of Charles and his mother.

'Together at last,' whispered Charles.

His mother smiled, her eyes glinting with sadness, just as the ceiling gave way in a massive explosion.

Farmers, fishermen and locals gazed across the skyline. Beyond the black towers of Castle Barry, the sky was a vast bank of ash-filled cloud. Beneath this grey swirling bank, licks of orange flame torn upwards like miniature volcanoes.

Fyre and Bertie reeled backwards, finding Stone

halfway along the courtyard.

'I tried to stop him,' said Stone, as Bertie gathered him to his feet, 'but he was too strong, like a man possessed.'

'Doesn't matter now, John, they're gone, all gone,' replied Fyre. The chaplain was lying on his back too, he sat up and rubbed his head. Bertie raced to gather the horses and led them away from the inferno.

Fyre helped Stone and the chaplain into the front garden. Once they were at a safe distance, they all fell against a low garden wall, and watched the building begin to collapse.

'There's no way that should have happened,' said Stone.

'It was planned, all planned,' replied Fyre, 'We've been interlopers in this all along; none of these people were meant to survive this.'

'So, by coming here, we didn't help anyone?' asked Stone.

In the distance Fyre spotted Cieran Murphy and Sean leading several inmates away into a side garden. He pointed this out to the others.

'Maybe we helped someone,' muttered Fyre.

'Thank God,' said the chaplain.

'Look, there's someone else,' Bertie gestured to a figure, half-falling across the lawn.

Stone felt Fyre's hand reach into his jacket. They made a knowing eye contact as Fyre retrieved Stone's silver pistol and secreted it under his own jacket. He wasn't sure what Fyre was up to, but he trusted him.

Bertie and the chaplain rushed to the stricken man's aid. He was so badly burnt that his face was unrecognisable.

They laid him down on the ground, beside the garden wall.

'He's dying,' said the chaplain.

'Who is he?'

'I think he was our chief surgeon, he must have been in his surgery when the first blast happened,' replied the chaplain.

Calmly the chaplain opened the man's jacket and shirt, placing his bag to one side. What was left of the chief surgeon tried desperately to say something, but his mouth was burnt beyond use. He gurgled a sound, struggled for air, and expired in the chaplain's arms.

'I can't say he was a good man, but he didn't deserve to die like this,' said the chaplain.

'Do you think he was involved in all of this?' asked Stone.

'I do,' said Fyre, 'Maybe his part, and the part of others will be revealed in that bag you're trying to hide behind your back.'

The chaplain gave a snort of derision, 'What on earth are you talking about, man?'

Fyre raised the pistol and aimed it at the chaplain. 'In my experience, the masters of puppets tend to hide in plain sight,' Fyre spoke deliberately. He could see in the chaplain's eyes that there was an understanding of the situation. 'If John Stone,' continued Fyre, 'were sent to kill a man, he would be dead by now. He was never meant to kill you, just a minor flesh wound would do, enough to divert any suspension while your lackies carried out your end game plan.'

Murphy reached the scene. He drew his pistol and pointed it at Fyre. 'Put the gun down!' demanded Murphy.

'No, Constable, I'm afraid not. This man is cause of all of this murder and misery. And all for a little chemical formula that changes people into whatever he wants them to be.'

'He's a man of God!' insisted Murphy.

'I don't think so,' replied Fyre with a menace in his voice.

The chaplain, all the while, had his eyes locked onto Fyre's.

'Oh, if only you knew how close to God I am, Sebastian,' said the chaplain, his voice losing his southern English accent and becoming harsher and more difficult to place, 'and if only it were John Stone holding that pistol.'

The chaplain grabbed the bag from the ground and

ran. Fyre followed his with the barrel of the pistol, but did not fire.

'Shoot him!' yelled Stone, getting to his feet.

'I can't' Fyre said honestly, as he watched the figure of the chaplain run toward the burning asylum.

'Bugger it!' yelled Stone, 'Come on.'

Fyre and Stone ran in pursuit. Murphy, unable to find any more strength in his legs, watched them go. The others huddled against the garden wall, trying to shield themselves from the intense heat. Their bodies exhausted, all they could do was watch the three men vanish into the billowing smoke. The chaplain reached the semi-demolished wing of the asylum. The heat blistering his skin, he turned and fired a volley of shots from a small pistol he produced from his jacket pocket.

Fyre and Stone dived for the ground as the bullets streamed over their heads. The chaplain tried to skirt the side of what was once the tall west tower, but the tower had collapsed all across the pathways and lawns. He was forced to scramble over the rubble.

Fyre and Stone were close behind him now. Trying to shield themselves with their jackets, they too reached the scree of rubble. The chaplain spotted an opportunity, his pursuers were so close he could fire what bullets he had at them at point blank range. He steadied himself on the broken masonry and raised the gun. He fired. A shot rang by Fyre's face, so close he could feel the air being disturbed as it passed.

The chaplain's left leg had been clutched by a blackened hand. What was once a man, now just a tortured shape, half rose from the rubble.

'Michael, let go!" screamed the chaplain, as he stared into innocent eyes he recognised.

Michael's grip was unshakable. The chaplain discharged a single round into his charred body, but the recoil of the weapon made him lose his balance. He fell, headfirst, down the pile of masonry. He rolled toward Stone, who dived to his right. The chaplain came to a sudden and violent halt, a large, twisted girder of iron piercing his body.

A brief fountain of bright red blood shot into the air, followed by the desperate cry of shock.

Fyre and Stone crawled down by the smoking pile of rubble. To their left more explosions could be heard across the building as the fire spread away from them.

The chaplain's hands clawed at the hot metal rod protruding from his abdomen.

'You think …. this is … over,' he sputtered, 'We … are close to becoming immortal … as God intended.'

'You can explain you actions to your God in person,' said Fyre plainly.

The chaplain laughed, but it sounded more like a death rattle.

'We can .. change the world, just look at your friend.'

Fyre followed the chaplain's eyes toward Stone.

'What about me?' asked Stone.

'You think … all those nice memories of your mother … are real, we put them there. John … Stone, we created … you.'

The chaplain's head fell backwards, limp on his neck. His body slid, sickeningly, further down the metal spike.

Stone rushed forward, half-falling. He grabbed the chaplain's head and yelled into his face.

'What do you mean? What about my mother!!'

'He's gone, John. Come on, we have to go,' shouted Fyre.

'Talk to him, channel his spirit, you can do that!'

'We have to go, John!'

'Help me, Sebastian!!'

'It doesn't work like that, John, we have to go!'

The asylum burned as the figures of Sebastian Fyre and John Stone walked through the smoke.

EPILOGUE

'We have to go,' Fyre said to Murphy.

'You do know you're all under arrest?' asked Murphy.

'I'm sorry, but we will have to go. This is over here, but there are others,' explained Fyre, 'we're going to find them and make sure this never happens again.'

Fyre placed Stone's pistol down on the garden wall. Behind him the building was falling in on itself. Tremendous crashes of masonry could be heard.

'The only way you'll stop us is to shoot us,' stated Stone.

Murphy thought about this, then replied, 'I think there's been enough death for one day.'

'You'll make sure that Sean doesn't get any of the blame for this?' asked Fyre.

'He was an innocent bystander,' stated Murphy.

Bertie had released all of the horses from the Asylum's stable block, all but three, which he now led across the lawn.

'Where are you going?' asked Murphy.

'It's better you don't know. These people, the ones who caused all of this, who manipulated the Barry family and made monsters out of men, they're gone from your little part of the world now. But they exist in other places,' Fyre paused and looked to Stone, 'and they know secrets, things we have not yet considered.'

'Good luck,' replied Murphy, 'and please, whatever you do, don't come back here.'

Fyre smiled at him. 'I promise, you will never see us again.'

With the asylum gone from the skyline. Sean had spent several sleepless nights around Castle Barry.

Cieran Murphy hadn't slept much either. There had been surprisingly little fuss about the events of that last few weeks. There was an official enquiry into the burning down of the asylum, but a superior from Dublin Castle had told him it would find that all of this was a tragic accident.

Murphy knew a whitewash when he saw one. There were funerals, eulogies, and headlines about terrible tragedy, but no mention of murders, or Fyre and Stone. He wondered to himself what would happen to the big houses and the estates owned by the late Lord Barry. He supposed they would be divided up among interested parties. Lord Barry, it had been revealed in one of the Cork newspapers, had borrowed heavily over the last few years. It wouldn't really matter to the locals who was resident in the castle, one landlord was much the same as another.

Sean made a bird noise and pointed across the road to a small cottage that hugged the corner.

Murphy knew the lone resident, a middle-aged widow.

Murphy nodded and moved forward.

The woman was gathering turf from an outbuilding. Her black clothes made her blend in with the treeline behind her. Only her white pinny made it clear where she was.

Sean darted forward, the woman, alerted to his presence, dropped the sods of turf, and froze on the spot.

A single shot rang out. She let out a scream.

'It's alright,' Murphy turned up the light from a

hooded lantern, so that his face and uniform could be seen, 'constabulary. There was a dangerous animal in the area, but we've got it. Go back inside.'

Without a word, the woman fled into her home and barred the door.

'You got him,' said Sean.

'Took us long enough,' Murphy shone the light down on the dead twisted face of a man. He had once been a driver and assistant to Detective Holt.

'Do you think there are any more?' Sean asked.

'If there are, we'll get them too,' replied Murphy, his eyes scanning the black expanse of the forest around them.

Fyre collected the tickets from the station master and examined them as the man spoke.

'Mr Smyth and Mr Jones, we got your message yesterday, Holyhead to London.'

'Yes, that's all in order, thank you,' replied Fyre.

'Smyth and Jones? Whatever made you think they were good names?' asked Stone, as they walked away.

Fyre smiled, 'Do you want to be Smyth or Jones?'

'I'm not sure who I want to be.'

Fyre paused his amble toward the platform. 'We'll find out the truth, John, no matter what it is.'

Stone hesitated, 'That's what I'm afraid of.'

'There's something else we should be more afraid of right now,' said Fyre slowly, his eyes darting to just over Stone's left shoulder.

'Well hello gents,' said Mr Potts.

Stone made the slightly of movements forwards, but was stopped immediately by the sight of a pistol barrel protruding from a jacket thrown over Potts' arm.

'Let's not have any unpleasantness now, shall we? We wouldn't want any innocent people to get hurt in the crossfire.'

'And they would,' added Mr Grey, he flashed open his overcoat to reveal two guns hanging from strings inside.

Fyre and Stone both took a look around the busy

platform. There were families gathered in tight groups, some unruly children running up and down, and dozens of students wheeling suitcases toward the carriages.

'Of course not,' said Fyre.

'Then let's move on, gents, just down there, toward the sheds.'

The four of them walked, two by two, down the platform, through an archway and on to a gravel path that led to series of red brick engine sheds.

The wide open mouths of the sheds made them look like ancient and ruined archways of some long-forgotten cathedral. Only the overpowering scent of oil and industry reminded them they were in the modern world.

'You've got a plan?' whispered Fyre.

'No, but I'm working on one,' replied Stone.

Potts and Grey cleverly kept their distance, walking several feet behind.

'That'll do,' snapped Grey, as he opened his coat again and pointed a gun straight at Stone. They had reached an isolated spot, out of sight of any passengers or workers.

'You're tricky, gents, we've been told to take no more chances with you,' added Potts, 'time's up.' He raised his pistol to fire.

Desperately Fyre tried to stall them, hoping Stone would come up with something, 'Surely you have questions for us?'

A single shot rang out, echoing from the wide arches of the nearby sheds.

Potts looked down at his shirt as a large red dot expanded across his chest. He looked up at his partner. 'Did you do that?'

A second shot followed.

Grey's head violently flew backwards, and his body immediately crumpled to the ground.

Potts looked over to Fyre and Stone, his mouth moving as if to speak, but all he managed to do was fall forward, hitting the gravel with a sickening thump.

Fyre stood still, stunned into inaction. Stone darted

forward and tried to pick up Grey's gun.

A third shot echoed, the sound muffled by the noise of a departing train. The bullet ricocheted off the gun and flew harmlessly into the brickwork behind Stone.

'I didn't have to miss,' said a female voice, echoing in the bricks and metal and making it hard to pinpoint from where it came.

'I believe you,' replied Stone. He stood up and watched Melisa emerge from behind a water tank.

'What now?' asked Fyre.

She raised the rifle and aimed it squarely at him.

'I can fire. Or …' With her left hand she removed a thin leather case from under her workman's coat. The case was burnt in places, but largely intact '… we can be partners …'